THE FOURTH LEVEL
CONTAINMENT
BOOK TEN

NICHOLAS HUNTLEY

First Edition, August 2019

nichhuntley.ca

WHITEWOLF PUBLISHING

Paperback ISBN 978-1-988765-30-3

Digital ISBN 978-1-988765-31-0

The text of this book is set in Times New Roman.

"The tension of the soul in unhappiness, which cultivates its strength; its horror at the sight of the great destruction; its inventiveness and bravery in bearing, enduring, interpreting, exploiting unhappiness, and whatever in the way of depth, mystery, mask, spirit, cleverness, greatness the heart has been granted – has it not been granted them through suffering, through the discipline of great suffering?"

– Friedrich Nietzsche

Act 1, Scene 1

Three white projector screens hung side-by-side in a dark room. A bright light switched on and shined onto each of the three screens before producing three separate projections. On the first screen were a series of random movie clips. On the second screen were moving images similar to the ones in the first screen, but distorted, blurry and discolored. On the third screen was a recording of the human brain under a functional magnetic resonance imaging (fMRI) at four different anatomical planes: a frontal plane, horizontal plane, sagittal plane, and parasagittal plane.

The brain was displayed in a black and white image and displayed blood oxygen level-dependent brain signals represented through colored spots that ranged along the color spectrum from red to violet. The frontal plane in the top left corner displayed the brain seen from the front, including the lower half where the mouth and jaw reside. Here, the brain was seen with its gyrus, folds or bumps of the brain, and sulcus, indentations or grooves. The brain was outlined in a dark layer of grey matter that was separated from the inner white matter. The other points of view were similar, except that the horizontal section cut through the horizon of the brain to see from the top or bottom and sagittal cut vertically to see from the left or right. Parasagittal was parallel to the sagittal section, but apart.

The projection displayed brain activity in coordination with the random clips of film and the altered film in the middle.

"A truly remarkable demonstration," Charlemagne expressed from the front of a crowd of onlookers, arms crossed. "What we see before us, gentlemen, is a translation of brain activity in the occipitotemporal visual cortex taken when a subject was shown the various clips on the left, into what we seen in the center. Isn't it remarkable how similar the images are? We are a step closer to decoding the brain."

Charlemagne stood amongst a crowd of businessmen in suits and scientists in lab coats. Charlemagne himself was in a black suit with a black tie, standing next to Chief Scientist of Cabernet Laboratories, Bartholomew Lambert, who was in a beige suit with a white dress shirt, blue tie and brown shoes, and Richard Huxley, who was in a brown suit with a brown vest, grey tie, and crème colored dress shirt. On Charlemagne's left was an elderly gentleman with a long beard and balding head. The group was protected by two members of the Protection Squad dressed in the black-grey tactical gear. None of the members present with them were part of Charlemagne's personal squad and were instead local boys hired to provide security for Cabernet assets in Allabrese.

"Thank you, Dr. Paul Tarrant, for your and your team's remarkable efforts in the last years to come to such a point. Although I'm aware of the difference between vision and dreams, the sooner we close the gap, the better one can move on to visualizing dreams for others to see," Charlemagne explained to the crowd. "However, I do feel I should warn one and all that while dreams are pleasant, they are not items to be dwelled on, but inspire. Look around us and where we are at – Cabernet Laboratories, where one's dreams become realities, and the power of the mind to create comes true for us, ordinary men. Why, when I was a boy, none of what has been accomplished would have seemed possible. Of course," he added, scratching his nose and lowering his head before looking back at the crowd. "I was promised flying car by this time period, and while we have yet to get there, it is beside the point… We continue, at least in this facility, to aim forward."

The crowd chuckled and murmured happily to one another.

"Thank you, doctor, for your time and demonstration," Charlemagne said, shaking the doctor's hand.

Charlemagne then stepped aside to shake the individual hands of each fellow on Dr. Tarrant's team while Dr. Lambert stepped in to shake Dr. Tarrant's hand before Mr. Huxley. Once Charlemagne had finished expressing his thanks to the team of scientists, he left with the group of businessmen and came to the corridors of Cabernet Laboratories.

Cabernet Laboratories was much the same as always. The floors of the hallways consisted of rectangular linoleum tiles laid in a vertical direction. Next to the crowd of people were glass railings that looked down to the corridor below on the ground floor. The scientists and businessmen walked from one side to the other, entering another laboratory, which was dark and had two projections. At the head of the room was a young man with long, wavy brown hair and soft, fair skin. He was dressed in a suit underneath his lab coat and introduced as Dr. Johann Schreiber.

The film consisted of the flow of dark red circular translucent plates which existed in the hundreds, some stacked upon each other, and others independent or piled upon one another. These funny looking dots were of course erythrocytes, red blood cells. The red blood cells exited on a pinkish background before a greenish transparent liquid was injected into the mix, causing the blood cells to stick together, or coagulate. Afterwards, a reddish liquid was injected into the mix and caused the cells to separate.

Charlemagne's eyes widened and he gave a proud smile. Once the demonstration was finished, Charlemagne shook Dr. Schreiber's hand.

"Thank you, doctor, for this demonstration on a new anticoagulant to combat coagulating cytotoxins," Charlemagne said. "Although still in its clinical trials, this new synthetic compound of yours shows promise as a cheap alternative treatment to various snake venoms. Some of you amongst the crowd might remember Dr. Schreiber from last year where he was presented an award for his work on the recovery of burn wounds – a treatment that my own adopted-son went through last summer in his own recovery. Thank you, Dr. Schreiber for all your work."

Like in the other room, Charlemagne shook the doctor's hand again and then the hands of the doctor's fellows who worked with him. Dr. Lambert and Mr. Huxley followed before they left the room to come to another where Charlemagne met with Dr. Thaddeus Jameson. A middle-aged man with curled brown hair, a long beard and fair skin.

From him, they saw a fascinating demonstration on a new piece of hospital equipment before leaving and exiting the department. From biomedical engineering, Charlemagne took the businessmen to a large freight elevator where they went down into the basement levels of Cabernet Laboratories. The basement tunnels were large and made of concrete, organized in a grid-manner.

Charlemagne took them to see Dr. Matthew Reeves, who had been developing a supercomputer in one of the laboratories' restricted labs, and then Dr. James Grossmann, who had been working on a new experimental pharmaceutical drug.

After seeing these men, Charlemagne took the businessmen down a concrete ramp towards a large set of metal doors. There, he provided access for them to enter a large chamber where numerous scientists were working around a large device in the middle of the room upon catwalks that stretched around the perimeter.

The scientists were not alone but accompanied by engineers working with blowtorches to touch up the sides of the machine in the center, which held tinted windows to hide the artificial sun inside that glowed bright.

"Here is the pièce de résistance," Charlemagne said, extending an arm towards the machine ahead of them. "The A2 Fusion Reactor, completed and fully functional as of this morning."

The businessman looked forward in slight worry and horror.

"Charles," one of them said, "is that safe? What about the safety concerns?"

"It is quite safe," a scientist responded, walking towards them.

Charlemagne looked at the man in the lab coat, an elderly man with white hair and a white beard. They shook hands.

"Gentlemen, this is Dr. Simon Pierce, our team lead on the project since what happened in Allabrese two years ago, and a friend of mine. He's overseen the repairs to prevent any sort of radiation leaks through the use of an experimental alloy known as *mjolnium*. Dr. Pierce is an expert in these matters, with extensive experience from his work on the particle collider in Geneva."

"A pleasure to meet you all," Dr. Simon Pierce said, smiling and keeping his hands in his lab coat, "but I cannot take credit for all of this work. My team, Dr. Lambert, and even Charlemagne here are in equal responsibility."

"Actually, I'm in full legal responsibility," Charlemagne replied, causing the businessmen to chuckle, "but Dr. Lambert here is the innovator of the project."

"We both designed it," Dr. Lambert deflected.

"He introduced me to the idea," Charlemagne replied.

"You sourced the alloy that allowed us to make the repairs," Dr. Lambert argued in a friendly tone. "Charles went all the way to the Arctic to find this rare material from a special type of meteorite."

"At any rate," Charlemagne responded, "the fusion reactor is complete and operating without issue with zero emission of any toxic or radioactive substances, including one we could not detect beforehand and was responsible for the mass hysteria two years ago."

Charlemagne looked at the machine with a proud smile. He then looked to the businessmen with him.

"Anyways, I believe this concludes our tour for this afternoon. If you'll kindly follow me back upstairs, I believe Dr. Lambert has a presentation on how you, the investors, could assist us in realizing the further dreams of our innovators at Cabernet Laboratories. Afterwards, you're all invited to our Halloween Party fundraiser at Curtia Dawson Memorial Library where the generous donations of men and women like yourselves will go towards our research and development of these new innovations."

Act 1, Scene 2

Later in the evening, Charlemagne stood in front of Cabernet Laboratories with Dr. Lambert as they enjoyed some fresh air. Charlemagne looked across the large parking lot of the labs and towards the freeway where the occasional car passed along on either direction. Cabernet Laboratories had a large parking lot for all of the workers of the facility, which was surrounded by a chain-link fence and had lampposts spread around with bright LED white lights that shined down.

"I think that went pretty well," Dr. Lambert said with crossed arms. "I'm hopeful."

"Yes, well, hold on to that hope," Charlemagne replied. "I hate having to sell us out like this to these strangers, but with the recent negative publicity I've cast on Cabernet Industries, it feels like I have little choice... our stocks are at an all-time low."

"Don't feel so bad," Dr. Lambert reasoned. "You've held a stiff upper lip and should be proud for standing up to these parasites. I for one, am proud of you and the direction you've taken, this company has taken, and all that we're doing."

Charlemagne looked at him with suspicious eyes.

"What did those scientists at the GDP do to you?" Charlemagne questioned. "It seems like you time with them has shaped your mind too."

"I couldn't stand them, even under Ms. Black's leadership, I'm glad I resigned and came back here," Dr. Lambert said. "I'm surprised they let me resign... but then again, I did sign their ridiculous treaties and am sworn to secrecy like you."

"Yes, and on that note, I think it's time we both left," Charlemagne said, looking at his Swiss watch. "I have to see to it that the children are ready for the party and change into a different suit. I'll see you at the party..."

"Sure thing," Dr. Lambert replied, nodding.

Charlemagne walked off from the pavement where he had been standing and proceeded to walk across the parking lot of Cabernet Laboratories. He reached his black sedan, opened the door, but before he entered inside, he looked over to the building of Cabernet Laboratories, the brick structure to the left that was the warehouse, the grey structure in the middle with the glass panes over the foyer, and then the building to the right where the offices were and the entire exterior walls consisted of glass windows. The smoke stack over the warehouse no longer ran smoke with the completion of the fusion reactor, which now produced more power than the facility knew to do with. Charlemagne gave one last look at the labs and then entered his car to return home, change, and then head off to the party in downtown Allabrese.

• • •

Several hours later, Charlemagne stood on the ground floor of the public library in downtown Allabrese where he had once fought the spirit of Curtia Dawson. He stood behind a podium atop of a stage that looked down and over to a crowd of townspeople, many of whom he recognized, as well as the investors from the tour.

"Next up," Charlemagne said, speaking into a microphone, "I would like to award the Cabernet Laboratories Scholarship of Excellence to our very own resident currently studying at the University of Harlech's Kinesiology Program: Peter Wolf Huxley."

The crowd clapped as Richard Huxley's son, Peter, walked from the crowd and onto the stage to accept the award from Charlemagne and have his picture taken. Tristan and Diana looked from amidst the crowd with unimpressed eyes, Tristan more unimpressed than Diana given their last encounter with him a year and a half ago.

"What a stupid middle name," Tristan grimaced, crossing his arms. "Wolf…"

Diana looked at Tristan. Peter appeared to be much older than when they last saw him, but still young and handsome. His skin was a similar fair skin shade to his father, which was in likeness to Diana. He was dressed in grey trousers and a light blue dress shirt and smiled as he had his picture taken with Charlemagne.

Tristan looked at him with a grudge. He was dressed as a knight with faux grey chainmail, a leather belt around his waist like a weight lifting belt, and shoulder pads with gold rims. The chainmail included leather rims around the neck hole. The chainmail extended onto his arms with two leather belts around the upper arms and down over his hips to halfway over his thighs. He wore black trousers and boots. Since the summer, Tristan's hair had regrown slightly and he maintained it short, half an inch on the sides, and no more than two inches atop.

Diana was dressed as an angel with angelic white feathered wings and a white dress with a white satin ribbon corset lacing on bodice, bell sleeves with a silver braid, and a halo headband. Her hair was kept at a medium length with a rope braid around the back and the rest of her hair flowing down around the back.

Peter returned to the crowd after having his picture taken with Charlemagne. Charlemagne returned to the podium to continue to address the crowd.

"Lastly, we have a special award to the scientists responsible for one of the largest and most ambitious projects of the current century. I am speaking, of course, of the Cabernet fusion reactor which was completed this week and is guaranteed to revolutionize the energy sector. To Dr. Simon Pierce, and my old friend, Dr. Barry Lambert, please accept the Derby Cabernet Award for Monumental Feats."

The crowd clapped and Dr. Pierce, dressed in a suit, and Dr. Lambert, dressed in a different suit from what he was wearing earlier in the day, stood up onto the stage and accepted the award given to Charlemagne by a female assistant in a black dress. Charlemagne gave the trophy to the two scientists and then took his picture with them while people continued to clap.

Once Charlemagne was finished, he came off the stage and spoke with Dr. Lambert and Dr. Pierce before the two left him alone. Diana and Tristan moved through the crowd and rejoined their guardian who looked to them with smiles. Charlemagne then looked past them and over to Brandan and Lacplesis who were dressed in tuxedos and keeping a fair distance apart from the kids as they watched over them. There were additional members of the Protection Squad, dressed in tuxedos, spread around the perimeter and entire library.

"Nice speech," Tristan remarked. "Can we go home now?"

"Tristan," Charlemagne scorned, "the party has only just started. Enjoy yourself – the entire town is here and tonight is a moment to celebrate and be together. Not to return home and be on your own."

Tristan didn't respond.

"Look," Charlemagne encouraged, pointing into the crowd. "All of our friends are here, such as Lars and his wife, some of your teachers, Diana's former coach (Mr. Cavanagh) …"

Charlemagne stopped as he saw his own friend come towards him. Roy Hudson, a police detective with the Nattau County Police walked over, dressed as a Victorian detective with a brown coat and deerstalker cap.

"What are you supposed to be?" Mr. Hudson remarked to Charlemagne. "I thought this was supposed to be a costume party."

"The costume was optional. Besides, I didn't think it'd be appropriate if I handed awards and was dressed as a mad scientist..." Charlemagne replied. "You certainly appear to have the Halloween spirit through you, Sherlock."

Charlemagne looked at Mr. Hudson and then over to two similar looking men, one younger and the other older, one with curled black hair and the other with light white hair and a thick beard. The older man wore glasses and was dressed as a pirate, while the boy next to him, his son, was dressed as a greaser in a leather jacket, white shirt and dirty light blue jeans.

"Hello, Mr. Cabernet," the older man said in a deep voice, shaking his hand. "Hello, Diana; Tristan."

"Hi," Diana replied.

"Eugene," Roy greeted.

"Hello, Mr. Macmillan," Charlemagne responded. "Jock. Where's Moira?"

"Oh, I believe she's around," Mr. Macmillan responded. "It took her a lot to come, but I was certain Diana would be here, which changed her mind."

"Where are the little ones?" Charlemagne questioned. "Lila and Elliot?"

"With their mother in Edmonton," Mr. Macmillan replied. "A party like this is no place for them anyways."

"Right, fair enough," Charlemagne said, looking to Jock and offering his hand. "Congratulations on your graduation from the police academy and acceptance into the Nattau County Police."

"Thank you," Jock replied, shaking Charlemagne's hand.

"I'm sure your father's already told you to be careful around me," Charlemagne jibed.

"The entire police force, really," Hudson added.

The adults laughed while the kids stood awkwardly with them.

"Here comes the real danger," Charlemagne said, looking as Chief Phillips approached with his wife.

Sabrina and Cole Phillips were fittingly dressed as Mr. and Mrs. Addams from the Addam's Family.

"Charles," Mr. Phillips greeted. "Already in trouble with the law?"

"By the presence of three police officers?" No, not this night, I'm afraid," Charlemagne replied. "Hello, Sabrina."

"Hello, Charles," Mrs. Phillips responded. "Hello, kids."

"Hi," Tristan replied.

"Here we are in the hall of your ancestors; the Kingston family that is," Charlemagne remarked to Sabrina. "The home of the Dawsons is where your mother lives. How is she doing?"

"She's passed away, I'm afraid," Sabrina replied.

"Oh, I'm terribly sorry," Charlemagne responded.

"It's alright – it was last spring."

"Oh…" Charlemagne said. "How are the kids then?"

"Aaron was a little distraught, but no more than the twins…" Sabrina explained. "Thank you for asking."

"No worries," Charlemagne replied. "She was a town treasure… the Dawson family have an important link to this town, its founding…"

"It's ever long feud with the Medicis," Mr. Phillips added. "A family of which I'm surprised to not see here…"

"They were invited, but you know how they are," Charlemagne replied. "Sheltered. The Medici clan has always felt apart from Allabrese, like the French and the English in Canada; the divide of the English and Italians in Allabrese runs the same way."

"Yes, anyways, it was nice to see you, Mr. Cabernet," Mr. Macmillan remarked. "Diana, do keep an eye out for Moira when you get the chance…"

"Sure," Diana replied.

The Macmillans walked off with the Phillips, and before long, Hudson left as Mr. Huxley came around with a wine glass in hand. For the purpose of the awards ceremony, Mr. Huxley, like Charlemagne, was dressed in a simple, but elegant and high-end, suit.

"Shouldn't you be speaking with the investors," Huxley questioned. "You did such a good job this morning and afternoon."

"I'm exhausted, Ralph," Charlemagne replied. "Besides, isn't that what you're paid to do?"

"I believe they're on board," Huxley remarked, looking to the kids. "Children, how are you?"

"Fine," Tristan replied.

"How is school? Charlemagne barely talks of you anymore," Huxley remarked. "What are your preparations for university? Submitted your applications?"

"Yes," Tristan responded.

"Oh, and to which schools?"

"University of Harlech," Tristan replied. "Science Program."

"And you, Diana?" Richard asked.

"Oh… I've submitted to a couple different places…"

"Have you decided what to pursue?"

"Diana's still largely undecided," Charlemagne answered. "However, I've encouraged her that if she does have interest in attending university, she should focus on a STEM program rather than arts."

"A smart choice," Huxley replied, "but business is also a viable option."

"Please don't encourage that onto her," Charlemagne requested. "A business degree has no more worth than an arts degree."

"Vivian's decided to pursue psychology," Richard stated. "If there was an actual waste of time and money, it would be a degree in that… There's no changing her mind though."

"Yes…" Charlemagne replied, looking to the kids. "Children, why don't you go find your friends to speak with? You have no obligation to be beside me all day – please, go and enjoy yourselves"

"Sure," Tristan replied, looking towards Diana.

Act 1, Scene 3

Diana and Tristan walked away from Charlemagne and Mr. Huxley, going across the front of the stage to the other side of the room where Tristan looked back to his guardian. Diana paused as she noticed Tristan stop and she held a hand over the railing of the stairs going up to the second floor of the library. Tristan soon joined her as he continued to walk. The two went upstairs and went around to loiter by the railings that looked down to the party below. Diana sighed as she looked down to the townspeople.

"It's really depressing when even Charlemagne doesn't want to be near you," Tristan said, bringing his hands together as he looked down with Diana.

"He didn't *not* want to be near us," Diana corrected. "He was being nice. He's the one that doesn't know that we don't have any friends, at least other than Moira."

"Moira isn't my friend."

Tristan looked amidst the townspeople and saw his former love interest, Vivian Huxley, dressed as a provocative cat with Maia Grayson by her side, dressed as a provocative bunny. Maia was shorter than Vivian by about three inches. Her white skin was tanned and her brown hair was much lighter than Vivian's, but shorter. Vivian's hair was long, slick and straightened to display its deep brown color. Her fair skin, which was so much unlike Richard or Peter's as it was perfectly white and perfectly smooth. Tristan looked at Vivian for an extended moment before she went out of his sight and onto the balcony patio.

Diana was looking at Tristan's sunken expression. She moved her right hand over to bring it over his arm. Tristan looked at her as she gave a reassuring face.

"Everybody is down there with someone," Diana said, looking back down. "Peter is with Aaron. Jock is with Alex. Vivian is with Maia. I'm with you."

"You should be with Moira," Tristan replied. "Everybody is with their best friend. Haven't you noticed? Peter isn't with Vivian. He's with Aaron. You should be down there with Moira... because at least you have a best friend."

Diana frowned at him.

"You know I can't leave you to be with Moira – I see her plenty enough at school and when I go out with her. I told myself after what happened last year that I would divide myself appropriately between you two, prioritizing you because you're the love of my life and that would be something she'd have to understand if she wanted my friendship. Tonight, I'm with you."

Tristan was unmoved by what Diana had said as she continued to stare down to the crowd of people as if he wasn't listening. Tristan had moved his eyes away from the girls and towards the boys. Peter was with Aaron whose skin tone, which he inherited from his mother; white as snow, which acted in contrast to his hair as it was as dark as darkness. He was dressed as a baseball player. His eyes then went to Jock who was his own best friend, Alexander Grayson, Maia's brother who had auburn brown hair and blue eyes as well as fair skin. He was an athletic boy, which made his costume ironic as he was dressed as a stereotypical nerd with glasses, plaid plants and a tucked in white collared shirt.

"Tristan?" Diana questioned.

"What?" Tristan replied.

"Did you hear what I said?"

"Yes," Tristan affirmed in an annoyed tone, straightening up. "Just go be with Moira, please. I can handle being alone –

I'm no stranger to it. If I get lonely, I'll go find Charles and hang out with him and whoever he's with."

Tristan started to move away from Diana and walk down the balcony. Diana stopped him as she grabbed his wrist.

"Tristan," Diana said in a strict voice.

Diana looked at him with serious eyes. Tristan looked back at her and the tension with him dissipated. He gave off an embarrassed look and stayed with Diana. She took his hand and walked him away from the balcony.

"Come on, let's find somewhere else to be," Diana said, bringing him to the lobby again where they looked to the right and into the ballroom.

The ballroom had various couples dancing to the tune of fast-beat tune. Diana stopped as she looked in, easing her grip on Tristan as the two looked.

"Too bad we can't dance together..." Diana said in a saddened expression. "Well, we could, but..."

Tristan looked at her with distaste towards her suggestion and words. The two walked away without another mention and came to the opposite side of the library where it was much quieter. There, they came to the back where there were tables and windows looking outside. There, there were various attractions set up such as tubs of water with apples, a haunted house composed of some tents, and a pumpkin carving station.

Diana sat down on the table and looked out. Tristan brought himself to lean against the window and did the same.

"You know, it's not our fault we don't have friends," Diana remarked. "It's a small town. The only other people there are aren't even our age, and that's either Gus Rowan or his brother, Justin."

"What an option," Tristan remarked. "One of them can make people believe the rumors going around that I'm gay, and the other can possibly get me killed."

Tristan looked down and saw Justin, a boy who was a year younger than Tristan. He had a skin tone similar to Peter by his mother, who was Peter's aunt, Megan Huxley and Richard's sister. His skin was tanned however, smooth and well-kept. He also had long blonde hair that went to his neck like a surfer. He was a boy that cared about his personal appearance, which was in contrast to his brother who had a rugged statue, was tall, and had greasy brown hair as well as unkempt facial hair. He had fair skin that was like his father, Ronald Rowan, the fire captain of Nattau County. Justin was dressed as a cowboy and with a girl around his age who was dressed as a Cleopatra. The two were near a set of cut-outs where one could take their pictures with their heads poking out from behind these cut-outs. His brother was at the apple-bobbing station. Diana looked at Tristan as he made his remark.

"Don't be mean," Diana scolded. "Justin is a nice boy. He's a good lifeguard too, even if he is gay. He works hard."

Tristan rolled his eyes and shook his head. He then looked as someone who was more familiar to him appeared outside. She was dressed as a goth with deep eyeliner around her eyes and black lipstick. Her genuine red hair was tied back in a bun and she was in a black dress with mesh around her arms and legs. She wore leggings that made her legs look darker as well as black high-heels.

Moira walked around outside on her own. Tristan gave a sigh and then looked to Diana.

"Ow," Diana muttered, bringing a hand to her abdomen.

"What's wrong? Tristan questioned.

"Just a little stomach pain… I thought I was going to be fine, but… ow…"

Tristan brought his hands from out of his pocket and brought them over to Diana's face as if he was examining her.

"You look a little pale," Tristan observed.

"Cut it out," Diana replied, swatting his hands. "You're not a doctor yet – it's nothing. I've been feeling it all day…"

"Oh…" Tristan responded. "Right, I remember now."

Tristan looked around as Diana stood up.

"Can you take me home?" Diana questioned. "I don't want to be here like this if we're not going to do anything but brood."

"Sure," Tristan replied, helping Diana onto her feet, "do you want me to tell Charles to drive us back, or…"

"No," Diana said, "I don't want to ruin his time either. You have a license. You can drive me home."

"Um," Tristan hesitated as they walked down an aisle of bookshelves, "okay…"

Tristan took Diana back to the lobby and down a set of stairs to the ground floor. He looked over to where Charlemagne had been, but he was gone now. The couple walked out of the library and came to the tops of the steps. Tristan briefly looked ahead and towards central park, and then Cabernet Industries administrative offices on the other side. Allabrese Civic Center was on the right, at the head of the park, and on the opposite-end was a plaza with the town cinema, street corner grocery store, and a bookshop.

The night was dark and there was a thickness of clouds in the air that left the skies as if there was a wildfire close by, but without the smell of smoke. The area around town square was lively, not noisy, but lively. There was a slight chill in the early October air, which caused every breath that Tristan gave off to be able to see his cold breath. Tristan walked to the bottom of the steps and reached the valet at a podium.

"I need the car for Mr. Cabernet, please," Tristan said.

Diana held her hands at her stomach as Tristan maintained an arm around her.

"Is Mr. Cabernet okay with you taking his car?" the valet questioned.

"I'm his son, and she's in pain," Tristan argued. "He said he'd take a cab – he's going to have a drink or two anyways."

The valet didn't argue with Tristan, but had Tristan sign a book on the podium while the valet radioed for the car to be brought out. The couple didn't have to wait long until Charlemagne's black sedan was brought out and to the curb of the library.

"Thank you," Tristan said to the valets as he opened the door for Diana.

Diana got into the car which was still running and closed the passenger seat door. The car was nice and warm. Tristan went around and opened the driver's seat door, stepped in and then closed the door. He took off the shoulder pads of his costume and tossed them back. He then adjusted the seat, the mirrors, and looked to Diana as she held her head back.

Tristan finished adjusting the seat and then brought the car out of park and brought the parking brake down. He then pulled off from the curb and proceeded to drive Diana back home with haste.

Act 1, Scene 4

Charlemagne stood on the ground floor of the west wing of the library with Richard Huxley where the catering was supplied on tables with white tablecloths and atop of decorative pieces that were in the Halloween spirit. The catering was to the sides of the room and in the center were various round tables with chairs for people to sit, eat and converse. Charlemagne and Richard went and sat down at a table where they could continue to drink wine and talk. Charlemagne poured his friend another drink as he looked over and two of his other comrades came and pulled out a chair for themselves.

Dr. Joseph Gilbert (Ph.D. in linguistics) and Mr. McGarrick were two of Charlemagne's higher ups in the company, Gilbert being the Chief Communications Officer of all of Cabernet Industries, and Herman McGarrick being President of Cabernet Industries and Chief Executive Officer of Cabernet Air. McGarrick was a tall, stocky man with neatly combed blonde hair and blue eyes. He had a round, jovial face. Gilbert was much as he was in the summer, short stature and neat dark brown hair. However, in person, there was a dark complexion around his eyes, similar to Tristan, but darker. Mr. McGarrick was dressed as a commercial airline pilot, while Dr. Gilbert was dressed as a doctor in scrubs.

"Good evening," Charlemagne greeted to Dr. Gilbert and Mr. McGarrick with a smile. "Come. Sit."

"It seems that we're too late, and Charlemagne has already gotten himself drunk," Mr. McGarrick jibed.

McGarrick spoke in a deep, raspy voice.

"Ah, but the party is only beginning," Charlemagne responded. "It *is* a party after all."

Charlemagne motioned the men of his company to push their wine empty wine glasses before them towards him so that he could pour them a drink.

"Where are your wives, gentleman?" Charlemagne questioned.

"Together," Dr. Gilbert responded.

"My dear Emma is with Madi, and I believe the two went to find Jacquie," McGarrick explained. "The women are better together than with the men."

"Good evening, gentleman," Mr. Bowman remarked, pulling a chair for himself.

"Martin," Charlemagne greeted.

Charlemagne passed the bottle to McGarrick to pour a drink for Mr. Bowman who was dressed as an eighteenth-century French nobleman. Bowman was similar to how he appeared a year and a half ago, with short brown hair and fair skin. He was the Vice-President of Cabernet Industries and Chief Secretary of the Board of Directors in addition to being a member of the board.

"How is your wife?" Charlemagne asked.

"Glenda is fine," Bowman said in a calm tone.

"Did you pick out that costume yourself?" McGarrick questioned Bowman.

"No, my wife did," Bowman replied. "She insisted on being Marie Antoinette. Is yours a stewardess?"

"Actually, she wanted to be a movie star – I picked what was the least embarrassing for me."

The men chuckled.

"Perhaps we should not speak so much of our wives," Huxley remarked. "We don't want to upset Charlemagne too much."

"Sorry," McGarrick apologized. "A toast to Charlemagne and his persistent state of being a bachelor."

"Here, here," the men responded, raising their glasses.

"Well, it might be that way, seeing that there is no hope in returning with Manon given that our son is dead," Charlemagne replied with a sunken expression.

"I can't imagine the pain you must have felt, even since you never knew the boy, he was your son," Gilbert remarked. "If any one of my five children even came down with a flu, I would be stressed from the thoughts."

"Five kids…" Huxley muttered. "How do you manage your title and five kids? I get a headache from the two, and I run the entire company! I'm lucky they're leaving soon."

"I have one little rugrat. How do you intend to be mayor with that many kids, Joseph?" McGarrick asked.

"Easily," Gilbert answered. "Madi's work is at home and she takes care of them while I'm at the office. She is quite capable and doesn't even break a sweat."

"Let's not forget that Bowman has ten children," Charlemagne said, bringing his hands together and resting his elbows on the table. "The rest of you are amateurs."

The men looked to Charlemagne.

"On the subject of your electoral campaign," Bowman said, looking to Gilbert. "How goes the campaign?"

"Well, thank you for asking," Gilbert replied. "Two more weeks to election day."

"What is so great about Theodore Grayson?" Bowman asked with spite. "The man's only achievement in his life was owning his own small business; an accountant firm below our own offices."

Charlemagne looked over and saw Mayor Grayson with his wife, Grace Grayson, and Dr. Moore, a general practitioner in

Allabrese. Mr. Grayson was in his late-fifties with short grey hair and fair skin. His wife was in her mid-fifties with dark reddish-brown hair tied in a bun. She was a short woman, approximately five feet in height whereas her husband was average height. Dr. Moore was a large, overweight man. The Grayson couple were dressed as a royal couple, while Dr. Moore was dressed as Frankenstein's monster.

"Try not to speak so loudly," Charlemagne remarked, nudging his head. "The man is over there with Dr. Moore."

"How can he stand being near that man," McGarrick questioned in a hushed tone. "Dr. Moore I mean – the man has a foul stench."

"Dr. Moore is a respectable physician," Charlemagne explained, "and as for Mr. Grayson, he is loved by the townspeople, and Dr. Gilbert is coming between him and the love of the town. Not to mention, Mr. Grayson has maintained the status quo of the town, kept chain stores and restaurants away, and so on. He is a subscriber to *Realpolitik*s and not an ideological man."

"Well, he's more of a conservative," McGarrick said with a nasty tone. "A liberal looking to conserve people's money – that's the kind of man he is and the background he has. After all, he is an accountant. He reminds me of the fiends that used to run the company before us."

"What do you make of Gilbert then? They were both independent candidates," Huxley asked and said, "on the ballot, I mean."

"Gilbert is more of a right-wing populist, like Charlemagne, which this town *is* accepting of and needs before it becomes polluted, commercialized..." McGarrick explained. "Overrun."

"On that note, Charles..." Gilbert said, looking over to him as Mr. Heavner arrived.

The man greeted Mr. Heavner who pulled out a seat for himself while Gilbert continued to speak. He was not dressed in a costume and instead in a simple black suit. He had a similar appearance to when he was seen in France, with shortened hair and round glasses.

"When are you going to run for mayor of Harlech?" Gilbert asked Charlemagne.

"Let's not ask such impossible questions of me. You know I'm apolitical and don't give a damn about the sham that is democracy," Charlemagne replied. "Hello, Henry."

"Gentleman," Heavner greeted, dropping down a fresh wine bottle. "I saw that you were out."

"A lifesaver as always," Charlemagne replied. "Thank you."

"Has anyone seen Frank?" Gilbert questioned.

"Frank is on a business trip to Harlech," Huxley answered. "He has an important legal case regarding all of the defamation in the last year."

"A toast to him then," Gilbert replied, raising his glass.

Charlemagne turned his head at the sound of some loud stomps. He looked and saw Kristoffer Kristoffersen, dressed in a suit with his white-blonde hair combed back and same beard as last winter.

"Hello, friends," Kristoffer greeted in his loud voice and Greenlander accent. "A pleasure to meet you all here."

"Hello, Kris," Charlemagne greeted.

"A fantastic party by Mr. Cabernet, no?" Kristoffer questioned. "What business are we talking of here?"

"Typical business," Charlemagne replied. "How is your work with Cabernet Foundation? I haven't heard from Allodia in a while."

"Business as usual, as you say," Kristoffer replied. "A lot of work done. A lot of toys delivered to make happy children."

"Good," Charlemagne responded. "Do you know if my sister is here, Kristoff?"

"No," Kristoffer answered. "Allodia is in England. She is a very busy woman."

"Yes, that's my sister," Charlemagne replied. "She must be still working on the re-development of Northumberland-Berwick with Defra. She's been busy ever since the forest fire was put out by the blissful rain that came the following week."

Kristoffer went on to chat with the executives while Charlemagne took out his phone to see a text from Tristan mentioning that he was going home with Diana as she felt unwell. He stood up and looked to the men.

"Apologies, but please excuse me," Charlemagne said before leaving.

Charlemagne walked out of the west wing, replying to Tristan's message with simple message, 'Be safe,' before entering the lobby.

"Charles!" a young voice shouted.

Charlemagne looked forward and saw a young boy with silk-like light brown hair and dark fair skin rush towards Charlemagne. Charlemagne intercepted the young boy and picked him up, hugging him with a smile. The three-year old boy was dressed in a Winnie the Pooh onesie with face paint blackening his nose.

"Hello, Mathias," Charlemagne said, hugging the boy and looking over to Miklos and Tanya. "I'm glad you made it. I wouldn't have considered you official residents of the town until you went to one of our all-time famous parties."

"Thank you, Charles," Miklos replied, taking his son in to his arms. "We wouldn't feel a part of the town unless we participated in your traditions and spent time with the community."

Charlemagne smiled to Miklos and then to Lukas next to him. The two were off-duty. Lukas was with his own wife, Marjeta, a beautiful Slovenian woman with dark blonde hair. Miklos was dressed as a lumberjack and Lukas as a Roman legionnaire. Tanya was dressed as some sort of tree nymph with a green dress whereas Marjeta was a Roman goddess.

"Please enjoy yourselves," Charlemagne insisted, "and if you'll excuse me. I'll catch up with you in a minute."

Charlemagne walked past them and around the lobby to get to the opposite side where there was a corridor that led to some washrooms beneath the east stairs. He entered the washroom and went to the urinal. At a moment's notice, Charlemagne heard the door open behind him. His ears twitched, but he didn't turn his head.

"Mr. Cabernet," a voice greeted.

The masculine voice spoke in a thick, deep German accent. Charlemagne flushed the urinal and then turned around. He looked at the man and saw he was dressed in a trench coat with a cap over his head like some sort of inspector. The man removed his cap and revealed his tired face. He had medium fair skin and was unshaven. He also had blue eyes and ginger hair.

"My name is Maximillian Bauer," the man introduced himself in a coarse South German accent. "Is it okay if we talk?"

"We're speaking now, aren't we?" Charlemagne replied, walking over to the sinks.

"The matter is of most urgency and concerns Zimmerman Corporations," Bauer explained.

"What of them?" Charlemagne questioned. "I have no business with them. They're my mere rivals."

"The subject is not of your company's rivalry, but of a matter of greater importance – one that threatens the stability of our world and current status quo; one that threatens your precious town."

Charlemagne turned to the man with a serious look.

"In exchange for what I know, I ask that you provide me transport to Switzerland so that I may go into exile," Bauer requested. "They are looking for me."

"Are you mad?" Charlemagne asked. "Who's looking for you?"

"Zimmerman Corporation and the Global Defense Project," Bauer answered.

Charlemagne's eyes widened at mention of the secret organization.

"How do you know of them?"

"I know lots, Mr. Cabernet," Bauer replied. "I know that you collaborated with this organization last year to save the world from an apocalyptic war as well as that you have a good heart and are right to trust. If you will listen to me, I can tell you of the secret documents that the former director of that organization stole and brought to Zimmerman Corporation. The documents of which concern the development of a dangerous technology that can power a dangerous artefact you also know of, the Amulet of Ra, as well as another that is currently missing and whose whereabouts are unknown."

"Alright, you have my attention," Charlemagne replied, walking towards the man, "but this isn't the place to talk about this sort of things. They might be listening."

"Of course, Mr. Cabernet," Bauer agreed.

"Come, I'll take you to my manor where you will be safe. It is protected by my own trusted men and you can breathe easy," Charlemagne said, walking with Bauer out of the bathroom. "I'll take you there at once."

Act 1, Scene 5

Tristan drove across the Nattau River in the dark of the night, driving around the roundabout at the end and coming down to the cliffside road that led to the manor. The gates of the mansion opened as the car got close, allowing him to drive up the hill and then down towards the garage annex. The doors of the annex opened as the car approached, and once inside, he parked the car and shut the engine off.

The couple got out of the car and Diana set off to go see Zephyr in his stall. Tristan looked at her as she went to see her horse. The garage had some renovations completed in the last year to expand Zephyr's stall and provide more room and some heaters. Zephyr's stall was straight across from the stall with the Tiger tank, which was next to the stall with the grey pickup truck. Diana went to a mini-fridge at the end of the aisle to retrieve some carrots before bringing them to Zephyr as a treat. She then pet him on the nose while Tristan retrieved his shoulder pads from the back of the car. He then closed the door and continued to stare at the two.

Diana looked over to Tristan and then walked over to join him. She blushed and walked with him to the elevators where they rode up to the kitchen store room. Diana entered the kitchen and adjusted her hair. She picked up the kettle and placed the handle atop of the faucet, turning on the sink to fill it with water. Diana then brought the kettle to its plate and started to boil some water.

"Do you want some tea?" Diana questioned.

Tristan looked at her. She brought a hand on his cheek.

"You didn't have cramps, did you?" Tristan said. "You just wanted to get out of there."

Diana looked at him. She shrugged.

"I did, but at the same time, I didn't want to be there," Diana replied. "Neither did you. Why should we have stuck around when we could be here, together?"

Tristan sighed.

"Do you want to watch a movie then? A horror movie maybe?" Tristan sheepishly asked.

"Okay," Diana smiled. "I'll make some popcorn too."

• • •

Charlemagne left the library and went down the steps to the valet.

"Mr. Cabernet," the valet greeted. "Shall I call you a cab?"

"No, where's my car?" Charlemagne replied.

"Err, your children withdrew your car and said that you'd be taking a cab home…" the valet responded, showing the book. "I'm sorry…"

"Damn," Charlemagne responded. "Nevermind."

Charlemagne turned around, looked at Bauer, and then went back up the steps and into the library. He looked around and then went into the east wing where he saw Barry drinking and chatting with some of the scientists employed at Cabernet Laboratories.

"Barry," Charlemagne said, grabbing his arm. "Can I have a word with you? In private?"

"Sure," Barry replied, walking away from the scientists with him. "What's up?"

Charlemagne walked him away from the crowd and towards a bookcase where Bauer was. Charlemagne quickly explained the situation.

"I need you to drive me home," Charlemagne requested at the end of it.

"Yeah, sure," Barry replied, taking out his ticket. "Come on."

Dr. Lambert, Charlemagne, and Bauer left the library again and went down to the valet podium where Barry presented his voucher. In a short minute, Dr. Lambert's vehicle, a brand new luxurious grey electric car, was brought out and parked on the curb.

"Hop in," Barry said, going around to the driver's seat.

Charlemagne opened the door for Bauer to enter in the back before going to the passenger seat in the front. Once they were inside, Barry switched gears to drive and set off to drive towards the manor.

Barry parked at the top of the hill, in front of the main doors. Tristan noticed a beam of light enter into the living room through the blinds behind him. He was lying down on the couch with Diana atop of him. Tristan moved his arm to poke a blind down and see outside. He noticed Dr. Lambert's car and saw Charlemagne exit the passenger seat before opening the passenger seat door behind.

"Charles is home early…" Tristan said in a depressed tone.

Tristan lowered the blind and looked to Diana. He took the bowl of popcorn into his hands and helped her sit up. The couple heard the main doors open and Charlemagne rush in with Barry. Diana saw the two come inside and then go towards the library.

"They're gone," Diana said, lying back down and bringing herself atop of Tristan's lap.

Tristan brought his hands up as Diana rested her head over his lap and brought them down so that he could continue watching the movie.

Charlemagne rushed Bauer and Barry towards his study, entering and closing the door behind him. Charlemagne then turned around to look at Bauer as he examined the inside of

Charlemagne's office. He looked at the painting on an easel and then to the aquarium next to the fireplace. Immediately in front of the door into the study was a display case, which inside contained a recovered Panzerschreck robot from the Arctic. At its side was the StG44 and Walther pistol Charlemagne had used and taken back with him. Bauer looked at the robot and then over to Charlemagne.

"German, isn't it?" Bauer pointed out. "You can tell by the high quality."

"A priceless artefact from the war," Charlemagne replied, walking over to his desk and sitting down. "Please, have a seat and let's discuss what needs to be discussed."

Barry walked over and sat down in front of Charlemagne's desk. Bauer came around once he was finished looking at the various items in the room and sat down. He took off his hat again and set it in front of him. Charlemagne looked at the man with intent, focusing on his green eyes and fair skin.

"Who are you? Other than your name," Charlemagne asked, "what is your relation to Zimmerman Corporation? Are you some sort of mercenary or… assassin?"

"No," Bauer denied. "I was… a scientist who has had enough of Zimmerman Corporation and their inhumane projects. You see, Zimmerman Corporation is currently conducting human experiments on a group of four specimens in an effort to develop supersoldiers through intensive gene and drug therapy met with the combination of certain advanced technologies to create a small army of supermen who will not only be of peak fitness, but possess abilities that would be deemed by some to be unnatural. I am speaking, of course, of psionics."

Bauer paused for a moment.

"One year ago, Fuyu Selebi left the Global Defense Project and took with him a briefcase containing documents and blueprints reserved in case of the outbreak of war between our world and the extraterrestrial, which would see the implementation of an initiative, or project, in a last resort to win the war against these technologically, and mentally, superior beings. Less than 1% of humans on this Earth possess such extraordinary skill, but none amongst us, except for those in Zimmerman's captivity, have been able to become awakened to these skills and trained to use them. It lies within a certain percentage of the world's population, and even then, it takes a tremendous amount of willpower to go through the training to be able to use these powers that in this small percentage is an even smaller percentage. From what I have seen, it takes a certain soul, and such souls are only found in people with iron wills. From these powers, one develops the powers of the mind, ability to speak telepathically, implant thoughts in those able to receive them, receive thoughts from those that can speak without speaking, move objects with a mere thought, and control the weak-minded. And this is only the basics of what is possible based on a year of progress and what I have seen to date..."

"What does all of this have to do with the Amulet of Ra then?" Charlemagne asked.

"The amulet, as you know, is nothing more than a rock wrapped in that extraterrestrial alloy – it is the rock that Zimmerman concerns himself with, because from that rock, these psionic supersoldiers gain the ability to teleport anywhere on a three-dimensional plane."

Charlemagne's face went pale.

"Just like in the myths..." Charlemagne remarked, scratching his head. "It makes sense."

"The ability to teleport is found only with this crystal in the hands of the gifted, which makes them a necessary accessory," Bauer explained.

"But there is only one rock in that crystal... thus only one user," Charlemagne said with hope. "Only one can use the rock at a time, so there is a limit."

"Not unless they divide the rock," Barry interjected. "Can they divide the rock?"

"They have divided the rock into smaller pieces," Bauer confirmed. "A total of almost forty smaller pieces to be exact..."

"Good Lord," Charlemagne remarked, bringing a hand to his forehead and sitting back. "An army of forty genetically-enhanced psionic supersoldiers... What are Zimmerman's intentions with that?"

"I am not sure," Bauer replied. "All that I know, is that in the next phase of the project, there were to be thirty-six more soldiers, and these men...!" he added, "are dangerous, because they, although men of deep souls, have been brainwashed to eliminate any consciousness, any sense of empathy, and any emotion from within them. In other words, they lack freewill and are rational animals. In another sense, they are cold-blooded killers, but with an intelligence greater than the average man."

Charlemagne looked to Bauer with worry.

"How troubling," Charlemagne simply said. "And, of these crystals, did you at least take with you a specimen?"

"No..." Bauer denied. "I'm afraid not."

Charlemagne didn't respond. Both him and Dr. Lambert were silent.

"Now that I have told you this, please, make an effort into locating the twin artifact with the other crystal," Bauer said. "The other crystal is far more dangerous and contains powers related to time. If Zimmerman were to capture this, it could spell certain trouble."

Charlemagne scratched his head.

"I'm having a hard time imaging what sort of trouble Zimmerman has in mind, especially since he's a mysterious figure," Charlemagne said, sighing. "Nonetheless, thank you for telling me all this, but I feel hopeless and uncertain what to do with all this information. I have no doubts that it is true, but I'm just one man... I can't overturn what has been set in motion."

"You have the power of connections and your own company," Bauer remarked. "I am certain you will think of something, unlike me. Currently, both by former captors and by extension, the Global Defense Project, are looking for me, which is why I need you to grant me passage to Switzerland where I have some contacts that can provide me refuge in a monastery..."

"Right, yes," Charlemagne replied. "I will honor the deal and provide you with that transport... The earliest I can have you flown to Switzerland is tomorrow morning when my personal pilot is available. In the meantime, you will have to stay here..."

"Is there no faster method?" Bauer questioned.

"I'm afraid not," Charlemagne responded. "I will go and see to it that we can get you some sheets for you to sleep in our guest room upstairs..."

"Thank you," Bauer replied as Charlemagne stood up.

"Thank you," Charlemagne said, nodding to him. "I appreciate you have chosen me to confide this information and trust that I will do all that I can do deactivate this threat from Mr. Zimmerman."

Charlemagne walked around his desk and left the room. He began to walk down the corridor when he heard the door open behind him. Barry exited and walked to Charlemagne. The two stood in the library.

"What the hell was all that?" Barry questioned. "Psychics? Supersoldiers? It all sounds insane."

"It is insane, but that man, is not insane. He knows about the GDP, what we did last summer, and the Amulet of Ra. If he's insane, then so are we…" Charlemagne remarked, "and all of this would be nothing more than a hallucination… a fever dream."

"What are you going to do?" Barry questioned as Charlemagne attempted to leave.

Charlemagne let out of a deep breath.

"I'm not sure," Charlemagne responded. "Do you have any means of contacting the GDP?"

"You want to contact them? Are you actually crazy?"

"What else do you want me to do? I can't raise my own army and develop research into psionics. Something like that is far out of my capabilities, and resources! May I remind you that Cabernet Industries is suffering a financial crisis right now? I know that the objectives and intentions of the council of nations behind the GDP aren't the nicest and most honest people, but they have resources to combat this clear threat that Zimmerman is posing. What troubles me the most is not knowing what his intentions are in raising an army as powerful as this…"

Barry crossed his arms.

"I'm going to go find some sheets," Charlemagne said. "Keep that man company, and tomorrow morning we'll fly to Switzerland with him before we start to plot our next course of action. Okay?"

"Fine," Barry replied, turning around and walking back.

Charlemagne looked to him with a worried face and then took a deep breath. Once he exhaled, he walked out of the library and went to find some bed sheets and blankets for his guest.

Act 2, Scene 1

The next morning, Charlemagne woke up in his bed and got out to use his washroom. He then exited and dressed himself for the day in his traditional three-piece grey suit. He fixed his bowtie and then exited to enter the north wing. He turned to the right, crossed the foyer, and entered the foyer of the north wing before where his makeshift lab used to be. He knocked on the door. No answer came. Charlemagne tried again, but no answer came once more. He then opened the door and entered.

Charlemagne looked ahead to the double bed in the corner of the room he had allowed Bauer to sleep on and saw that it was deserted. The blankets and sheets were left in a mess atop and the man was nowhere to be seen. Charlemagne looked around the room for a moment before returning to the sheets. He looked around the emptied room. Almost all of Charlemagne's equipment, tables, and tools had been moved from the room. The room appeared to be bare almost. All that there was, was the double bed propped in the far left corner of the room, next to the table with Charlemagne's computer (which remained), and behind the computer was one of the tables propped against on the other side of the wall. Charlemagne looked around and then he went to the library and his study. He didn't see anything out of the ordinary in either rooms.

From his study, Charlemagne went to the other side of the house and into the kitchen where Mavis was making some tea and preparing breakfast.

"Good morning, Mr. Cabernet," Mavis said. "I'm just working on an English breakfast for us all. How did you sleep?"

"A little trouble sleeping…" Charlemagne confessed. "Have you seen my guest from last night? I set him up in the library to sleep and took some sheets from the laundry room."

"What guest?" Mavis questioned.

"A man who was at the party… a colleague of myself and Dr. Lambert," Charlemagne explained. "He isn't around and I'm worried where he might have gone off to. You haven't seen anything?"

"I'm afraid not, Mr. Cabernet," Mavis replied. "Sorry."

"No, it's quite alright, love," Charlemagne said, stepping back. "Carry on."

Charlemagne brought a hand to his head. He then left and searched the house again. Once he confirmed that Bauer was nowhere to be seen, he retired to his study where Mavis came with a tray of food and tea for Charlemagne. She set the tray on his desk and then left him. Charlemagne was on his computer, rewinding footage from the CCTV camera system around the perimeter of the house but did not see anyone leave after Barry had left. Charlemagne scratched his head and sat back.

"How perplexing," Charlemagne muttered under his brief, picking up his cellphone.

Charlemagne shot a text to Barry, asking '*Do you remember what happened last night?*' to him. Barry didn't answer immediately, so Charlemagne set off to have his breakfast before picking up the phone and dialing a number. The phone rang for a moment before someone answered.

"Hello?" Barry questioned in a groggy voice. "Charles? What's up?"

"Good morning," Charlemagne greeted. "Sorry to disturb you, but do you remember what happened last night?"

"Yeah, of course," Barry responded. "Aren't we going to Switzerland?"

"Yes… and with who is it that we're going to Switzerland with?"

"With the German man? Bauer, I believe his name is."

"Right!" Charlemagne replied. "Right. I do remember, I'm just checking because, well, he's not here, Barry."

Charlemagne explained what he found earlier. He also explained that surveillance footage around the house did not show anyone leaving.

"Well, that means one of two possibilities. Either, you have some sort of blind spot in your security system, or he's still in the house somewhere," Barry said. "Have you checked everywhere?"

"Well, not everywhere," Charlemagne replied. "I've checked everywhere except the children's rooms to avoid disturbing them as well as the basement."

"Well, it sounds like you haven't checked everywhere then..." Barry responded. "He might be hiding somewhere, I don't know. He didn't sound like a perfectly stable man. I wouldn't be surprised if he's extremely paranoid."

"The cameras in the garage didn't yield any results," Charlemagne said, "so the only possibility is the storage."

Charlemagne sighed.

"I'm going to take another look," Charlemagne then said. "I'll keep you updated."

"Thanks."

Charlemagne hung up and then picked up the phone again. He dialed a four digit number and kept the phone to his ear.

"Good morning," Charlemagne greeted. "I need Mr. Heavner to give me a call as soon as possible and for you to send a small squad of men to the house. I have a special assignment."

Charlemagne stood up from his desk after dropping the phone and went across, back to the kitchen, and into the basement. He entered the storage room under the foundations of the house and looked around for a brief moment, but did not see anything or anyone. He then returned upstairs and went into the east wing. He checked his lab, but didn't see anything. He then checked Tristan's room, but saw it was empty. Charlemagne walked down the corridor and opened the door into the gym where he was bench pressing a sum of two-hundred twenty-five pounds towards his bare chest. The boy was dressed in dark blue soccer sweatpants that he sleeps in, his golden necklace, and nothing more. A scar was noticeable on Tristan's right shoulder, a burn scar that was quite large, circular and in a peculiar shape. Charlemagne looked at the scar for a moment with an uneasy face.

"Tristan," Charlemagne greeted as the boy brought the barbell up and onto its handles.

"Yeah," Tristan replied, sitting up and looking to Charlemagne. "What's up?"

"Is everything okay here? Is Diana okay?"

"Yeah, everything's cool," Tristan responded, wiping sweat from off his face with a towel he had on the floor. "Why?"

"No reason," Charlemagne responded, looking around. "Is Diana sleeping still?"

"I don't know," Tristan responded, panting light pants. "She's fine though. Trust me. Please don't wake her."

"Right," Charlemagne replied, nodding. "Very well. Carry on."

Charlemagne left and returned to the foyer of the house where he heard a knock. The Protection Squad team consisting of Lacplesis and Brandan stood on the other side of the door, in uniform. Charlemagne let them in and then took them to his study.

"What appears to be the problem, Mr. Cabernet?" Lacplesis questioned.

"Sorry to drag you from your regular duties, but I have a special assignment for yourselves and Mr. Heavner. I need you to run a background check on individuals from German-speaking nations with the name Maximillian Bauer, with an age range from my age to about your ages. There should be a small handful – from them, I need you to reduce them to people with red hair and blue eyes, and if possible, focus on those with a military background."

"Yes, sir," Lacplesis replied, taking notes. "Anything else?"

"No," Charlemagne responded, shaking his head. "That is all."

"We'll get back to you when we're through doing what we can, and then we'll leave the rest to Mr. Heavner and his investigators."

"Thank you," Charlemagne nodded.

The boys left the study, leaving Charlemagne at his desk. He looked at his computer and back at CCTV recorded footage. He proceeded to rewind from the camera at the front of the house to when he arrived with Dr. Lambert. Charlemagne then paused at the exact moment the car turned off.

Charlemagne got out of the vehicle first followed by Dr. Lambert. Charlemagne opened the door behind the car, and then seemingly closed it. Charlemagne paused, brought the footage back, and then replayed it. Charlemagne opened the door to the rear passenger seats behind his seat for a moment and then closed it without anyone exiting. The two, Barry and Charlemagne, then went up the steps and came into the home alone.

"No…" Charlemagne replied, shaking his head. "Impossible."

Charlemagne picked up his cellphone and was about to text Barry, but he stopped himself and put the phone down. He then stood up and walked to the other side of his study, looking outside to the dull grey morning before turning back around. He simply shook his head.

Act 2, Scene 2

Diana opened her eyes and stretched her body in her bed before bringing an arm down next to her. She then tilted her head to the side and looked depressingly to the empty space next to her. Her eyes then wandered over to the shelf over her dresser. The shelf contained mementos from her adventures in the last two years, including the box of cigarettes, a vial of ectoplasm taken from 1136 Elmwood Crescent, the head of the robot from the Ural Mountains, her victory ribbon from the Nattau Derby, the small Anubis statue she had bought in Giza, the piece of her and Tristan's wishing star she had gifted to Tristan, the nutcracker Tristan salvaged for her from Kristoffer's workshop, the film reel gifted to her by a boy named Sebastian, and Tristan's broken watch. Behind these mementos were some framed pictures, including a picture of her with Tristan, Allodia, and Charlemagne in St. Petersburg, a picture of her and Zephyr at the Allabrese Equestrian Center, a group picture of her, Tristan, and Charlemagne with his old expedition crew in Alexandria (minus Manon), a group picture of the Guardian Initiative at the Cabernet Outpost in Kennte, a group picture of the RV Ingstad, including Kristoffer, and a picture of Diana and Tristan with Manon in front of the River Seine in Paris prior to Judith's death and funeral. Atop of Diana's dresser were jewelry boxes, a small cabinet for keeping necklaces inside, and a Bible laid out and open with a cloth underneath. At the corner of the cloth was a green candle on a steel candle holder. Behind the Bible was a picture of her mother and father together, before they were parents.

On and around Diana's desk were further memorable photos, including a photo of her mother with her blonde hair and light blue eyes, and of Diana and Tristan together, at the Allabrese

Winter Festival last December, which replaced the one of them in front of the Neva River in St. Petersburg. These two pictures had been placed in a double-frame that fit two pictures the same size. Behind the desk were random photos taken on Tristan's phone, including selfies of her and him, her and Moira, and some of her with Charlemagne, the Protection Squad, and others dear to her, posted on a corkboard with thumbtacks. The photos of her with Tristan outnumbered those without. In front of the picture of Diana's mother and her and Tristan was Diana's latest read, *Call of the Wild* by Jack London.

Diana's room was not too messy. Her closet, next to the dresser was open and the laundry basket was out with various clothing piled around. Above the door, Diana had nailed a cross with a steel figure of Jesus Christ crucified on the cross. The blinds of the room were drawn and it was dark due to the gloomy weather. The door into the bathroom was open, which gave way for the sound of clashing metal coming from the gym.

Diana rolled out of bed and put on a blue-green flannel shirt tucked around the chair of her desk. Diana had gone to sleep in a nightgown. She put the shirt over her back and then made the trip, barefoot, from her bedroom, through the bathroom, and opened the door to the gym. There, she saw Tristan working out just as he was when Charlemagne had seen him, but instead of bench pressing, he had moved the barbell to the matted ground and increased the weight load to almost three-hundred pounds, including the barbell. Tristan wore a weight lifting belt around his lower back to brace it.

Tristan leaned over, grabbed the barbell by the middle grip and stuck his rear out. He placed one hand on the left grip so that his left palm was facing him and his right hand on the right grip so that his palm was facing away from him. He then tightened his hands around the bar and pulled the bar upwards, straightening his posture and extending his arms out. Tristan looked at himself in the mirror, at his right shoulder where there was a burn scar imprinted into him in the shape of a wild beast, and then dropped the weights down. He repeated this five times.

Diana looked at him as he exercised and examined him. Tristan held a serious glance with darkened, exhausted eyes. He had slight bags. Her eyes then moved down to his physical form. Tristan had broad shoulders, defined triceps and broad forearms. He had a low body fat and trimmed figure at his torso, which left his abdomen muscles visible and defined his pectoral muscles of the chest. He also had a well-formed muscular back. Tristan lacked body hair on his chest and back, something which he was self-conscious of. He only had hairs on his arms and legs up to his thighs, and what hair he did have was golden blonde so that it blended with his natural skin tone. By his legs, Tristan had moderate calf muscles, thick thighs, and well-rounded, muscular glutes. Diana tilted her head as she looked at him with an extended gaze – not at his body, but at his face. She leaned against the door frame with a saddened face of her own. She then sighed and left the room.

Tristan finished his reps and looked over to Diana as she left. He picked up his water bottle at the bottom of the bench and took a drink of water. He then lightly panted and sat down as he recovered from his last set. He looked out to the door and then tilted his head down to the carpet floor. Once a minute had passed, he stood up and went to the barbell where he started to take apart the weights from the bar, removing the safety clip and then pulling each plate off. Once they were all off, Tristan picked up the forty-five pound bar and brought it over to a squat rack in the back of the room. He gently brought the barbell around the frame and then landed it on the handles. Once the barbell was secured, he went to his weights and loaded two forty-five pound plates on either side met with an additional twenty-five pounds to make the load two-hundred and seventy-five pounds.

Once the plates were on, Tristan secured them with the safety clips and then brought himself under the bar, securing the bar behind his neck and on his shoulders before grabbing the bar with his hands and picking up the entire bar. Tristan then took a step back and looked at himself in the mirror with the weight in hand. He then started to lower his legs, reaching down to the ground in the squat position until he was all the way down and the back of his thighs touched the back of his lower legs. He then brought himself up and went again, picking himself up with his thigh muscles. At the third rep, his legs began to shake. Tristan cut himself short and stopped, bringing the full weight up and stopping.

Tristan walked over to the bench and picked up his water bottle. He was panting hard. He looked at himself in the mirror with a glare and then away to the ground. He shook his head and then sat down where he rested for almost three-minutes, in motionless and audible silence. Once the three-minutes had passed, he walked over to the barbell and picked the weight up, feeling the coldness of the barbell on his shoulder. Tristan picked up the weight and then stepped back. He took a deep breath and brought himself up on the tips of his toes before bringing himself down.

With eyes on himself in the reflection of the mirror, Tristan squatted down and then brought himself up. He went again and felt his legs shaken. He brought himself up and then went down again, struggling to raise himself up at the third rep. Tristan gritted his teeth and groaned. He brought himself up and then dropped the barbell onto its handles.

"Dammit," Tristan muttered, turning around and walking towards the bench.

Tristan brought a fist down onto the cushion of the bench. He held a deep frown. He then let out a sigh and picked up his water bottle and phone. He took both into his room and then stepped across the gym to enter the bathroom. He turned on the showerhead and looked at himself in the mirror. He brought a hand to his right shoulder and touched gently with his fingers. He then moved his hand away and brought it to his left cheek, touching there as if there was something there to be touched.

The shower let off steam and covered the mirror in condensation. Tristan removed his sweatpants and went into the shower, washing himself from his sweat and cleaning his hair. He stayed in the shower for almost fifteen minutes, ten of those minutes were spent simply standing and letting the water fall down while he did nothing but stare at the tiles. Tristan finally pushed himself to turn off the water and stepped out. He grabbed his towel, covered himself, and took another towel to dry his face and then his torso. Once those were dry, he walked towards the door, turned on the fan to air out the room, and then stepped across to enter his bedroom.

Tristan closed the door behind him and sat down on his neatly made bed. He looked out the window across from him, through the blinds and to the grey clouds above. He then looked at his own dresser and at the picture of him and Diana, which was next to the most recent one of the couple that had raised him, Mr. and Mrs. Merrick, his parents as they were in autumn clothing, in front of the old family home. The man, Mr. Merrick, in the picture had a dark reddish-brown beard, was in his forties with crow's feet and balding head of hair underneath his knit cap. Mr. Merrick had a firm build and fair skin. He was with a woman who had a skin tone similar to Tristan's, but with light brown hair. She was slim, and her facial features were unlike Tristan's. Her face was skinnier and she had a taller nose and bonier cheeks. Her eyes were green though, while the man's eyes were blue. She was beautiful. Tristan's eyes then went to the wardrobe across from the foot of his bed, and then to the desk behind him.

Atop of Tristan's desk was a brown notebook with no markings on the front but made of leather. It was a thick book. In the center of Tristan's desk was his laptop, and above his desk was his own corkboard, with seldom posted. Diana had posted a picture of him with the catfish he caught in Henshaw Forest, but that was about it. Above Tristan's bed was the only memento in the room. It was, of course, Finn's longbow, mounted above carefully so that he didn't chip or cause damage to the polished yew wood.

Tristan looked around his room and then scratched his head. He was eerily alone. He then heard a knock on his door.

"Hello?" Tristan asked.

"Breakfast is ready," Mavis announced.

"Thank you," Tristan replied, going to his dresser and taking out some clothes.

Tristan exited his room, dressed for the day, and went downstairs to have breakfast alone. Once he was done, he took his plate into the kitchen, opened the trash bin under the sink, and saw that it was almost full. He scraped what was on his plate into the trash can and then set his plate onto the counter. Afterwards, he grabbed the black trash bin by the rims and pulled it out, setting it on the side. Tristan finished washing his plate and then loaded it onto the dishwasher. He then returned to the trash bag, picked it up, and went into the store room with it.

Instead of taking the elevator, Tristan went into the attic of the garage and with the trash bag around his back, went downstairs via the ladder to dump the trash in the trash can. He then climbed back upstairs and entered the store room, stopping in front of the shelves as he saw what was there. Charlemagne had various alcoholic beverages, cases of wine, hard liquor, beers, and other assortments of items stored in addition to cans of food, herbs, spices, bags of flour and rice, and other foods. Tristan looked at the cans of beer. His head then jerked at the sound of Mavis greeting Diana in the kitchen. He quickly left and didn't return.

Act 2, Scene 3

On the following Monday, Charlemagne woke up mid-morning at around nine o'clock. He opened his eyes and looked out to his thick red blinds that blocked out the daylight. He brought a hand to his forehead and then slowly awoke. Charlemagne showered and then dressed himself, coming downstairs to see it to be quiet. The children had left for school an hour ago and Mavis was vacuuming in the foyer.

The kitchen was neat and tidy. Charlemagne took a bowl from a cupboard and turned the kettle on. He prepared himself some oatmeal with some various berries he found in the refrigerator. He also made himself some coffee with some cream and sugar. He placed his breakfast on a tray and took it with him to the dinette, setting it down and dining on his own. He ate at his own pace, slowly, looking at his tablet while he ate and read the morning news.

Once he was done, like Tristan, he took his plates and cutlery and returned to the kitchen to scrape what was leftover into the trash bin and then wash his plates to bring them into the dishwasher. Afterwards, he left the kitchen and went to his study to check his emails, answer some, and stop every so occasion to think, bringing his hands to his chin or stroking his moustache.

At about noon, Mavis brought Charlemagne's lunch for him and set it down. She had made some chili for him. He ate and then brought the tray to the kitchen, washed the bowl and cutlery, and then brought it into the dishwasher. Charlemagne then returned to the lobby, but not his study, instead going upstairs to change into a business suit. He then went downstairs, went through the kitchen, and entered the living room so that he could enter his car.

Charlemagne drove out of the manor and made his way towards downtown Allabrese, parking his car at the back of the office, and then walking around and into the main lobby. He made his way towards the elevator and then went up to the top floor. Charlemagne walked past his secretary's desk but took notice that she was not present. He didn't make much of it and continued down the corridor to his office, looking into other offices and seeing them to be empty. Charlemagne came to his office, brought his hand to the doorknob, and then turned around to go the opposite direction.

"Perhaps there's a meeting I might have missed," Charlemagne whispered to himself.

Charlemagne passed the secretary desk and went into the meeting room. It was empty. Charlemagne then returned to the third-floor lobby and hit a button to go to the second-floor. The elevator went down and stopped. Charlemagne stepped out and looked ahead to the secretary desk, which only had one person at it.

The man greeted Charlemagne by waving his hand then continued to attend the receiving calls. Charlemagne wandered around the offices and saw there to be an unusual lack of people than their typically was. Once he was done looking around, he returned upstairs to go to his office and sit down at his desk.

Charlemagne tapped his fingers as though he was waiting for someone or something. He then turned around and looked out to the town. The skies continued to be grey without a raindrop in sight or even the sun for that matter. There were seldom people outside, walking the streets, and seemed unlively in comparison to last Friday night. He stayed in his office with a bored expression on his face for almost an hour, doing much as he was doing at the manor, but at the head office.

At a quarter to two o'clock, Charlemagne stood up and left. He went downstairs, walked to his car, and then drove out of the office and around town square to drive towards the hospital. Allabrese General was towards the outskirts of downtown, between the suburban homes and commercial center, on the same road that went north towards Linz Mountain and the abandoned mineshaft. The hospital was set on a hill with the emergency department facing the major street with a causeway for ambulances to pull in and out. At the same road, further ahead, was the entrance into the large parking lot. Charlemagne entered and looked for parking in the parking lot. He couldn't find any, so he left and parked his car on the curb about a block away on a residential street. He then walked towards the hospital, entering the parking lot and taking the side entrance.

The main lobby of the hospital was moderate for a Monday afternoon. There wasn't too much commotion, which allowed him to walk to reception and wait in line for only a couple minutes until he was seen by the admitting clerk.

"Good afternoon," Charlemagne greeted, pushing forward his driver's license, "I have an appointment with Dr. Moore."

"One moment," the admitting clerk typed at her computer. "I'm sorry, Mr. Cabernet, but Dr. Moore has cancelled all his appointments today and asked to re-schedule. There's been an intense overflow in the emergency department and due to short-staff, he's been pulled to help."

"Really? Charlemagne questioned. "Is it really that bad that they'd pull him?"

"ER has been busy since around six this morning," the admitting clerk explained. "Seems to be some sort of flu outbreak."

"Oh dear…" Charlemagne replied.

"If you'd really like to see him, you'll have to check in downstairs, but wait times aren't looking promising – they're about an hour or two more than expected…"

"No, I think that'll be alright," Charlemagne remarked. "My check-in with him can wait until next week when the good doctor is not busy."

"Would you like to reschedule then?"

"Yes," Charlemagne said.

Charlemagne set an appointment for next week and then made his way towards the exit. He stopped beforehand and turned around, walking down and taking a set of stairs to the basement level, following a red line that took him into the emergency department. Upon entering, he saw that it was packed with people, stretchers being driven along the corridors, necessitating him to move out of the way, and nurses and doctors rushing around. Charlemagne walked down a corridor and came to the triage area where there was indeed an overflow of people on stretchers, in pain, vomiting, and appearing sweaty and feverish. Charlemagne picked out a mask from a box and brought it over his face. He looked around for another moment before exiting.

Act 2, Scene 4

Diana and Tristan attended school and arrived at eight o'clock on the same Monday morning. Mavis had driven them and set them off at the front of the school. The couple walked down the main walkway and towards the steps inside. Upon entering, they noticed that the halls were quieter and that there were less people than usual.

Since the start of school in September, the couple had the habit of separating upon arriving to go to their lockers where Moira would typically met Diana at her locker and Tristan would spend his time alone re-arranging his books. Diana and Moira would talk and then go to the cafeteria to continue talking to each other, while Tristan would take his books and go upstairs to the library to do whatever he needed to do. The first bell, a warning bell, rang at twenty minutes past eight o'clock, setting people to go to their first classes, which started at twenty-five minutes past eight o'clock and didn't end until twenty minutes to ten. Almost seventy-five minutes for each class, four classes each day, the series of classes changing every other day for the eight courses they had.

Today, Tristan's first class was chemistry, which he had with Diana. Moira had her computer science course in the basement computer room. Chemistry was the only class the couple had together that she wasn't present. Afterwards, Tristan had physical education, which left him isolated with the others boys while Diana was at English with Moira. Between the two classes, they had a ten minute break, ten minutes for Tristan to get changed and then ten minutes after the class for him to change back into his regular clothes for history class, which all of them shared. Tristan simply sat alone while Moira and Diana stuck together. Every once in a while, Diana would leave Moira be and sit near Tristan, but these were rare occasions.

At twelve-thirty, the school broke for a seventy-five minute lunch break. Tristan stood up from his desk and proceeded to pack his things. Diana packed hers and then left with Moira, stopping at Tristan's desk beforehand.

"Do you want to spend the last thirty-minutes together and work on our lab for chemistry?" Diana questioned. "Moira has to work on a project for comp sci."

"No," Tristan replied in a distracted tone. "I mean, I can't. I have intramural basketball. We can work on it later tonight."

"Okay," Diana responded, taking a step back.

Diana left Tristan alone and left with Moira. Tristan stopped putting his things away and then looked to the side. He then continued after the short pause and left. Diana and Moira walked down the hall and went to Moira's locker. Moira arranged her books while Diana leaned on the locker next to hers. She held a sunken look.

"What's wrong?" Moira questioned as she put books away.

"Nothing, it's just Tristan as usual," Diana replied. "It's the same old with him ever since he got back from England. He's been distant like he was before we started to date, but even then, he would usually crack a joke or two, smile, and laugh. Now, he's just serious almost all the time."

"He'll grow out of it, hopefully," Moira responded, shrugging. "From what I remember you telling me, he had an intense trip being kidnapped by Charlemagne's Nazi son and held hostage by him. He's probably just traumatized from the wild experience… I would."

"He wasn't held hostage," Diana replied. "I mean, I'm not sure about it, but from what Tristan told me, he stayed with Charlemagne's son to keep an eye on him to make sure he didn't do anything crazy and bring him to Charles, but he got pulled into the madness and at the end, the kid died. Really, that's all Tristan said there was to it."

"Yeah, it sounds like he's traumatized," Moira responded, closing her locker and walking with Diana downstairs. "If you think he needs some sort psychiatric help, there's always the student councilor and the psychiatric office at the hospital."

"I don't think it's that serious… or even anything like that," Diana replied. "I don't know what it is."

"Have you tried asking him what's wrong?" Moira questioned.

"Yes, and he denies there's anything wrong," Diana said. "The last time I asked was mid-September, and he said he was only stressed about university and his course-load, which I'll admit, is reasonable. He's taking a heavy-load compared to us."

Diana and Moira arrived to the cafeteria and sat in line to have lunch. Moira was rummaging through a wallet.

"Dammit, I forgot my debit card," Moira cursed.

"Don't worry, I'll buy for you," Diana replied.

"You don't have to do that…" Moira responded.

"Dude, I work as a lifeguard and we get overpaid by a lot," Diana reasoned. "It's okay."

Diana and Moira got their food and then went around to find a seat, which wasn't hard given that the cafeteria was almost empty. Moira sipped one some soda and then brought her hand to her throat. She coughed into her arm.

"Sorry," Moira apologized. "I think I'm getting that nasty flu that's going around."

"Yikes," Diana replied. "Stay away from me. I don't want to get sick. If I get sick, Tristan will get sick, and he has it rough enough."

"You're so considerate," Moira responded in a dull tone. "No offense."

"You put up with hearing me complain about my relationship with Tristan non-stop every day," Diana replied. "You have nothing to apologize for…"

"Touché," Moira agreed, going back to eating her lunch.

"I'm scared Tristan might breakup with me," Diana expressed. "It gives me anxiety – the fear of him leaving me, but at the same time, it's my biggest fear, but also seems like an impossible fear. We live together. We see each other every morning of every day. Not to mention, we've become so intimate. We're a part of each other's lives, even if we've grown emotionally distant from each other… I'm scared he might leave me because of whatever might be bothering him, but I'm also scared that my own fears and anxieties will bring us apart. Oh, this is maddening."

"Girl, relax," Moira replied to her. "You need to stop worrying. If Tristan isn't doing anything to hurt himself or you, I don't see what there is to worry about. Just let time flow, enjoy your time with him, and like I said, maybe it'll pass."

"I hope you're right," Diana responded, holding her hands at her head and elbows at the table.

"Alternatively, if you think it's too much, maybe you should talk to him about taking a break or something," Moira suggested.

Diana glared at Moira.

"Separating myself from him is the last thing I want to do or that even sounds reasonable," Diana barked. "I'm not a coward – I'm just a coward to confront him about what I think are issues between us but am not sure if they really are. I would rather suffer with him than suffer without him. If there's anything I've acquired in my life, it's the iron skin to suffer."

Moira rolled her eyes.

"Sorry," Moira apologized, "then confront your fears and talk to him. Ask him what's wrong and demand to know. If he insists, then believe him and move on from these fears. He should trust you and not be keeping secrets. Remind him of that too. I wouldn't be with a man if I knew he was being dishonest with me... it's not good practice."

"You're right..." Diana replied in a cold tone. "You're right."

"Not to mention the fact that you keep your relationship a secret because of some schizophrenic fears that people are going to judge you about it," Moira remarked.

Diana looked at her.

"I don't care what anyone here thinks of me," Diana pointed out. "You're my only friend here and you know. It's Tristan who's afraid. Not that he should since people currently think he's gay thanks to Peter and Aaron, but apparently, in Tristan's weird logic, people thinking he's gay is better than thinking he's committing incest... not that it even is incest since we're not blood-related. It's an imperfect, perfect relationship right now. It has its drawbacks to make up for its privileges."

"Sounds balanced," Moira simply said, "as all things should be."

"The world is a naturally imbalanced place," Diana said.

Diana poked a French fry into some ketchup. She then ate it and looked at the rest of her food.

"Alright, well, I've lost my appetite with this dull talk," Diana said, sighing. "Sorry."

"No worries," Moira replied with her mouth full, finishing her food.

The girls picked up their lunch trays and then took them to the garbage bins. They then exited the cafeteria and looked to each other.

"I've got to go downstairs to work on my project. You can come if you want," Moira said. "I could use the company."

"I'll pass," Diana replied. "I need to do some homework."

"Suit yourself."

Tristan dribbled a basketball in the gym and then jumped to make a shot. The ball went into the basket, scoring for his team. Tristan ran his hand through his sweaty hair as he walked back to his side and then looked forward to some girls on the sidelines. He gazed at them for a moment before jerking his head towards the bleachers.

Diana was sat there, alone, looking down towards him. Tristan looked back to her. A whistle blew.

"Merrick, get back on-side!" a couch shouted.

Tristan moved his head and went back to the other side of the court. At the end of the game, he showered and quickly changed to meet Diana in the gym. He stopped in front of her, holding a hand to his gym bag and looking to her. They kept approximately a foot between each other.

"Hey," Tristan said, giving a light smile to her.

"Hi," Diana greeted in a shy tone, blushing.

Act 2, Scene 5

Charlemagne woke up on the following Monday, in bed, in the same position as yesterday morning when he woke, in his room with the thick curtains that blocked out the daylight. He brought his hands to his head and looked at the time on his alarm clock. It was currently seven o'clock in the morning. Charlemagne got out of bed, went to the washroom, showered, and then got dressed in his traditional suit. He then went downstairs and came into the dinette where the children were having breakfast.

The television was on in the living room, playing national news, while the kids did some homework together and ate. Charlemagne went into the kitchen where Mavis was washing some dishes.

"Oh, good morning, Mr. Cabernet," Mavis greeted. "Can I interest you in some French toast?"

"Oh, yes please, Mrs. Quinn," Charlemagne replied. "Let me just set a pot of coffee."

"There's a light bit of rain out right now," Mavis said. "I don't know if you noticed. I was thinking of calling the gardeners to trim the lawn, but I'm not sure now. They were busy yesterday apparently."

"Busy? Or unavailable?" Charlemagne questioned, putting some coffee beans into the coffee machine. "Apparently there's quite the epidemic at the moment."

"Probably unavailable," Mavis replied. "I'll give them a call when I return from taking the kids to school."

"Oh, don't worry about driving the children to school," Charlemagne said. "I believe it's my turn to drive them. I haven't driven them to school in quite a while and have to go in for a meeting at Cabernet Laboratories anyways."

"Are you sure?" Mavis questioned.

"Yes, I'm quite sure," Charlemagne insisted.

"Oh, thank you," Mavis replied. "I'll be able to start on some laundry then."

Charlemagne continued to arrange his breakfast before sitting down at the dining table in the dinette. The kids had left and the TV had been turned off. Charlemagne looked through his tablet as he ate and then stood up to return to the kitchen to return his plate.

At approximately eight o'clock, Charlemagne put on his overcoat and waited for the kids at the foyer. Each of them walked down the stairs and joined him to walk down to the car, which was parked at the front of the manor. The car was currently running so that Charlemagne could run the heater. The kids entered in the back of the car and Charlemagne came to the driver's seat. Once they were ready, he shifted gears and brought the parking brake down to drive down the hill of the manor and out the gate.

Charlemagne drove towards the hill that led up to the bridge across the river, and he came up and then around. Charlemagne saw ahead as he faced the narrow road that was bridge. There were parked police cars blocking the pathway at the end. Charlemagne drove forward and as he made his approach, some police officers moved themselves in front to signal him to stop. Charlemagne slowly made his stop and opened his door window.

An officer walked over and looked into the window. He was young, had a medium white skin tone, curled brown hair and brown eyes. Tristan poked his eyes out towards Charlemagne's window as the police officer arrived.

"Sorry, Mr. Cabernet, but I'm afraid I can't let you through," the man said. "The town is under quarantine due to an unknown, but life-threatening pathogen that has taken seven lives overnight. We've been instructed by the Government of Alberta, who have announced a quiet state of emergency, to prevent any travel in or out of the urban center."

"Good Lord," Charlemagne remarked, "seven lives? Are classes suspended then for the children?"

"A public notice went out that has canceled classes at Lord Phoenix Secondary School and Prince Albert Elementary School until further notice," the police officer informed.

"And how far does the quarantine zone extend? I have to attend a meeting at Cabernet Laboratories in Champions Plains that I cannot miss."

"The quarantine zone extends to the Carella, the south marshlands, and north mountains," the officer explained. "I'm sorry you had to hear this from us…"

"No, that's quite alright," Charlemagne replied, looking forward.

The police officer straightened up and was about to leave before looking to Charlemagne.

"Please, Mr. Cabernet," the officer added. "Your reputation is well-known, so please take this advice and don't attempt anything. Go home, stay there until the quarantine has been lifted, but please don't attempt to worsen the situation or place yourself, or loved ones, in danger."

Charlemagne looked at the police officer who took a step back. He then left. Charlemagne put the car in reverse, drove backwards by a bit, and then made a three-point turn to go the way he came.

"No school," Tristan said. "I'm cool with that."

Diana looked to Tristan. Charlemagne drove them back to the manor and then got out. They returned inside and removed their extra layers. Charlemagne looked to the kids.

"I'm going to make some phone calls to a lot of people," Charlemagne said. "I need to see if Mr. Huxley has fallen ill and take census of who is healthy and who is not. If you need me, I'll be in the study."

Charlemagne then quietly left while the kids returned upstairs.

• • •

Tristan sat in the living room with Diana, watching television in the late morning. Tristan kept his face turned outside to the window, looking over to the opposite side of the river. Diana had her feet up on the coffee table and her laptop on her lap. Tristan turned his face to the side as he heard the unforgettable sound of rotors flying from the distance. The noise got louder. Tristan looked back out of the window and up. He couldn't see anything.

At the left corner of his eye, however, he saw some trucks driving down alongside some armored personnel carriers with the Canadian maple leaf on the side. The convoy of vehicles parked in front of the manor. A group of uniformed personnel in digital woodland camouflage got out. They were not uniformed in tactical gear, but some of them had assault rifles.

The group of army personnel followed a leader, an elderly, slim man with fair skin and white hair. He wore a cap and had two gold leaves on each of his shoulders, designating his rank. The man walked up the steps and across the driveway of the manor. Tristan's face went pale and he stood up. The doorbell rang.

"Who is that?" Diana questioned.

"Not anything good," Tristan replied, looking out the window towards the front landing atop of the steps.

Diana looked with him, through the curtains. They then stepped back and looked at each other. Diana turned off the TV and closed her laptop, setting it on the couch. The couple then moved to step out and into the foyer when they saw Charlemagne on the opposite-side, walking over and towards the door. He did not look happy. He was accompanied by Mavis behind him.

Charlemagne went to the door and opened it. The kids went over and stood behind.

"Good evening, Mr. Cabernet," the high-ranking officer greeted. "My name is Major-General Howell, and as you know, the Province of Alberta has announced a silent state of emergency for the ongoing epidemic in the Nattau County. Now, the Canadian Forces Base of Edmonton has been mobilized to oversee and provide security for the quarantine to assist the Public Health Agency of Canada with the investigation into the deadly virus that has taken seven lives as of yet and infected upwards to seventy-percent of the town's population."

Major-General Howell took an envelope from a female next to him. Diana looked at her. She had short red-hair, similar to Moira and light skin. She also had green eyes. Major-General Howell presented the envelope to Charlemagne. Charlemagne took them with great care. It was sealed and unopened.

"I have orders from the province and federal government to temporarily seize your private property for operational and administrative use, and to set up a base of operations to oversee the quarantine from a safe distance," Howell explained. "Over the next twenty-four hours, my division of troops will be busy establishing primitive defenses in order to safely contain the epidemic from spreading."

Charlemagne looked at the envelope. He then gently opened it and pulled out the papers inside. The papers were not from the Government of Canada, but from the Global Defense Project and Committee of Concerned Nations, signed by the Canadian representative. Charlemagne read through them with difficulty, squinting and then putting them away.

"Well," Charlemagne said with a red face, "I believe I have no choice in this matter… You can set up your base of operations on the field around my manor…"

"I'm afraid we will need more than that," Major-General Howell remarked. "I will need a place for my officers to quarter for the night – I take it that a rich man like yourself will have no problem providing for them, feeding us, and the sort."

"That is outrageous," Charlemagne remarked. "You cannot simply occupy my home – there is plenty of space on this side of the river. You can establish camp near the airfield – it's a much more optimal location. There even used to be an air force base there!"

"Mr. Cabernet," Howell paused, "may I remind you that this is a state of emergency, and your refusal to comply will result in your arrest and forcible seizure of your property anyways."

Charlemagne looked at him and shook his head. He then stepped out of the way.

"You can use the ground floor," Charlemagne said with a sigh. "The foyer and ballroom are the most spacious, and there is additional space in the living room, dinette, and library if you need it, but please… let my children and I have the second-floor. These are where our bedrooms are…"

"Very well," Howell agreed. "I appreciate your cooperation, Mr. Cabernet."

A small group of officers entered into the foyer and set off, looking around.

"Mrs. Quinn, please see to their needs," Charlemagne said before turning to the kids. "Why don't you go upstairs?"

Tristan moved to the side and then went towards the staircase. Diana followed, looking behind and towards the woman with red hair. At her right breast was her surname, 'Hughes,' in capital letters. Diana stopped at the bottom of the staircase as the woman was with a colleague, reading some sort of document.

"Ms. Hughes," Diana shouted to her.

The woman looked over to her and tilted her head.

"Is Moira okay?" Diana questioned. "Your daughter? Your kids!"

Ms. Esther Hughes looked away and back at the paper before looking over to Diana.

"Moira will be fine," Ms. Hughes replied. "I've been told that everything will be okay."

"Come on, Diana," Tristan suggested, tugging her arm. "Let's get out of here."

"One second," Diana replied, turning back around and going into the living room.

Tristan followed. Diana picked up her laptop and then went back with Tristan upstairs. The couple walked down the hall and all the way to Diana's bedroom. They then entered and Diana went to her bed, sitting down and bringing her feet up. She opened her laptop and went back to what she was doing. Tristan paced the room with a degree of anxiety.

"What the heck…" Diana muttered. "I have no Internet."

Tristan looked at her. He took his phone out from his pocket and checked.

"Neither do I," Tristan replied. "I don't have any signal either."

• • •

Charlemagne returned to his study and picked up the phone. He dialed a number and then brought the phone to his ear.

"I need whatever on-duty of my protection squad to come to Cabernet Manor," Charlemagne stated. "I also need Mr. Heavner and Mr. Frank to contact me as soon as possible."

Charlemagne put the phone down and then went to the cabinet to the left of his desk. He crouched down and opened the cabinet doors at the bottom, revealing the safe inside. Charlemagne brought his hands to the top and pulled out a piece of wood that came down and hid the safe, leaving a small space for him to stack some small pieces of wood he had on the side on some nodes to create small shelves. Charlemagne then closed the doors and stood up. He went to a table on the right of his desk and picked up the quad-helicopter drone, placing it in a briefcase, and then closing it. He then picked it up and left the room, locking the door behind him, and then coming upstairs and going around to go his makeshift lab. The lab was still emptier than usual with a lack of equipment, projects, and specimens lying about. The room was clean, however, and the bed in the corner of the room was neatly made.

Once inside, Charlemagne set the briefcase down on the table in the middle of his room, opened it, and then took the drone out. He turned the drone on and walked out of the lab and onto the balcony between the lab and Tristan's bedroom. He held the drone over the balustrades and lifted it up. The drone's rotors began to rotate and it gently lifted upwards. Charlemagne left the drone hovering as he went inside and logged on to his computer.

Charlemagne took remote control of the drone and set it off to fly past the convoy of vehicles and head towards the town. The door behind Charlemagne opened. Charlemagne quickly looked over and saw that it was Tristan. Tristan looked around the room with a saddened face and then looked to Charlemagne.

"What are you doing?" Tristan questioned.

Charlemagne looked back at the computer screen.

"Someone has to find out what is going on," Charlemagne remarked. "I just received an affidavit from the Canadian Representative of the Committee of Concerned Nations stating that if I meddle in the epidemic in Allabrese, there will be consequences. Meanwhile, they send the Canadian Armed Forces to occupy my home. I don't believe it…"

"You're not going to do anything… stupid," Tristan then questioned.

"No, my dear boy," Charlemagne replied. "I won't. In fact, I can't quite recall when I have done anything deemed 'stupid.' I have only done what nobody else has dared to do."

Act 3, Scene 1

On the following Friday evening, Charlemagne looked out from the balcony and towards the sunset. He was dressed in his own Protection Squad tactical uniform in its greenish-grey digital camouflage. A minor wall had been built along the beaches of the east coast of the Nattau River out of concrete barriers. The Nattau Bridge had been reinforced and turned into a fortress. The telephone landline had been cut and only water and electricity were being supplied to the manor as these were independent sources anyways. Charlemagne returned inside his lab and looked at the mess atop of the table and he moved to the center of the room.

A large white sheet of paper had been planted and Charlemagne had drawn in marker a rough outline of the county with the Nattau River, the Carella River, the mansion, and included Highway 40, which was the freeway that ran from the east, over the Carella River, and through Champion Plains towards downtown Allabrese before crossing the Nattau River as the Nattau Bridge, and then going north. The cliffside road that went south, in front of the manor, was not a part of the freeway. Charlemagne had also drawn and labelled other parts of the county, including the creek behind the fields that belonged to him, which was the Scruton Creek. He also marked the forest between the Cabernet Field and the airfield as well as the mountain next to the airfield, which was known as Tolkien Mountain. Charlemagne drew the road that went west towards the airfield as well as the offshoot road that went off from Highway 40 and towards Allabrese Cemetery where Charlemagne fought Nero Medici almost two years ago.

On the east coast, Charlemagne drew two off-shoot roads that ran along the coast, one that went north towards the Nattau

Water Treatment Facility behind Linz Mountain, and the one to the south that went to the Allabrese Equestrian Center and the southern inhabitable marshlands where the Carella and Nattau River joined. In the north, next to Linz Mountain, Charlemagne had labelled Huntley Mountain, and next to this mountain was Graziani Mountain. Graziani Mountain loomed over Champion Plains. Both Champion Plains, and the plains to the west, beyond the smooth, but steep cliffs that downtown Allabrese sat atop of, known as St. Allan Plains.

Charlemagne had drawn a rough outline of Downtown Allabrese, marking locations in pen. He made a note of Central Park, the Civic Center, Curtia Dawson Memorial Library, Cabernet Head Office, Allabrese General, the Allabrese Art Gallery, Nattau County Police Department, and Lord Phoenix Secondary School. The high school was two blocks behind the civic center, to the right. Charlemagne also made a mark of Nattau County Recreational Center where Diana worked at as well as St. Allan's Church to the left. In the east of the town, Charlemagne marked where Prince Albert Elementary School was, and in the south, he marked where the popular Broiled Buffalo Pub was. Between Linz Mountain and Huntley Mountain, Charlemagne made a note of where the abandoned mineshafts were and extended the road to go towards the industrial mills where Diana had been kidnapped and taken to by the Medici gang on Charlemagne's 56th birthday. Towards the Carella, Charlemagne labeled where Cabernet Laboratories stood and drew offshoot roads with one going to the Medici Manor at the opposite-side of town.

Lacplesis and Brandan stood across from the table, dressed in their own tactical uniforms.

"I'm glad the two of you weren't inside the quarantine zone and instead at the observatory when the quarantine went into effect," Charlemagne said to the boys. "However, it means that the rest of the team, including Miklos and Lukas, are stuck inside and will need to be brought out if not already ill. I've been able to use Lucky as a delivery pigeon and have been receiving correspondences with him to rally his team for exfil tonight. In addition, Lucky has done some surveillance and deduced the primary patient care center to be situated at the children's school. Our mission tonight, gentleman, is to extract our comrades and get me some material to test and do some research on the supposed respiratory virus that has contaminated up to seventy-percent of the town's populace. I will need blood, an oropharyngeal swab, and if possible, a live specimen. I have a quarantine cell ready for use in case we are so fortunate. Any questions?"

• • •

Diana lay on her side at the side of her bed, looking out with a worried face. Tristan held on to her and had fallen asleep despite the light in the room from Diana's desk lamp. Diana turned around, coming onto her back and bringing her hands onto her abdomen. Tristan woke up and moved his arms, bringing them closer to him so they had some space. He continued to try to sleep as he kept his forehead against the side of her head.

"Why don't you read your book," Tristan suggested, keeping his eyes closed.

"I finished it already," Diana said in a saddened tone. "It was good. You can have it back if you want."

"Mm, just take it down to the library and add it to the collection," Tristan replied. "I don't keep books in my room. I just add them to the collection."

Tristan took a deep breath.

"If you want, you can read what I'm currently trying to read, even though I haven't really touched it in a while or finished it," Tristan said, keeping his eyes still closed. "It's *The Island of Doctor Moreau* by H.G. Wells."

"You *still* haven't finished that?" Diana questioned. "You've had it since the start of the month."

"I've been busy," Tristan replied. "It's in my backpack. I haven't even been able to read it in English because of that stupid book we have to read for Mrs. River's class."

"Okay," Diana responded. "Thanks, I'll take a look at it tomorrow. I appreciate you recommending me books to read. It's nice…"

Tristan didn't respond. Diana moved to her opposite-side so that she could look at Tristan. She brought a hand to his hair and began to groom it. The couple's foreheads touched and their noses were side to side. Tristan opened his eyes and looked at her. He had a sunken expression, but Diana appeared to be anxious, especially as her hands ran through Tristan's hair.

"What's wrong?" Tristan questioned.

"I'm worried about Moira," Diana replied. "They said seven people died last night because of the virus. What if Moira gets infected? What if they don't find a cure?"

"The people who died last night were most likely senior citizens with defunct immune systems," Tristan explained. "If what they've said about the virus so far is true, it was most likely death caused by a rapid onset of pneumonia, which led to them drowning because of the fluid in their lungs."

"Oh my God," Diana remarked, "that sounds awful."

"If it wasn't this virus, it would have been the flu," Tristan replied. "I know it's sad, but you're not doing yourself any favors by worrying about it. We're lucky we're across from the river and that none of us are displaying any sort of symptoms."

"Moira complained about having a sore throat the last time I saw her…" Diana said.

Tristan looked at her with an expression of disbelief.

"How has this happened to our town? We're such a small, sheltered community," Diana expressed. "I don't see how it's possible for a virus to just take us by surprise. There must be a patient zero, or something… someone who brought this upon us, but even then, how come we're the only town? Where did patient zero get his virus from?"

"Viruses can originate from a lot of places. For example, the H1N1 virus that caused a scare when we were eight was thought to come from pigs, hence the name Swine Flu. The same virus took millions of lives in 1920 when it was known as the Spanish Flu and also was thought to come from pigs. The same virus also clings to birds and causes Bird Flu. Albeit, all three of these examples come from different strains or variations of the H1N1. There are different variations of these just like there are different variations of the Rhinovirus (common cold) and influenza viruses that come around."

"Can they produce a vaccine?" Diana asked.

"A vaccine could be possible, if the strain of the virus infecting everyone is the same. The problem with vaccines is that they only cover the strains of the weakened virus they contain. For example, influenza vaccines are limited in their capacity because there are so many variations of the influenza virus (just like the common cold), which accounts for their low efficiency rates. However, with the epidemic that's going on, we might be lucky since it's more than likely one common strain that's going around. The downside is that it might take some time to formulate a vaccine. If I had to guess what Charlemagne was up to, it was probably to create a vaccine."

"How come you didn't take your vaccination shots when we went to France?" Diana then asked. "Don't you believe in vaccines?"

"I believe the process of vaccinations, where we introduce weakened or dead strains of viruses into our system, as an ingenious method. But I don't trust the people who make these vaccines, especially since they have a history and been known to carry carcinogenic materials such as thiomersal, an organic compound that contains mercury, which was quietly removed from most vaccines in the United States since 1999. You might ask, 'Why do they carry these chemicals?' and I don't think it's because pharmaceutical companies do it on purpose to harm people, but perhaps maybe because of their own ignorance if not laziness, or frugalness to not find a safer alternative. These are corporations after all," Tristan explained. "I'm only cautious and think other people should be more curious and cautious as well, in addition to being self-informed rather than trusting the media and big pharmaceutical companies who thrive on their own greed. Also, I never get sick, so as far as I'm going, I seem to being doing something right."

Tristan gave a proud smile. Diana rolled her eyes and dug her head into Tristan's chest. He brought his arms around her and then hugged her as the couple fell asleep together for a brief nap.

Act 3, Scene 2

Once the sun had set, Charlemagne and his elite guard set off on tying a rope down the baluster of the lab balcony and setting it down. Lacplesis and Elegast went down first before Charlemagne joined them and set foot onto the bushes below. The team paused there for a moment and then crossed the causeway to reach the opposite side and enter some bushes there before reaching the outer fence.

Lacplesis and Elegast helped Charlemagne climb up the fence, giving him a boost before Lacplesis helped Elegast over, followed by Lacplesis climbing over with Elegast bringing his hands through the grates of the fence. Once out of the manor perimeter, the team snuck along the sides of the fence and came to the cliffside street, crossing over with hunched backs to reach the other side and then go down a set of stairs to the beach below.

Charlemagne and the team walked down the beach for almost a kilometer to reach a small boathouse on the sides of the river. There, they entered and took out a long rowboat and some paddles, carrying the boat to the river, and setting it down. Charlemagne entered the boat first followed by the others, and they proceeded to row their way away from the shoreline, and forward.

Once the boat was a fair distance from the west coast of the river, they steered the boat south towards the Allabresian Trail and Allabrese Equestrian Center. The night was dark and the clouds persisted to block the moonlight from exposing their movements. The team steered the boat towards the peninsula that stuck out in front of the forest. They rowed with gentle strokes, avoiding excess movement to blend with the flow of the large river and sneak behind the hill ahead.

Once they were around, they intensified their rows to make their landing on the coarse beach and then get out into ankle-high waters. The team carried the boat with them as they exited the river and set it upon the grass. They then looked around and saw that it was quiet. The coldness of the night exposed only their cold breath as they breathed quiet breaths.

"Right," Charlemagne said, "we're in enemy territory now, lads. We have a ways to go to reach town on foot, so let's not waste any time. I'll lead the way."

Charlemagne stood up and proceeded to head down a field to reach the road that went to the Allabrese Equestrian Center and marshlands at the southernmost part of the county. There were no vehicles travelling along the road, which allowed them to move forward by following the roads.

Within a short distance, the team could see the Nattau Bridge and small outpost built by the army with bright lights around the perimeter of the horrendous cubical structure. The team stopped to examine the structure with binoculars. At the current hour, almost midnight, the team could not see any soldiers outside, on the rooftops, or anywhere except on the bridge to provide controlled access where the police were.

"The government worked fast to set up a checkpoint and minor perimeter," Charlemagne noted. "However, it appears that their caution levels are low."

Charlemagne put his binoculars away and then saw ahead at the site of a police car belonging to the Nattau County Police Department.

"Out of the way," Charlemagne warned the boys, going towards a fence to hop into some bushes.

The team hid in the bushes and watched as the patrol car passed by them. Charlemagne followed the car with his eyes and saw it head south. He then stood up and climbed over the fence again.

"We'll need to be cautious even if they're not," Charlemagne suggested. "From here until we reach the outskirts of the town, we'll travel from farm to farm."

"Yes, sir," Lacplesis confirmed.

The team moved forward, down the road and towards the fence of a farm ahead. They hopped over and then proceeded to blend into the tall crops to make headway towards the town. Once through the field, they used what was around them, tractors, bales of hay, the exterior walls of barns and farmhouses, to continue onwards.

Charlemagne and the team soon reached the main freeway where they travelled along the sides, along a ditch in the earth to reach a tube that ran under the road and came to the other side. They then continued along a similar ditch on the opposite-end, and when that came to an end, they travelled up and proceeded into the farm on their left.

The team travelled along the rest of St. Allan's Plains through the interconnected farms, spreading out and away from the freeway to reach the cliffs that downtown Allabrese sat atop of. Once they had reached the cliffs, they moved back towards the freeway and stopped by some bushes.

A patrol car drove upwards and into the town. Charlemagne looked up and could not see what would be coming towards them from down the hill. He also looked at either side of the cliffside and saw that although smooth, it was too steep of a hill to climb, which meant their only option was the sidewalk of the road. The road going up the hill was approximately fifty meters in length.

Charlemagne took off his backpack and opened it. Inside, he had the quad-drone, a tablet, and a remote controller. He took out the drone and turned it on, letting go and letting it rise up. He then squatted down with the tablet on the floor, receiving a live feed from the drone's camera and the RC remote in his hands. Charlemagne had the drone go up higher so that he could see oncoming traffic headed downhill. The feed showed the road that went towards the city center, the houses on the outskirts of the town, and the lack of traffic and general motion around.

Lord Phoenix Secondary School was not too far and visible from the camera's range with its large field towards the right. Charlemagne could also see the various vehicles parked along the sides of the road that bordered the school property, which included various trucks including military vehicles. From the top of the hill, the school was approximately three blocks away. The school property was approximately two blocks in length.

Charlemagne did a sweep around them and did not see any incoming traffic. He kept the drone in the air but put the tablet away and grabbed his backpack.

"Let's move," Charlemagne said to the others, leading forward.

The team moved quickly up the hill and to the top, entering the suburban neighborhoods on the west side of Allabrese. The drone followed them as they crossed the street and continued forward for two streets, stopping inside the front garden of a house and the bushes there. Charlemagne took his tablet out to set the drone to stay close to them.

Another patrol car passed the road and went west. The team moved out of the bushes and travelled down the street of the neighborhood they were in to reach the chain-link fence that led into the field behind the high school. Charlemagne diverted the team through a path that led to a road on the left-side of the school from where they were and to get them away from the military vehicles.

Some bushes on the right-side blocked their view of the field and gave them cover to rush towards the road that faced the front of the school. The team stopped at the corner of the crosswalk and sidewalk of the kid's high school. The lights outside of the school were bright and there was military personnel at the front entrance of the school providing controlled access into the building with gas masks equipped and assault rifles in hand. Some of the personnel had German Shepherds and were patrolling around the perimeter of the school. A wooden sign had been built on the paddock of dirt in the front of the school, but at the angle the team was at, they couldn't see what it read. Charlemagne could see two men in white hazmat suits in front of the school, with their masks off and having a cigarette. Once they finished smoking, they put their masks on and then returned inside. The military personnel didn't bat an eye at them.

"I'll need a hazmat suit to enter, as a disguise and for my own safety," Charlemagne noted. "I imagine the only way to get one would be from the outside, but where?"

Charlemagne led the team back and towards the opposite-corner of the gymnasium annex. The gym had a set of one-way doors with no handles on the exterior side. Further ahead, there were doors that went into the rear hallways. Charlemagne looked around and then towards the trucks. He led the team towards the trucks and they helped him unlock the rear doors so they could climb inside and look at what was set around.

Within a few minutes, they managed to find Charlemagne a white hazmat suit to don. Charlemagne put on the suit, removing his smock and placing it in his backpack, but keeping the rest of his uniform underneath. He gave his backpack to Lacplesis and then put on the gas mask that went with the suit. Charlemagne then looked at Lacplesis and Brandan.

"I should be okay from here on out," Charlemagne told them. "Miklos and the others will be waiting for you in town behind the cinema. According to him, there is a curfew that forbids citizens from being out after 10pm, so he'll be in hiding with the others. Go and find him and I'll work on what I need to work on here."

"Yes, Mr. Cabernet," Lacplesis replied. "We'll be in contact with you."

"Good," Charlemagne responded. "Now go."

Lacplesis and Brandan left Charlemagne on his own. The drone followed them as they left while Charlemagne stayed in the truck for another moment. He picked up his backpack left on the ground and then got out. He rushed forward and came to the bushes that led to the path, which led to the street adjacent to the school. Charlemagne placed his backpack in the bushes, took out a small black messenger bag, placed the strap on his shoulder, and then walked back towards the school.

Charlemagne walked down the sidewalk in front of the school, keeping calm, especially as he came to the steps up to the path headed to the main entrance. The military personnel looked at him as he walked towards them. Charlemagne continued forward with confidence. The soldiers moved to the side as he was about to head past them. They reached out and brought their hands to the door. Charlemagne stopped in front of them with a bit of surprise. A drop of sweat fell down the side of his head. The soldiers opened the door for him. Charlemagne nodded to them.

"Thank you," Charlemagne responded in an urbanized North American accent.

Charlemagne entered the school and then looked behind him as the doors closed. The lights of the school were dim. Ahead of him was a wooden frame covered in white plastic sheets on the side and with a door in the middle. A sign on the door read, 'Decontamination Zone' at the top and at the bottom, 'Access Control Point.' Charlemagne went towards the door and entered the decontamination zone.

A variety of hoses with wands were set down for off-going personnel. The floor of the room was wet. The space set for authorities to decontaminate themselves was small and there were only two hoses coming from the bathroom to the side. Charlemagne walked across the room and entered the other side. He entered a small antechamber with another door that finally led into the school corridor. Charlemagne continued forward and proceeded to walk down the halls of the school, reaching the end and turning to the left to go towards the gym. He could hear the moans and groans of people echo as he got closer. In the immediate corridor outside of the gym, there were various crates and carts with medical supplies.

Charlemagne pushed against the gym doors and entered into a crowded space with various stretchers parked around with people atop of them. He looked around with sadness and could see various personnel attending to his townspeople, offering plastic cups of water, ice packets, and wet towels on the foreheads of patients. Charlemagne stood where he was as he looked around with hesitation and horror.

Immediately, Charlemagne could recognize at least two people who worked at the office, some scientists, and even some parents from the parent-teacher conference he attended last month as well as some teachers. In total, there were less than one-hundred people crammed in the room and about ten personnel attending to these people. Charlemagne took a step forward and began to walk through the narrow aisles as he observed the people in their feverish pains. Some people were crying out in the corners of the room in agony. Their faces were wet with sweat and hair amess. Their eyes were red and by their words, Charlemagne could notice that some of them were having delusions, persisting that they were with the devil, while others pleaded for their lives and shouted out that they wished to live.

Charlemagne had walked to the opposite-corner of the gym from where he had entered. He looked forward and began to recognize someone with red hair, coughing into a towel. Charlemagne made his way towards him and took off his messenger bag to set it against the stretcher the man was on. Charlemagne looked at the red-headed man in blue pajama bottoms.

"You…" Charlemagne said in a neutral and cold tone. "What are you doing here?"

Bauer looked at Charlemagne through the suit. He relaxed his body.

"I couldn't stay," Bauer simply said in a wheezy tone. "They- they knew I was there and I had to leave… for the sake of yourself and your children. I couldn't put them in harm's way. I came to the town and came down with this horrible illness… police found me on the streets and I was brought here when the hospital ran out of space…"

Charlemagne brought his gloved hand to his forehead. Bauer was hot. His skin was wet. His eyes were red and pupils-dilated. Bauer coughed into his towel again, lurching forward as if he was sitting up, and then lied back down when it was over.

"Let me get a swab from you," Charlemagne requested. "I need a specimen of this virus so that I can create a vaccination of some kind…"

"If you can get me out of here, Mr. Cabernet, you can run as many tests as you see fit," Bauer responded, grabbing Charlemagne's suit. "I cannot stay here. They are close…"

"Who are?" Charlemagne questioned.

"Zimmerman and his men…" Bauer responded. "Do you not notice where all this equipment is coming from? The boxes either state 'Next-Gen Pharmaceuticals,' or 'Fletcher Accessories,' both of which are a subsidiary of Zimmerman Corporation. I have been in this room for the past twenty-four hours, and all these government doctors have done is monitor and control people's fevers and pains. None of them have asked for saliva, or even blood or run any tests on any of us… There is no effort to cure anyone or do any sort of research, which tells me that there is something more going on here than we know about…"

"I will figure out what is wrong, but I need test samples," Charlemagne explained.

"I will make you a deal then, Mr. Cabernet," Bauer replied. "If you help me escape this room and come to your home, you can run your tests *and* I will help you when the time comes to fight Zimmerman Corporation…" he paused to cough, "and that time might be closer than both of us estimate…" he coughed again. "I cannot escape to Switzerland without your help, so I will not escape at all, and instead stay and fight."

Charlemagne looked at him.

"What if the virus is contagious? I can't bring you out of the quarantine zone," Charlemagne explained. "I'll be placing others at risk…"

"Human-to-human transmission has not been proven in the last twenty-four hours…" Bauer explained, "you will need to make your decision based on that fact and trust me."

Charlemagne looked at Bauer. He straightened up and then looked around the room.

"I'll be right back…" Charlemagne said, walking towards the exit, leaving and stopping at the carts and crates in the outside corridor. He searched around and saw there to be various pharmaceutical drugs in small jars that varied in their small sizes. He grabbed a vial that was labeled 'Ketamine' and then closed the drawer.

"Perfect," Charlemagne remarked. "A little Special K should do the job nicely."

Charlemagne turned around and looked at the various containers of equipment behind him. He searched for an intravenous syringe as well as a nasal cannula kit. Once he found both, Charlemagne extracted contents of the vial into the syringe and then walked back towards Bauer as he was coughing.

"Do I have your promise that you will assist me? No matter what I ask or what must be done?" Charlemagne questioned.

"Of course," Bauer replied.

Charlemagne took the syringe and placed it into the intravenous needle in Bauer's arm. He then pressed down and gave Bauer the medication. Once he was done, he placed the syringe onto a tray and then looked to Bauer.

"What have you given me?" Bauer questioned.

"Don't worry," Charlemagne answered. "I know what I'm doing."

Bauer looked to him and then tilted his head to the side. He had fallen unconscious with his eyes open. Charlemagne checked his pulse and then assessed his airway. He then gently closed Bauer's eyes and looked to the doctors in the room. Charlemagne came down to his knee and began to fiddle with the oxygen tank below. He connected the tube from the tank and then brought the nasal cannula up and into the nose of Bauer so he could breathe easier. Charlemagne took some blankets and rolled them up, propping Bauer up so that his head was better supported. Once that was set, Charlemagne took a single blanket and placed it over him as if he had died.

"Time of death, 2225 hours," Charlemagne announced to the room in his fake accent.

"Take the stretcher to the cafeteria," a doctor stated. "We'll process in the morning."

Others in the room looked to him, including doctors. The patients seemed mortified. Charlemagne took the brakes off the stretcher and pulled the bed out, pushing it down the aisle for a short distance so he could get around and push the stretcher down the corridor and then out of the room. Charlemagne took him down the hall, picked up a portable vitals monitor pack, walked down the main corridor, and towards the cafeteria corridor. He then stopped and proceeded to monitor Bauer for the next hour or so.

Act 3, Scene 3

Charlemagne brought a syringe to Bauer's intravenous needle in his right arm and injected him with another substance. He then looked at the vitals monitor at the end of the bed and saw Bauer's heartbeat rise to ninety beats per minute. Various wires were plugged into the monitor, including electrocardiogram nodes on his chest, a pulse oximeter probe on his index finger, and the nasal cannula that wrapped around to the oxygen tank attached to the stretcher. Bauer began to awaken and move about in the bed. Charlemagne stood up and looked at him.

"Take it easy, you're starting to come out of anesthesia, so it's typical to feel a little groggy," Charlemagne warned. "I'm sorry, but the only way I saw getting you out of there, or really, any one in that room, was if you were, or at least appeared to be, dead."

"No," Bauer replied, bringing a hand to his head, "it was a good idea... How long has it been?"

"Less than an hour," Charlemagne replied. "I gave a small dose, but you'll feel the effects of the drugs for the next twenty-four hours in the least... I just gave you a shot of Ritalin, which should make you a bit more focused as we make our escape."

"Where are my things?" Bauer questioned. "The paramedics said that my things would be near..."

Bauer attempted to get out of the bed. He removed all the tubes, wires, and nodes attached to him and pivoted himself out of bed. Maximillian Bauer was a fit man with a lean build, muscular and his body with a moderate amount of body hair. He had a rugged, mature appearance of an adult male at his age, early forties or late thirties He only wore the pajama bottoms and nothing more.

"Are these them?" Charlemagne questioned, picking up a white plastic bag beneath the stretcher. "Here's another."

"Thank you," Bauer said, taking them. "I just need to get changed."

Charlemagne gave Bauer some privacy to change into the clothing he was wearing. Once he was done, he walked past Charlemagne. Bauer wore the same trench coat and hat from the night the two met.

"What is the escape plan?" Bauer questioned.

"I have a team of my best men waiting for me in town at the local cinema," Charlemagne replied. "The plan is to return to the manor undetected. I will tell them to meet us behind the school and we'll proceed from there together."

"Understood," Bauer replied.

Charlemagne led Bauer towards an exit. He brought his hands to the push bar and pushed against it, opening the door. Bauer immediately stepped forward and in front of Charlemagne, bringing a hand in front of him. The two cringed as they heard an alarm set off.

"There's a device attached to this door, most likely to detect movement," Bauer said to Charlemagne.

The alarm was followed by the ringing of a different alarm from the front and the shouts of some military personnel.

"We need to leave," Charlemagne said, removing the hood of his hazmat suit so he could see better. "We need to cross this field."

Charlemagne and Bauer exited the school and came to the patio behind. The two stopped as they looked at either side and saw the soldiers with their weapons pointed towards them.

"Don't move!" a soldier yelled. "We have authority to open fire! Stand down!"

Charlemagne and Bauer looked to the soldiers on the left. There were two of them with assault rifles pointed forward, same as on the right, but with canines barking towards them. Each of them looked at either side.

"Charlie-Seven, this is Charlie-Actual," Charlemagne communicated over the radio. "We're in a tight spot... I need you to come to my location ASAP."

"Copy that, Charlie-Actual," Lacplesis responded. "We're enroute."

"What is the plan?" Bauer questioned as the soldiers began to get close to them.

"To wait for help," Charlemagne replied. "There's too many of them."

"That is not a plan," Bauer cursed, bringing his arms to the back of his head and getting on his knees.

Charlemagne mimicked. Bauer kept his eyes on one of the soldiers in particular.

"Do you see this young one? He is nervous," Bauer stated. "Perhaps too nervous."

Charlemagne looked to the left and saw the soldier Bauer was speaking off. He was shaking.

"Let them come close," Bauer simply said. "I have an idea."

"It best be good."

"Trust me."

The soldiers stood two meters from them at a safe distance. Bauer kept his eyes on the youngest soldier who kept his assault rifles pointed. Suddenly, Bauer raised his arm towards him.

"Get down!" Bauer shouted to Charlemagne.

Charlemagne ducked down to the ground. The nervous soldier shot his rifle up into the air in a panic, startling the others to duck, especially with Bauer's words. The dogs squealed and ran away as the altercation took off. Bauer lunged forward and tackled the young soldier to the ground, grabbing the rifle of the other soldier by the barrel and elbowing him before he could react and bringing him to the ground before picking him up. Bauer span the man once and then threw the body of the soldier towards the others, causing them to flinch and delay their reaction further.

Bauer ran towards them and kicked one of them to the ground before engaging the other as he attempted to strike at him. Bauer blocked and countered, bringing the soldier to the ground and breaking his arm in the process. The soldier shouted. Bauer picked up a rifle and hit the other in the face, knocking him out. He then went over to Charlemagne, helping him up so they could run across the field as the alarms continued to trigger.

"Charlie-Actual, this is Charlie-Seven," Lacplesis reported. "Police are on high alert and are enroute to your location – I suggest we regroup at an alternative rendezvous point."

"Copy that," Charlemagne replied. "Stand-by for location."

Charlemagne continued to run and reached the end of the fence. The pair then ran down the sidewalk with Charlemagne stopping by the bush to pick up his backpack and then continue down the street. Charlemagne and Bauer stopped at the sight and sound of flashing sirens. Charlemagne could also hear gunfire in the distance, most likely coming from behind.

"This way!" Charlemagne recommended, redirecting them towards one of the houses on their left.

Charlemagne and Bauer ran towards the house and proceeded to climb over the fence and into the backyard of the house. From there, they continued through the neighborhood from house to house until they reached the end and Charlemagne picked up his radio. The sound of gunfire in the distance persisted.

"Charlie-Seven," Charlemagne said with a pant, "this is Charlie-Actual. Have yourself and the others brought to the downhill slope west."

"Negative…" Lacplesis responded.

Charlemagne could hear some gunfire on the other end as well as some sirens.

"We're under fire in town square," Lacplesis added.

"Damn…" Charlemagne muttered. "We need to go back to them. I can't let them be captured or killed."

"Standby, Charlie-Seven," Charlemagne answered over the radio. "I'm on my way to assist."

No immediate response came through.

"Charlie-Actual, this is Charlie-One," Miklos said over the radio. "Do not. I repeat, do not come towards town square. Have yourself return to the exfil site. Myself and the others can handle ourselves."

"I won't let you all die!" Charlemagne argued.

"We won't," Miklos simply responded.

"Hey," Bauer said to Charlemagne, nudging him.

Charlemagne looked to him and then towards the house they were at. The lights had turned on inside the house and Charlemagne could hear the mutter of some words.

"We can't stay here," Charlemagne said, moving towards fence.

Charlemagne and Bauer hopped over the fence and entered the house behind the previous home. They then went through the gate of this house and towards the front to cross the street and make their way across. The pair came into the next backyard, which was unideal due to a large hedge that blocked the fence into the yard behind. Instead, they went to the next house, moving away from the freeway, and then came over to house behind. Charlemagne and Bauer exited and reached the front of this house, stopping at the corner of a fence to look ahead and towards the top of the slope.

Two police cruisers were parked with their sides exposed, blocking the road. The police car sirens were flashing red and blue, and there were approximately four police officers in total.

"Our exit is past those men," Charlemagne said.

"I can easily do that with the one magazine I have," Bauer stated, checking the assault rifle he has, "but I have a feeling like you won't like that."

"No," Charlemagne responded. "I have had a lot of run ins with this local police, and the thought of harming or putting at harm's risk to any of them has never crossed my mind."

"I thought so," Bauer replied. "What is your alternative plan?"

"I need a better view... I need to see who these men are being led by, but the lights are blinding me."

"We'll need to cross eventually," Bauer stated. "Let's take a step back, move further down the street then cross, and then move back down towards the house at the corner."

"Good idea," Charlemagne replied.

Charlemagne and Bauer moved back into the backyard of the house they were at and proceeded to move south for three houses before they came to the front yard again and crossed over to the house at the other side. From there, they came into the backyard of this house and crossed all the way to the end so that they were at the house right next to the freeway and police blockade. The two hopped down from the fence and looked around this yard.

Charlemagne saw that this yard had a separate garage annex from the house with the end pointed towards the freeway. He went to the door of the garage and took off his backpack to rummage through.

"One of my kids gifted me a nifty little tool for my last birthday," Charlemagne quietly said, taking out a metal case with various pointed tools. "She said she thought of me when she saw it."

Charlemagne proceeded to attempt to unlock the door into the garage, taking about a minute to do it successfully so they could hide inside. Charlemagne walked to the end of the garage holding the handle of his backpack and looked out the window outside. He looked forward and saw Captain Macmillan, Moira's father with these men.

"Perfect," Charlemagne said under his breath. "Mr. Macmillan is a reasonable man. I'll speak with him and he'll help us."

"He looks to be nervous," Bauer cautioned. "Are you sure?"

"Macmillan isn't one to be nervous over conflict," Charlemagne responded.

"He isn't nervous about the conflict ongoing right now, but perhaps, about the epidemic…" Bauer clarified. "He seems like the type that would do anything to prevent the spread of an epidemic to safeguard other people."

"We're not harboring the virus," Charlemagne replied. "Human-to-human transmission has not been proven as of yet…"

"He won't understand that."

"He'll see to reason," Charlemagne insisted, standing up. "I'm going to speak with him, father to father."

Charlemagne exited the garage and went outside. Immediately upon stepping outside, Charlemagne heard and saw a glimpse of an armored car pass by the blockade and stop. Charlemagne went to the fence and kept down. He listened to the sound of footsteps walking away from the blockade. Macmillan went out of sight and towards the front of the house.

Charlemagne came around the back of the house and kept to the sides of the exterior of the home.

"I understand that you are in charge for the night, captain," an officer spoke to Macmillan. "Do you care to explain to me why you refuse to have your men search the surrounding homes for the suspects?"

"I'm sorry, but that is a violation of the privacy of our residents," Macmillan replied, "and legally, a violation of their charter of rights and freedoms."

"We are in a state of emergency, captain," the officer explained. "You do not need a warrant to search homes – all civil liberties have been suspended in this county until further notice. If you cannot do your job, then we will have to remove you from your position."

Charlemagne peaked around and saw Macmillan speaking with the officer. Macmillan had his face turned towards Charlemagne with the back of the officer to him and face to Macmillan.

"Am I understood?" the officer questioned.

"Yes," Macmillan replied.

"Good."

The officer walked off. Charlemagne leaned forward from where he was hidden. Macmillan saw him. He took a step back and turned away. Charlemagne stepped away and waited. The armored personnel carrier left and Charlemagne heard some encroaching steps his way. Macmillan appeared around the corner and crossed his arms.

"What are you doing here?" Macmillan questioned. "Please don't tell me that you have something to do with the manhunt."

"They're not researching the virus, Eugene," Charlemagne instead said. "All they're doing is comforting the ill, but not running any sort of tests or making any sort of effort to find a vaccine. There's something more going on here than is being let on."

"What do you mean?"

"I'm not sure what it is that is really going on," Charlemagne clarified, "but what I do know is that our town has come under occupation for mysterious circumstances due to this mysterious illness, and I will not let them bring harm to our people. I've smuggled a colleague of mine who I found at the high school and intend to run tests on him to develop a vaccine if possible, and learn more of this illness."

"Charles, this sounds crazy," Macmillan replied. "I can't help you. I shouldn't even let you leave with this ill person."

"We cannot trust these government officials," Charlemagne insisted. "It is in our hands to safeguard our children's health and safety. What will you do if Moira or Jock come under? Rosa or Elliot? The state will not ensure their survival, but instead accommodate them so that they can have a comfortable death."

"What do you want from me then?" Macmillan questioned.

"I need you to suspend the blockade, even if it is for a minute or two, so I can escape and return to my manor. I already have arrangements made to cross the river, but just need to get away from the plateau."

"I can't simply tell my men to leave," Macmillan replied. "At least not without a good reason."

"Leave it to me," Charlemagne stated. "I'll provide a good reason, and you will see them off. Okay?"

"Fine," Macmillan responded, "but only because this is a dire situation, Charles. I trust you more than I trust these strangers."

"Thank you."

Charlemagne rushed away and back into the backyard of the house they were at. He went into the garage annex and met with

Bauer. Charlemagne ducked down. He rolled up his sleeves and proceeded to rummage through his backpack to take out his tablet.

"Charlie-One, I've reached the new rendezvous point, but police have set up a blockade," Charlemagne announced. "What is your situation?"

No response came. Charlemagne turned on the tablet to find out for himself. The tablet provided a live feed of the chaos in town square. The Protection Squad was not fighting the police, but instead the army who had driven into the city center with their armored vehicles and blocked the two intersections headed south. The team was held up at the library based on Charlemagne's analysis of the area. Miklos, Lukas, Holger and Hardrada were there with Lacplesis and Elegast, hiding behind the pillars in front of the library entrance. All of them were armed with their assault rifles and in uniform.

"Charlie-One, you don't have enough ammunition to outlast a fight with them," Charlemagne warned. "Retreat."

"We're pinned down," Miklos stated. "We won't surrender."

"You won't need to surrender if you retreat," Charlemagne repeated. "You... you need some sort of distraction... An explosion."

Charlemagne paused for a moment and took the RC remote into his hands. He drove the drone out of the way and towards the city center to look around. He then looked down towards the armored personnel vehicles and flew down towards them. Charlemagne hid the drone beneath them and gave himself a light to look at the mechanics of the car. Charlemagne fiddled with the drone and found a tank. He got the drone to drill a hole into the tank, spilling a brown liquid down. He then moved the drone over to the next vehicle to do the same before coming out on the side opposite from where the troops were taking cover from. He proceeded to fly the drone over to the next blockade at the other intersection to repeat this.

Once Charlemagne was done, he flew the drone back towards the other side to see that a large puddle of gasoline was forming. The soldiers had barely reacted to the buildup of gasoline. Charlemagne brought the drone towards the pavement and had the gasoline ignite with the flamethrower the drone had. The fire quickly spread, going under the APCs and catching them on fire as well as the feet of the soldiers who quickly panicked and ran off as they caught on fire. The fire caught on to the other puddle and both vehicles were instantly in flames. Charlemagne drove the drone to the other intersection to repeat this, and just as he set the second fire, the armored cars exploded.

Gunfire stopped between the two parties. Charlemagne flew the drone towards the team as they made their escape and returned the quad drone to autopilot as he turned off the tablet and stood up. Charlemagne heard the second set of explosions and saw a minor fireball rise up in the distance. He looked out of the window and saw Macmillan ordering his men to go investigate. They got into their cruiser and drove off. Macmillan then looked over to the garage.

Charlemagne and Bauer exited and confronted Macmillan. Macmillan looked to Charlemagne.

"Please, find a cure, Charles so that this terrible chapter in our town's history can come to an end… for the sake of our children foremost…" Macmillan pleaded.

Charlemagne nodded to him and then set off downhill with Bauer. The two didn't look back and once they came to the bottom of the hill, they entered the ditch on the side of the freeway and continued to make their escape back to the beach.

• • •

Charlemagne helped Bauer out of the row boat once they reached the west shore of the Nattau River. Bauer had grown weak from the long walk they made from downtown Allabrese to the southeast coast. Charlemagne helped him walk and reach the tops of the cliffs where the manor was. He noticed that the area around the mansion was quiet and there was a lack of presence of the army, especially in the fields behind. They had all vacated.

"I- I can barely move," Bauer exclaimed with weak breaths. "What a damn illness this is."

"Take it easy," Charlemagne replied. "I have you, friend. We're almost home."

Charlemagne helped Bauer cross the street and they came to the gates of the mansion. Charlemagne pushed through and went up the steps to the top of the hill, and then up the steps of the front of the house. Luckily, the front door was unlocked, or left unlocked, so they could enter the foyer. The foyer had been cleared from all the equipment set up earlier. Charlemagne looked around.

Bauer collapsed onto the ground and fell unconscious. Charlemagne immediately attended to him, checking his airway and breathing before proceeding to perform CPR as he was unresponsive. Within less than a minute, Bauer let out of a cough and Charlemagne fell backwards. He took a deep breath, wiped the sweat on his forehead, and then took a deep sigh.

Act 3, Scene 4

The next day, Charlemagne sat in a dark room, looking to Bauer in a quarantine cell as he rested on a bed in a pair of pajama trousers borrowed from Tristan, which he never wore anyways. Like in the high school, Charlemagne had a set of electrocardiogram nodes set on Bauer's chest, an oximeter probe at his finger, and a face mask providing oxygen to him. In comparison to when he had brought him to the manor, Bauer looked healthier. His skin had returned to its light color, his body temperature had returned to normal levels, and he displayed no other symptoms. A total of twelve days had passed.

Charlemagne sat in front of a large computer monitor, which had two additional, smaller monitors on either side. The larger monitor displayed a live feed of an electron microscope as Charlemagne looked at a slide of Bauer's blood. The monitors on the left displayed a live feed of the security cameras around the perimeter of the manor. It was dark out. Charlemagne returned to examining the blood. He was dressed in his traditional suit, but without the blazer. The sleeves of his shirt were rolled up.

The depictions of the biconcave erythrocytes, or red blood cells under the high-powered microscope were incredibly in depth, about the size of cantaloupes on the monitor. The smaller plate-shaped objects were platelets and the larger spherical-shaped objects with an uneven surface were leukocytes, or white blood cells. In all of the blood Charlemagne had collected, he was unable to isolate any pathogen in the bloodstream.

"How bizarre," Charlemagne remarked, closing his eyes and bringing a hand to his temples. "I haven't found anything."

Charlemagne turned off the microscope and span around in his chair. He looked to Bauer in the quarantine cell to his left.

Next to the quarantine cell was Charlemagne's former multi-use device that was in his makeshift lab, in the corner, and next to various reinforced crates stacked upon each other along the entirety of the left wall with shelves above, holding containers with samples of various objects. Some of the items included specimens of ectoplasm collected by Charlemagne, the canister that Charlemagne kept spirits entrapped in, vials of certain shavings of metals and elements, ingots stacked upon each other, gems, and bottles of compounds, acids, and synthetic drugs. Charlemagne had an entire collection of items stacked around, not on display, but in storage. At the end of this side of the room, in a display case, was Charlemagne's jumpsuit and equipment from when he used to hunt ghosts.

In the middle of this side of the room was a platform with a rectangular object under sheets. Next to the display case was a short corridor that led to a set of reinforced doors, and on the right-side of the room was another display case with a piece of raw alien alloy collected as a meteorite in the arctic – the same meteorite that Charlemagne had found in the mines.

The right-side of the room didn't have shelves, but instead two sets of doors set apart from each other. The ceiling of the room had light fixtures, but they were of course turned off. Charlemagne stood up from his chair and walked over to Bauer. He brought a hand against the glass and looked inside.

"I'm sorry," Charlemagne confessed, "but your blood, like the slides of your epithelial cells from your palate show nothing, and what is more curious than this, is the fact that your symptoms have completely disappeared since you came to my home. What is good, is that I haven't developed symptoms as I expected I would – it has been almost two weeks, which just about proves that this virus does not transmit from human to human, which means that there is a common source that is infecting the other people… What that is, I'm not sure…"

Charlemagne thought for a moment.

"I need to return to the town," Charlemagne concluded. "I need to find someone else, someone who is displaying symptoms so I can isolate this pathogen. You've made a full recovery from this ailment, which is good, but not good for my research into producing a vaccine or remedy."

"Can you give me some more pain medication?" Bauer questioned. "I… I need more."

"I'm sorry, but you've maxed out… anymore could put you under cardiac arrest again…" Charlemagne explained. "Your immune system is still active."

"How long do I have to stay in this chamber of yours?" Bauer then asked. "If you say I am cured, then surely I can come out now."

"I'll considerate it tomorrow, but I want to be absolutely sure and wait until your immune system settles down," Charlemagne replied, "which could take a while. I'm sorry."

Charlemagne sighed.

"Without a sample of the pathogen, I cannot run any proper tests. I cannot develop any cures or any vaccines. I have no idea of what is going on in the town since we left, but thankfully, the army have not returned to bother us, ask questions, which… come to think of it, actually bothers me more. After all the commotion, I dread to think of what happened to Miklos and the others too. It *has* almost been two weeks… I haven't seen any military vehicles in the local area, which could mean they've moved over the river or perhaps to the airfield. In truth, I haven't left the manor and only my housekeeper has gone south to pick up groceries from the next town. I'm curious of what the death toll could be like, or what kind of damage the virus has done to the people. For their sake, I hope I am wrong about the federal government and figures alike. I hope they are treating the people well. A virus like this… is deadly. I haven't seen such one since the outbreak of Swine Flu almost a decade ago or the SARS outbreaks in China."

Bauer groaned.

"What is it?" Charlemagne questioned.

"My head aches…" Bauer complained.

"Really?"

"Yes, but not because of the illness, but because of all this talk of the virus…" Bauer replied. "Talk to me of something else, please…"

"What do you want me to talk about then?" Charlemagne questioned.

"Where did you grow up, Mr. Cabernet?" Bauer asked.

"Please, you don't need to call me, 'Mr. Cabernet,' Charlemagne responded. "You can call me Charles. I think we've familiarized ourselves enough to be able to address one another on a first name basis."

"Very well, Charles," Bauer replied. "You can call me as my peers called me once: Maxim, but please, tell me. Where did you grow up?"

"I spent my early years in East Anglia in England," Charlemagne answered, "and from there, I lived in a boarding school in London until I became a teenager and my parents enrolled me at a prestigious boarding school in Harlech. I spent my summers here, in Allabrese, with my mother and siblings, and at times with my father as well. He was quite fond of the equestrian culture in this town and used to take me to see bronc riding, horse racing, horse jumping, all sorts of events which mildly amused me. I had other, greater passions from my father though," he said with a sigh.

"Your relationship with your father sounds indifferent," Maxim noted. "Have you suffered because of him?"

"Fortunately, no," Charlemagne replied. "I love my father and mother, but not equally."

"What is your suffering then?" Maxim questioned. "What have you suffered over in your life, Mr. Cabernet?"

Charlemagne frowned.

"Tedious things…" Charlemagne generally said, scratching his head.

"How so?"

"Well, the little details of my early life… a life that seems like a lifetime ago were fixed with menial sufferings…"

"I don't want to know of those then," Bauer responded. "I want to know of your true sufferings… the moments in your life that have left you in pain, questioning the universe and God, questioning your existence…"

"Well, I lost my grandfather when I was about eight years old," Charlemagne sighed. "He was my grandfather, but he was also my father figure… My- my biological father neglected me, and I never respected him. He was a weak man and a stain on our family history. By the time I had gotten over my grandfather's death, I was about twelve years old, and by then my grandmother died of sorrow, and I suffered again for another two years until I was fourteen. Unfortunately, these sufferings took a negative turn on me as I said, my father neglected me and there was no one more in my life to steer me in the right direction. I was not a religious man either at this time. I didn't question God, because I never considered God. I was not one to be taken to Mass or be taught anything to do with spirituality. All the death of my grandparents put onto me was an inspiration to be good, kind and curious. My grandfather did pass on to me to be skeptical. I maintain that. No, all my sufferings did onto me at this time was inspire me to be like my grandfather. By the time I had healed, I didn't think less of the world because I did not blame the world. I didn't think of any deeper meaning behind my grandfather's death and left it where it was. I didn't come to truly think and question the purpose of all this until I was at a very late age."

"How old?"

"Fifty-one to be honest," Charlemagne said with a sigh. "For most of my life beforehand, I explored, travelled, met the people of the world and all they had to offer. I pillaged graves and robbed tombs. I invented gadgets and I synthesized compounds. I researched. My father, a man who hated me, my grandfather, and our family company, resigned as chairman in 1989, making me the new leader. I used the riches I had acquired to live a life of leisure and fuel my extravagant lifestyle. At the age of thirty-eight, I almost married, but... it wasn't my obsessions on the unknown that steered me away from her, it was my obsession with another woman – lust, as it were. I lied to many for years that it was because of her discovery, but no. It was because of her. I was still interested in her, but at this time, she was in a relationship to my best friend."

Charlemagne sighed.

"From 2000 to 2012, I primarily lived here as a serious businessman. I continued to invent, research, but I seldom left the town except to travel for meetings, tours, etcetera. In 2012, I injured myself in an unfortunate accident in South America where I had fallen down a cliff. The accident left me in a serious depression because for once, I had realized my mortality. I had also realized that I had lost my youth. For two years, I lived a secluded life and rarely even left my home. I spent a lot of my days thinking... for the first time in my life, I thought about the nature of the world and what it meant to live – the purpose of life as it were, and all I could see was that there was no point in anything and nothing had meaning."

Charlemagne sighed again.

"Two years ago, I had made arrangements to liquidate the assets of my family's business and kill myself," Charlemagne confessed. "I never did kill myself, because God had placed two children in my path, Diana and Tristan, whose innocent hearts inspired me to see the world in a different light. Unbeknownst to them, of course. I learned that there was more to life than the material desires I had or wanted to know. I didn't care about being the grandmaster of science, the greatest explorer and scientist who ever lived. I had found humility. I became a father, and that was the joy that my grandfather had because I realized, my grandfather didn't care to become a grandmaster of science either. His joy was me. He enjoyed being my inspiration in face of my father's degeneracy, perhaps to compensate for his own failure in raising him so, and it was when I became Tristan's inspiration, I had awoken. I had become like my grandfather as I had wanted. Diana and Tristan, they're an interesting pair… I see myself in both of them, Diana more than Tristan, even if Tristan and I have a closer relation. I respect Diana's privacy and only wish she had a mother around. Mind you, they both need a mother in their life."

"And how did you eventually find God?"

"Diana," Charlemagne replied. "She pushed me in the right direction and I found faith. At the same time, the experiences I had with the extraterrestrial life that you somehow know of, or angels as I prefer to think of them, influenced me heavily. I've spent the last two years since my attempted suicide readjusting my world view based on my life experiences, and I have been happy, even if it hasn't been permanent happiness. Last spring, that woman I told you about, not my fiancée, but the other, had died. Before she had died, she had told me that I had killed her long beforehand because she had developed ovarian cancer due to the experimentations I had her conduct for me to create that stupid fusion reactor. I was responsible for her miscarriage that broke the marriage between herself and my best friend. In addition, my fiancée had told me beforehand that she was pregnant when we had separated and that she had given birth to our son, my own son. I spent the following months in search of him and when I had almost reached him, he escaped and died in a tragic fire. Other than the fact that he died, the fact that I had almost placed two of my other sons, Tristan and a man named Miklos, both of whom I consider to be my sons even if they aren't... that I had placed them in harm's way out of my obsession. It took a toll on me. I realized that my own demons still lingered; my selfishness; my obsessiveness. I wanted to find him, not only so I could reunite and attempt to end this urge within me to love my own flesh and blood, my own son as my grandfather had loved me, but also because I thought if I found him, my former fiancée would forgive me and we would come together again and love each other as we once loved each other. It was another display of my lust to be with her sexually... and also romantically. It... it keeps me up at night even now, all these vice, and the torment that I will never change, that my sins have consequences on others, but... but I have strength to endure even if I am not in peace. I never had the strength like this to endure sufferings before... before I found God. Indeed, I do feel as though I have transformed, and I owe it to the children who have helped me become human."

"Yes," Maxim simply said. "Suffering develops the soul, and with the proper guidance, one can come to know God, but the choice is within us to either accept God and understand our sufferings, or turn away from him and be ignorant forever. Only a foolish man sees suffering as a problem, but the tests of life are different for everyone."

"What of you?" Charlemagne questioned. "I've told you my entire life story, but what about you? Where did you grow up? I recognize your accent to be German…"

"I am Swiss," Maxim answered. "Swiss German. My father's father had fought in the Second World War under the Waffen-SS. At the end of the war, soldiers of this elite unit were placed in camps where most of them starved and died. My grandfather was a fortunate man who escaped and went to Switzerland. There, he met my grandmother and established a family of his own. He worked as a farmer, changed our family name to reflect that change of lifestyle from soldier to peasant, and I was raised by his youngest son, who had to make his living in a different trade. My father went to school, studied, worked hard, and became a lawyer. Like him, I was the youngest child of four, but we were a middle-class family and I had more options than him. When I was sixteen, I travelled to Rome where in the Vatican City I met the most beautiful woman of my life. She was an American girl. Her name was Sophia and we talked for hours for the three days we were together. On the last day, she confessed to me that she wished to become a nun. I didn't understand. She told me to pray about it, so I did. All I ever thought about was her and because of her, I prayed. She was the only woman I ever loved, and it both confused me and hurt me that she didn't love me as much as she loved God… but despite this, I continued to love her. I sought to take a vow of chastity, but not as a priest. The priesthood was not for me. Instead, once I had completed my mandatory military service with the Swiss Army, I applied to be a Swiss Guard and there I worked, at the Vatican where I had fallen in love. I suffered so much out of my own desire for her, for years and years until we met again in my first year as a guardsman. I confessed my love for her, but she told me her heart belonged to God. I asked her, 'Isn't it an expression of God's beauty if we come together to be one flesh?' and she replied, 'It is an expression of our love for God that we devote ourselves to Him and only Him through our sacrifices.' I then, with little thought in my head, asked her to marry me. She refused, of course, but she told me this, that 'When we are at the right age and you believe you still love me, I will be ready to start our lives together.' Unfortunately, this was the last I saw of her..."

"What happened?" Charlemagne questioned.

"The next year, I was transferred to work with an interesting man named Bishop Tristan Williamson. He was an eccentric man, obsessed with history and the ancient. He was quite like you, in some manners. He was unfortunately assassinated in a car accident in the Middle East, in which I was injured and taken prisoner by the assailants, a group of Islamic extremists, of the Brethren of Islam, who kept me as a slave. I didn't stay with the same group, but changed hands quite a few times until Zimmerman's mercenaries found me in Africa and took me for their own."

"And at what part of this life story did you become a scientist?" Charlemagne questioned.

"I am not a scientist," Maxim replied.

"Who are you then?" Charlemagne asked.

Maxim sat up.

"There's trouble around," Maxim stated.

Charlemagne and him looked to the footage of the security cameras. A convoy of three armored personnel carriers had driven forward and parked on the road outside of the manor. Charlemagne stared at the APCs. They were different to the ones utilized by the Canadian Army.

"What on Earth…" Charlemagne said, standing up and going over. "I'm sorry, but I need to leave. The kids may be in trouble."

Charlemagne typed into the computer console.

"I thought it was strange that the army had left so sudden after we infiltrated the town, and I expected some sort of retaliation for what we did… this might be it."

"Can I help?" Maxim questioned.

"Stay here," Charlemagne cautioned. "I'll be right back."

Act 3, Scene 5

Charlemagne returned to the library of the manor and exited to reach the foyer. He looked out the front entrance and saw the vehicles ahead, parked outside. The engines of the vehicle were running and their headlights were switched on. Charlemagne looked at them for a moment and observed nobody to be outside, exiting the vehicles, or to even be in sight. He looked for another moment before crouching down at the sound of shattering glass. Suddenly, an object zoomed from the vehicles and landed inside the manor foyer. Charlemagne looked at what it was and saw that it was a canister. Another two were shot from the vehicles and landed inside. The canister let out a haze of a greenish-brown visible gas.

"Children!" Charlemagne shouted at the top of his lungs. "Children!"

Charlemagne rushed upstairs and went around to go after them as the gas spread. From where he was, without passing through the cloud of gas, Charlemagne could already smell the foul odor of the gas.

Diana heard Charlemagne's screams and sat up in her bed. Tristan was passed out next to her, on his stomach with his head on its side atop of the pillow.

"Tristan, wake up," Diana said, nudging him.

"What?" Tristan questioned.

"Wake up," Diana said again. "Charles is coming."

Tristan pushed himself off the bed and got off from the foot. He stood up and moved to go to his room through the bathroom. He then stopped as he heard glass shatter behind. Diana let out a scream of surprise. Tristan looked at the canister and saw that it resembled a grenade of some kind. The grenade began to emit the same gas from downstairs.

"Oh God, it stinks," Diana stated, bringing her hands to her nose. "Get it out of here!"

"Holy crap, yeah" Tristan remarked, picking up the canister and opening the door.

Tristan quickly threw the canister out and then turned around.

"Oh my God!" Diana shouted, pointing to the balcony.

Tristan looked as a pair of commandos in black uniforms and gas masks rappelled down from the roof and onto the balcony in front of the bathroom. They were armed with assault rifles. The pair bashed their bodies into the French window into Diana's room, opening the door and pointing their weapons towards them.

"On your knees!" the men shouted in American accents. "Get down! Hands on your head!"

Diana picked up the chair at her desk and instead threw it towards them. The men covered themselves as the chair hit them. Tristan picked up the chair and pushed a man back, forcing him into the window and out while the other one fell back into the balcony. Tristan used the chair to keep the man down. He was disarmed from his rifle. Tristan kept the man pinned with the chair.

"Diana, get out of here! Go to Charles!" Tristan shouted as he kept the man at bay.

Diana attempted to go into the bathroom, but she took a step back.

"There's more of them coming from your room!" Diana yelled, closing the door to the bathroom.

Tristan looked over to the door as he continued to struggle with the man on the balcony floor. He looked to Diana and quickly gave her the chair to barricade the door before dropping down to pin the man on the ground with his own body.

Charlemagne came into Tristan's room and saw that it was empty. The door onto the balcony connecting his room and the lab was open. Charlemagne looked and saw some rope hanging from the ceiling. He then looked to the other side and saw a pair of commandos attempting to bash the door into Diana's room open. Charlemagne backed out of the room and went down the hall towards the other doorway. He opened the door and entered the room.

Diana let out a scream as Charlemagne appeared. Tristan turned around and the commando he was atop of pushed him off. Tristan was pushed against the footboard of Diana's bed. The commando resumed control of his assault rifle. Charlemagne intervened and struggled with the man, bringing the rifle up and away from being pointed towards the kids. Tristan quickly got out of the way as Charlemagne pushed the man back. Tristan helped Diana barricade the bathroom door by pushing her dresser into the pathway while the chair jammed the door.

Charlemagne kept control of the assault rifle and readied it. He then came to the hallway and knelt down, taking cover under the door frame. The commandos gave up on attempting to get through the door and stopped bashing their bodies against it. Charlemagne waited for them to come down the hall. He then opened fire on them, maiming one while the other took cover. The two exchanged fire with each other.

Tristan and Diana brought their hands to their ears as they crouched near him. The other commando stopped firing and began to retreat. Charlemagne stood up and looked to the kids.

"Hide until I say it's clear," Charlemagne said, walking forward with the rifle pointed.

Tristan nodded and looked to Diana's closet. Diana opened the closet and the two got inside. Charlemagne walked forward with careful steps as came to the home gym. He took cover at the door way and looked inside. It was clear. Charlemagne then looked back into the hall and towards the door into Tristan's bedroom.

The commando got out of cover and fired towards Charlemagne. Charlemagne got out of the way and hid in the gym. The commando then came around the corner. Charlemagne hit him in the mask with the butt of the rifle, causing him to be pushed back. Charlemagne then shot him in the leg, causing him to fall over.

"Clear!" Charlemagne shouted.

The kids got out of the closet and came into the hallway. Charlemagne examined the gas mask the commando was wearing as he passed out and saw that the visor had broken. He then went to the body of the other who had passed out. He took his mask and brought it over his face. Charlemagne also collected ammunition so he could reload the rifle. The kids looked at the mess. Charlemagne could not see any insignia on the shoulders of the soldiers.

"Huntsman?" Charlemagne said, leading them to the makeshift lab. "Follow me."

Charlemagne went into the small bathroom next to the lab and took two towels. He wet them in the sink and then gave them to the kids.

"Don't inhale the gas," Charlemagne warned. "We don't know what kind of poison it is. We need to get to the library."

Diana and Tristan took the moist towels and brought them to their faces. They then left the room with Charlemagne and came to the foyer. Charlemagne set foot into the foyer, and instantly, the glass of the windows facing the causeway shattered with the gunfire that came from the APC turrets. The cloud of gas had gotten worse and filled the room with the greenish-brown haze.

Charlemagne looked forward and towards the door on the other side of the foyer second-floor. The rapid fire of the turrets was focused on the ground floor and not the second. The windows on their right then smashed open with additional canisters of gas and further commandos entering with assault rifles pointed.

Charlemagne opened fire towards them. The closest commando fell to the ground as he was shot in the thigh. The others backed up to retreat into cover. Charlemagne took some shots towards them before the windows on the other side of the room smashed open with additional commandos who fired towards him.

"Dammit!" Charlemagne cursed at the volley of fire that suppressed him.

Tristan took a step back and exited. Diana followed and looked as he fetched the other rifle. He then readied it and pointed it towards the commandos in the foyer from the hallway. He opened fire through the windows and shot a man hiding in the corridor that led to the library. Charlemagne noticed the hellfire of bullets towards him had stopped and turned to open fire at the others.

"Now's your chance. Move!" Charlemagne shouted.

Tristan ditched the rifle and ran off with Diana, across the hall with their towels to their face, and into the opposite corridor. Charlemagne neutralized the commandos in the foyer and went after the kids, closing the door behind them. He reloaded his rifle and then went into the library with them.

The kids rushed down the spiral staircase and came to the ground floor of the library. Charlemagne followed and led them towards the aisle that went to his study, but stopped at a bookcase against the wall on the left. Charlemagne tipped a hardcover novel to the side and then pulled against the bookcase to reveal a hidden room on the other side.

"Get in," Charlemagne said to the kids.

Diana and Tristan walked into the hidden room and saw that it was small and contained a similar freight lift to the one by the kitchen.

"Where does this go?" Tristan asked.

"To an emergency bunker beneath the house," Charlemagne explained. "Hide here and wait for me. I have to go rescue Mrs. Quinn who is almost certainly in danger."

Charlemagne closed the bookcase door and left the kids in the darkness of the room. Tristan held onto Diana as they stood in the darkness alone while Charlemagne went to his study, opening the door and going to a window. Charlemagne let out a cough and rubbed his neck. He cleared his throat and proceeded to remove the blinds of his study window looking out to the patio. He smashed the window open and got out, but stopped as he noticed commandos on the roof. Charlemagne opened fire towards them, noticing the sky to be a dark reddish hue. He hit one on the leg and caused them to fall over, roll down and fall off the roof. The other retreated. Charlemagne continued forward and stopped as he saw that the pool water was a brighter shade of red, almost like cranberry juice by the lights in the pool. Charlemagne then heard the growls of an unknown creature. He fell to his side and looked up onto the roof of the opposite wing of the house.

Stood atop of the roof was an unpleasant naked creature with daunting yellow eyes looking out from black sockets. They had a leathery brown, mutilated skin and were bald. The creature was anthropoid, but ghoulish in tattered clothes, hunched over and walking erratically. They seemed like zombies.

Charlemagne quickly stood up as they ran over the rooftops and then hopped down. He went to the French window into the trophy room and attempted to open it, but the door was locked. The zombies ran towards him, causing Charlemagne to point his rifle towards and open fire.

A single bullet caused the zombie to stagger, and a couple caused them to fall over. Charlemagne shot two to the left and was then ambushed by a third on his right. The zombie brought its hands to Charlemagne's face and shoulder. Charlemagne bashed the end of the assault rifle into the creature and caused them to back off as it tried to bite his neck. He then shot at the zombie and then bashed his body into the French window to force it open.

An additional couple of zombies appeared from over the roof while others came from the gardens. Charlemagne ran off and came into the kitchen. He then went towards the freight elevator, but saw that the gates were closed as it was on the sublevel. He instead went into the attic of the garage and heard Mavis shout out. Charlemagne climbed down the ladder and went to her bedroom

"Let go of me!" Mavis yelled.

Charlemagne came to her bedroom and stopped at the open door. He looked inside and could hear a struggle. He went down the corridor into her suite and entered the small living room and kitchen. The walls were pink and the room was well-decorated. Charlemagne went to the door into the bedroom and looked inside. Mavis was struggling with two commandos who were attempting to apprehend her.

"Stop right there!" Charlemagne shouted.

Charlemagne shot at one commando in the knee and at the other in the arm. Mrs. Quinn ducked down and screamed.

"Take it easy, Mrs. Quinn," Charlemagne said. "It's me."

"Oh, thank goodness," Mrs. Quinn responded, standing up and rushing towards him.

"Come with me," Charlemagne stated. "I've come to get you out of here. The manor is under attack."

Charlemagne and Mrs. Quinn returned to the garage. They climbed the ladder up to the attic and then came into the kitchen. Charlemagne could hear the patter of zombies around.

"It's not safe out there," Charlemagne cautioned, avoiding the trophy room. "Come with me."

Charlemagne took Mavis into the dinette and then the living room. Each of the rooms were amess from when the Canadian Army were stationed with their equipment. The APC had stopped firing into the foyer, which allowed them to quickly dash across and come to the library. Charlemagne stopped in the middle and saw some commandos above. They opened fire at him, but he quickly went across and into the corridor outside of the library.

The two entered the library. Various windows shattered as canisters were volleyed in. A group of zombies were also atop of the balcony above. Charlemagne immediately brought Mavis to the bookcase next to the study as the zombies jumped down. He quickly opened the bookcase door and had Mavis go in. Charlemagne then looked behind has he saw a zombie face towards him. He rushed himself into the hidden room and closed the door behind him just as the zombie was about to get him.

Charlemagne locked the hidden door and took a deep breath in the darkness. Diana and Tristan took steady breaths. Charlemagne reached around his body and brought out his phone, turning it on and then switching on its flashlight to give them some light.

"Sorry about that," Charlemagne said, taking a deep breath. "Come on."

Charlemagne took them to the lift and opened the gates forcibly with his hands. He then had them load onto the platform before closing the gates and switching the lift on to go down into the depths beneath the manor.

Act 4, Scene 1

"This sublevel has existed for quite some time, since my grandfather constructed the house in the forties upon returning from the war, but this lift, like the lift to the garage, was my own addition. Before this, there was a ladder that went down to a nuclear shelter in case of nuclear war. My grandfather was a cautious man…"

"How far down are we going?" Tristan questioned as the lift continued to delve down.

"I've estimated it to be approximately fifty meters below," Charlemagne stated. "I've added my own additions over the years. Before Tristan moved into his room, it was a storage room for all sorts of items I had collected. I moved those items down here after he moved in, and since last year have moved more and more equipment down here, including my own lab equipment to convert the immediate space to be my new laboratory. With… imprudent eyes always watching my moves, I thought it safer to move out of sight. The original shaft we're going down originally didn't include an elevator, but ladders. The ladders remain on the struts in case of a power failure and we need to escape."

The elevator reached the bottom of the shaft and the gates opened for them to step out. Charlemagne was in the room from earlier where Bauer was. Tristan looked around. The room was dark and only lit by the light coming from Charlemagne's computer. Bauer was in the corner of the room, sleeping. On the right, between the two doors, Tristan saw an air conditioning fan spinning to provide fresh air into the room.

Charlemagne walked over to the first watertight door on the right. He turned the valve, opened it and turned on a light with a light switch on the side.

"The bunker is connected to power upstairs and has a series of batteries with emergency power in case of an outage as well as a backup generator room at the end of this room," Charlemagne explained. "In here are enough supplies to last us quite some time… I have various non-perishables, fresh water, canned fruits, vegetables, meats, powered milk, oats, rice, flour, and all sorts of items. I also have other items such as batteries, lighters, and…

"Assault rifles…" Diana pointed out, looking over to the small arsenal of weapons in the corner of the room.

"Yes," Charlemagne replied. "I've made careful preparations in case of a situation where civilization might collapse, or in our case, the manor is invaded."

"What kind of things are over there?" Tristan questioned, pointing to the shelves on the opposite side of the main room.

"Less useful items," Charlemagne replied. "That's my collection of various metals, gems, chemicals, compounds, acids, organic compounds, drugs, seeds – I suppose those last two are of use in an apocalyptic scenario…"

Charlemagne led them into the second door, which was a large room, square room with various bunks. There were approximately twenty-four bunks in total lined against the wall. A separate door at the end.

"There are twenty-four beds, four for us, the rest for our loved ones in town," Charlemagne explained. "The door at the end leads into a bathroom with showers. The waterworks of the house are separate from the ones in town. Our water isn't filtered by the county, but by its own filtration system in the laundry room that sifts out fluoride and has the capability to also remove radiation in case of nuclear fallout. Thus, the water is drinkable as long as there is power to run the filters.

"What do we do now?" Tristan questioned. "The manor's been invaded, and…"

The lights in the bunker flickered for a moment. Charlemagne took a step out of the living quarters and went to his computer. He checked closed-circuit footage and could see commandos searching around the house for them. The lights of the house were turned off. Charlemagne coughed into his arm. He then cleared his throat as he looked to another screen that displayed power levels.

"Just as I thought," Charlemagne said. "The main power supply has been cut off, so we're using backup power. Damn…"

Charlemagne coughed into his arm again.

"Are you okay?" Diana questioned.

"I'm fine," Charlemagne replied, "it's just that I was exposed to that poisonous gas at the start and it's done a number on my throat – it feels as if I had acid reflux."

"Shall I get you some water?" Mavis questioned.

"Please," Charlemagne replied, clearing his throat.

Mavis went into the storage room and returned with a bottle of water. She opened it and handed the cap and bottle to Charlemagne who drank.

"Who were those people upstairs?" Diana then asked. "Were they with the government?"

"I'm not sure," Charlemagne responded, setting the bottle on his desk and walking across the room. "I doubt they could be with the Canadian Army special forces, but they appeared to be from this continent. I don't believe they were Huntsman."

Charlemagne picked up the assault rifle he had been using and examined the rifle.

"I don't recognize this model of rifle," Charlemagne noted with a frown. "I'll have to do some research…"

Charlemagne uncocked the rifle and removed the cartridge. He took it to his desk and set it on the side. Charlemagne then sat down in his desk chair.

"I'll have to search through my files to see if I can find anything, but it'll take a while," Charlemagne expressed. "Why don't you children have a rest? You've been through a lot just now and it'll be better if you take it easy for the rest of the night. Hopefully tomorrow, we can come out and make plans on what we do next."

Diana nodded and looked to Tristan. Tristan entered the living quarters and looked around. Mavis entered the room with some blankets from the storage closet. Tristan went to a bed at the corner of the room and sat down. Mavis gave him some blankets. It was cold in the bunker. Diana left to the washroom and then returned to take the bed perpendicular to Tristan. The couple looked to each other and held saddened expressions.

"I'm going to take Charles' advice and get some sleep," Tristan said. "I don't see anything else for us to do and just want to sleep."

"Okay," Diana replied, nodding. "Goodnight."

Tristan kept his hoodie on and lay down on the bed. He spread out the blankets and then kept on his side to sleep. Diana did the same, but didn't close her eyes immediately as she thought to herself. Mavis took the bed behind her and walked around for a moment, going between the bathroom and the main room. Upon her return, she started to close the watertight door.

"Please just leave it ajar," Diana requested, sitting up. "I don't want it to be too dark in here... The light from Charles' computer is comforting."

"Okay," Mavis replied, nodding.

Diana continued to keep her eyes open and looked to the light as Mrs. Quinn went to her bed and lied down to sleep.

Diana continued to look until naturally, her eyes closed and she fell asleep on her own.

• • •

Charlemagne brought his head up from his desk and looked around. He was in his office at the Cabernet Industries head office. He looked around and stood up. He looked out the window and towards central park and the rest of the town. It was morning and the sun was out. People were walking around and there was life in the town. Charlemagne looked at it and smiled. He took a deep breath and turned around as Huxley walked in and set a folder on his desk.

"Financial report for this quarter," Huxley announced. "Shares have risen and profits are the highest they've been in over a year. That reactor of yours has really turned the tide."

Charlemagne looked to him. He nodded.

"Yes," Charlemagne agreed. "I suppose it has."

Charlemagne looked back outside and sat on the corner of his desk. He smiled. Charlemagne's eyes wandered around the park until he noticed a red-haired man staring at him from next to a tree. It was Bauer. Charlemagne looked at him and then away as he heard air raid sirens come on.

A squad of jets flew over the town and a massive explosion detonated before him. Charlemagne covered his face as he felt the heat of the fire, glass shattered at his window and he was torn back.

Charlemagne jumped up as he awoke. He was sat at his desk in the bunker. Charlemagne brought a hand to his reddened cheeks, which were warm. He was flushed. He looked to Bauer in his quarantine cell, but he was gone. Charlemagne then felt a hand on his shoulder. He instantly turned around and stood up, looking at Bauer.

"What? How did you get out? You're not supposed to be out," Charlemagne said to him.

"I have healed," Bauer said to him. "If this illness were contagious, you'd already have fallen ill or been infected, but you haven't become ill thus the likelihood that you are infected is low. We need to return to the town for the sake of the townspeople. It's imperative, Charles."

Charlemagne paused for a moment.

"We do need to return," Charlemagne agreed, scratching his head. "I need another test subject given to run tests on. I'll never be able to work on a vaccine if I can't identify the pathogen to cause all this."

"The men above, they work for Zimmerman," Bauer stated. "I recognize this weapon behind you... it is a weapon produced by his company. The men in your home, searching for you, are members of his elite guard."

"Huntsman?" Charlemagne questioned.

"No," Bauer denied. "An even more elite guard, but smaller than the Huntsman Legionnaires. The Huntsman are a multinational mercenary group of fighters and soldiers leftover from the nations of the Soviet Union. They are as venomous and deadly as the spider they take their name from. Although they are not directly owned by Zimmerman, but by a callous and shame of a man named Bogdan Alexandrov, they do his bidding nonetheless. The group that attacked your home works directly for Zimmerman."

"You know each of them well, I take it," Charlemagne said to him. "Were you a part of either of their teams once?"

Bauer looked to Charlemagne. He didn't respond.

"I despise all of them," Bauer instead said, looking to the closed-circuit footage on the computer screen, "but I do know much of them as I was instructed to."

"What are they doing here?" Charlemagne questioned. "I can believe them to be here to make an attempt on my life now that I'm exposed, without my own men protecting me, but at the same time, are they here for you?"

Bauer didn't respond again. He continued to look at the screen.

"What if all of this, the epidemic included, is about me?" Bauer questioned.

"What do you know that is so valuable to them?" Charlemagne then asked with skeptical eyes. "What is it about you that makes you valuable to them to want to reclaim?"

"I know it all," Bauer replied, "and if they suspect I am with you, then Zimmerman is afraid that you might come to know what I know, which is no small problem. I shouldn't have come here…"

"And yet you came," Charlemagne responded. "You owe it to me and this town to set it all right. In your time with Zimmerman, was there ever experimentation with biological weapons?"

Bauer didn't immediately respond.

"Of course," Bauer finally said after a pause, "Zimmerman Corporation has experimented with a variety of viruses, bacteria, micro-organisms, however, I've been vaccinated for them all, and so have these men. If Zimmerman had unleashed a man-made pathogen on this town, I wouldn't have come down with the illness… and if it were novel, I would never have gotten better."

"What then?" Charlemagne questioned, looking to the screen.

"We will have to find out, but first, we need to leave and return to the town. With the army vacated, the town infected and under quarantine, I suspect the Huntsman are here to assume control and search for me," Bauer stated. "If we resurface, we will need to disguise ourselves in their uniforms and infiltrate as one of them. There will be no other way…"

Charlemagne nodded and went to the storage closet. He fetched a pair of gas masks for each of them and then put on his tactical uniform and picked up his backpack. He then handed Bauer his clothes. Bauer put on the uniform he had been wearing underneath his clothes. The uniform was similar to the one donned by the Huntsman above, but had a dark purplish digital camouflage integrated into the black uniform. His uniform also did not have the standard patch on the shoulders of the huntsman spider.

"The manor is still contaminated with that deadly gas," Charlemagne said. "Here."

Bauer took the gas mask and put it on.

"The gas is a powerful hallucinogen," Bauer replied, "a product of Zimmerman's research and development into advanced chemical warfare."

Diana listened in on the conversation from under the frame of the watertight door. She saw Bauer and Charlemagne equip themselves with rifles and ammunition before leaving to the elevator. They boarded and then set off. Diana walked back into the living quarters and went to Tristan. She nudged him and caused him to wake.

"What is it?" Tristan asked in an annoyed tone.

"Charles and that man he rescued from Allabrese just left," Diana stated. "They're going back into the quarantine zone to help out… I'm going with them."

"What?" Tristan questioned, opening his eyes and squinting at her. "Are you serious?"

"Yes," Diana responded, "I'm worried about Moira."

"Do you want to get the disease and possibly die?"

"Look, you can either stay here and let your girlfriend go on alone," Diana replied, "or you can come with and protect me. I'm not going to force you..."

Diana turned around and left. Tristan got out of bed.

"You *are* forcing me," Tristan muttered, standing up and leaving.

Mrs. Quinn snored as the kids left the room.

Act 4, Scene 2

Diana and Tristan came into the main room. Diana went into the storage closet and got a pair of gas masks for the each of them to wear before they went to the elevator. She also got some flashlights for them. The lift had gone up to the ground floor and left the shaft vacant. Diana shined the flashlight into the space and saw a ladder on the side while Tristan looked around for a switch. He brought his hands towards the switch to call the elevator back down. Diana stopped him.

"If we call the elevator back down, they'll know we're behind them," Diana explained. "We need to follow them until we're at a point of no return, and then they'll have to bring us with them."

Tristan looked at her and then over to the ladder.

"How do you feel about climbing up a hundred meters?" Tristan replied. "Do you feel like overcoming your fears?"

Diana looked at the ladder with an unpleasant look.

"It'll be safer than climbing up the Urals without a safety line," Diana replied, opening the gate and stepping into the shaft.

Tristan followed and allowed Diana to go up first.

"I'll be right behind you," Tristan assured her.

The couple went up the shaft on their own without issue. On their ascent, Tristan noticed another air conditioning vent that filtered air. Once at the top, they entered the dark hidden room in the library. Charlemagne and Maxim had closed the door behind them. Tristan opened the safety gate so they could step out of the shaft and then closed it behind them. He then took out his flashlight with Diana from his pocket and looked around for the door release. Diana found it and opened the door, stepping out into the library. Tristan followed from behind and saw that the room was dark. A thick haze of the gas remained and slightly obscured their vision of the entirety of the room alongside the darkness.

"Which way do you think they went?" Diana questioned in a hushed tone.

Tristan shrugged and went to the door into the corridor before the foyer. He opened it gently and peaked out. The foyer was dark, but the haze had cleared out better. Lights from outside, possibly vehicles, shined in through the broken glass of the windows. The haze was clearer in these lights. The walls were riddled with bullets from the APC turrets. Tristan saw Charlemagne and Maxim pass into the dinette from the living room.

Diana and Tristan went out into the corridor before the foyer and hid in the corner of the archway in. Tristan stopped as he noticed some beams of lights coming from the second floor. A patrol of three commandos exited with flashlights mounted to their assault rifles. They exited from the north wing and came down the steps to stand in the middle of the foyer where they spoke with one another in Russian. These people were not the same black-clad commandos that had attacked them, but they instead wore a purple-digital camouflage and of course, spoke Russian.

A commando stepped towards the corridor where the kids were. Tristan leaped back and out of sight, maintaining his view and seeing that another commando had grabbed him by the shoulder to stop him. He negated his action and the three of them instead went out through the front door. Once Tristan was sure they weren't coming back, he went out with Diana, staying close to the east wall and staying low.

Tristan stopped again as they reached the open front door. He looked out and saw the patrol team talking with another team at the causeway. An APC was pulled in to the top of the hill and had its lights pointed towards them. They too spoke in Russian, so whatever they were saying was incomprehensible by either of the kids. Tristan stayed at the corner of the door and waited for them to either move along or come back, the former being the better option.

The commandos eventually moved towards the APC and boarded. The engine of the APC roared to life and proceeded to drive forward, and once the lights weren't shining towards the door anymore and it was clear, Tristan proceeded down into the living room where he saw the shadows of some commandos in the corridor towards the trophy room. The kids quickly went into the dinette and evaded them as they passed them and went into the foyer.

Tristan made sure that the commandos went out of sight before he continued with Diana out of the dinette and towards the kitchen. From the kitchen, they came into the store room. The freight elevator into the garage was sublevel and the gates closed. Tristan opened the door into the attic of the garage and went in with Diana.

Once in the attic, the couple looked down and saw Charlemagne with Bauer as they forcibly raised the garage doors into the rear pen. The sound of an engine could be heard running from the eastside. The kids hid behind a squared bale of hay and looked below. Tristan removed his gas mask. The floorboard at their feet creaked as Tristan leaned over. Bauer jerked his head over and looked towards them, looking to Tristan. Charlemagne followed in reaction to Bauer and saw the kids.

"What the hell," Charlemagne reacted as they were about to leave. "What are you doing out here?"

"I wanted to come with you," Diana replied, climbing down the ladder, removing her gas mask and joining them. "I'm worried about the people in town. I want to be sure the people we care about are okay."

Tristan followed and came downstairs.

"I won't allow you to come," Charlemagne denied. "It's far too dangerous for a pair of teenagers to come into a war zone. You are to stay here with Mrs. Quinn."

"Keep your voices down," Bauer instructed.

The four of them turned their attention to the garage door and the sound of Russian chatter from the other side. The garage door began to make noises as though it was being forced open.

"Keep behind us," Charlemagne ordered, exiting outside with Bauer to take cover around the corners of the doorway. The kids hid behind the wall of a stall in the garage.

The commandos managed to open the garage door by a bit and rolled a gas canister inside. At the sound of gas leaking out, Tristan and Diana put on their masks again. The door then opened wide and commandos opened fire towards them, using Charlemagne's sedan parked inside as cover.

"Damn," Charlemagne remarked, keeping cover.

Charlemagne and Bauer returned fire, triggering the alarm of the black sedan as its windshield shattered from the gunfire. Diana could hear Zephyr's neighing in the background as the two parties continued to fire towards each other.

Once the commandos in front of Charlemagne's car had spent their magazines, Bauer pushed in and got in close, neutralizing the enemies. Diana and Tristan got out of cover and stepped out into the aisle. Diana went to her horse and comforted him.

"The two of you are returning to the bunker at once," Charlemagne ordered, stepping towards Tristan.

The door into the kitchen storeroom burst open and another pair of commandos entered, firing towards them. Charlemagne brought Tristan to duck and got him out while Bauer fired up and then took cover below them. Another pair of commandos rappelled down and inserted from the east garage door.

Bauer took the fight to them while Diana hid in the stall across from Zephyr, near the tank. Charlemagne and Tristan hid outside in the pen. Charlemagne fired towards the commandos above who had spread out and taken out stun rods. Tristan saw as one approached Diana from above, jumping down and going towards her. He attempted to go in, but Charlemagne had to keep Tristan at bay whilst struggling to shoot towards the commando. Bauer took care of the two commandos from close quarters and looked over as the commando near Diana raised his stun rod towards her.

Zephyr stormed out of his pen and reared at the man, stomping down at him. Diana rushed out and rejoined Charlemagne. An additional patrol of three men had arrived at the back of the APC. Tristan saw the APC turret turn towards them. Bauer looked towards it and then towards Charlemagne. Another pair of commandos inserted from the kitchen store room.

"Run!" Bauer shouted. "Get them out of here!"

The family covered their heads as the APC burst into flames and exploded. Charlemagne didn't hesitate for another minute to lead the kids out, through the pen and over to the fence.

"Move, move," Charlemagne shouted, encouraging the kids to climb over the fence and to the other side. "We are leaving!"

Bauer moved back and provided covering fire as Charlemagne continued to lead the kids forward. Tristan looked back, through the fence on the right at the wreckage of the APC. Charlemagne pulled the kids forward and towards the forest ahead where they took refuge.

Act 4, Scene 3

Charlemagne continued to lead the kids through the forest until they had found themselves in the middle of it and far from the manor. They stopped for a moment to catch their breath. Charlemagne reloaded his rifle and then looked to the kids. Diana and Tristan removed their gas masks. Charlemagne removed his.

"I'm incredibly disappointed in you, children," Charlemagne scolded. "Not only have you placed yourselves in danger, but you've most likely jeopardized my mission to help the town."

"Why don't you stop treating us like kids," Tristan remarked back. "We can handle ourselves."

Charlemagne flinched at Tristan's response.

"I was in space, and Diana's been trained in combat by some of the Earth's most elite forces," Tristan went on. "She's seventeen, and I'll be that age too in twenty-four hours. We're not little kids like we were when we met…"

Charlemagne looked to Tristan with a frown.

"Until you turn eighteen, you will continue to be regarded as children to me," Charlemagne simply said, "because you will be my responsibility to protect and care for. I'm sorry, but that is how it is."

Charlemagne began to lead on.

"Was I a kid when you abandoned me with Finn?" Tristan questioned.

Tristan stood down and gave an ashamed look as soon as the words had left his mouth. Charlemagne turned around. His frown had sunken deeper. He shook his head at him. The kids followed Charlemagne onward and stopped in the midst of the forest. Charlemagne's ears twitched at the sound of footsteps. He hid behind a tree and the kids hid behind trees behind his.

Tristan looked forward and could see a man wandering forward.

"Charlemagne?" the man questioned in his German accent.

"Maxim?" Charlemagne asked.

Charlemagne got out of cover and went towards his friend. The kids got out of cover and joined him.

"Are you alright?" Charlemagne asked as the two united.

"*Ja*," Bauer responded, looking to him and then the kids. "Your children?"

"Unfortunately," Charlemagne replied with a bitter tone. "I'm terribly sorry, but they'll have to stay with us until I can bring them to somewhere safe to stay."

"No problem," Bauer replied. "Shall we continue?"

Charlemagne and Bauer led on with the kids behind them. They crossed through the forest and came to the edge of the forest, near the road on the way to the airfield. Charlemagne and Bauer followed the edge of the forest and came up to the top of a hill that looked down to the freeway. Bauer and Charlemagne went prone on the grass as they looked below. The kids followed.

The four of them observed the convoy of vehicles attempting to cross the bridge over the river. The convoy consisted of army trucks in a queue on the way to the bridge with their engines running, but vehicles in place and going nowhere at the moment. They were stalled and the drivers of the truck, armed mercenaries, were outside, at the sides of the convoy. The convoy was escorted by armored personnel carriers like those at the manor. A cargo helicopter flew overhead and towards the fortress across the river, at the entrance of the bridge on the eastern side of the river. The façade of the fortress was barely visible from where they currently were because of the transformations of the bridge into a checkpoint for traffic and the bright lights that were a massive contrast to the surrounding scene.

"Zimmerman's brought his entire army here," Charlemagne said, taking out his binoculars. "Whatever it is that you know, it must be incredibly of value to them to want to keep a secret."

Charlemagne passed the binoculars to Bauer to look ahead.

"They've thickened their defenses on the coast of the river," Charlemagne said. "There'll be no means of crossing on a boat like last time."

"I see the only immediate way in as across the bridge," Bauer replied. "Here is how we will enter: we will stowaway on one of the trucks below, get through the checkpoint, and then exit once across to continue on foot."

"Each vehicle is being checked before it enters," Charlemagne observed. "Why is that?"

"I'm not sure," Bauer responded.

"Do you think they anticipate us and this plan?"

"It's a possibility," Bauer replied, focusing for a moment.

Charlemagne took the binoculars again and observed as a patrol on the bridge examined a truck. A pair of mercenaries with a German Shepherd shined a flashlight into the back of the truck while another patrol had a dog sniff around.

"It doesn't seem like they're all too careful in their search," Charlemagne expressed. "We might have a shot… if we dare."

"Who dares wins," Bauer responded. "I do not think they're looking for us. It seems to be some sort of protocol they've pre-employed. Come."

Bauer went off and proceeded to go downhill under the darkness of the night. Charlemagne and the kids followed from behind and they came to the road below where they hid at the side of a truck. Bauer then led them to the head of the truck behind and examined the back of the truck in front of them.

"No use," Bauer said, seeing the cramped space inside.

Bauer turned around and noticed a patrol on their way towards them. He took a step back and went to the front of the truck behind. He then got down on one knee and began to usher them over.

"Hurry," Bauer instructed, pointing to the truck before him. "Underneath."

Bauer monitored the oncoming patrol from the right and then went first, going prone and crawling under the truck and leading the way forward as the others went under. The patrol passed them on the left as Bauer came to the other side and continued under the next truck. The mercenaries around them, like the ones at the manor, spoke in Russian to one another. They walked at a calm pace and were casually conversing with one another.

The team reached the end of the convoy where Bauer got out and helped the kids into the back of the foremost truck where there was space for them. Afterwards, Charlemagne and then Bauer entered inside and hid in the back of the cargo. Some chatter could be heard around them and the cabin of the truck's door opening could also be heard. The truck shook for a moment and then began to move.

The truck rolled forward. Charlemagne and the kids were able to peak outside through slits in the canopy of the army truck. Tristan watched as they drove forward and came under the bright lights constructed in the center of the bridge. The truck stopped before the gates inside and a canine patrol stood waiting at the corner of the vehicle while the driver turned the engine off and got out.

The driver presented a folder with documents to the officer, distinguishable by the short cape at his right shoulder and lack of a helmet. He looked through the documents and spoke with the driver in a relaxed tone, asking questions. The mercenary gave quick responses, mostly yes or no, which Tristan, as far as his knowledge of the Russian language went, could understand.

Once the officer was finished asking his questions, he had the canine patrol move over and begin to sniff the truck. Tristan moved away from the canopy and sat down. Bauer had his eyes closed while Charlemagne breathed quiet breaths. Tristan's ears twitched as he heard the sound of the dogs whining. He quickly peaked out to see what was happening.

The German Shepherd was refusing to go near the truck to the point where his handler was getting angry. The officer was questioning the handler and the handler was answering him in negatives. The officer then looked to the driver and began to question him. The driver shrugged. The officer then moved over to the truck and began to walk to the rear. Tristan lowered the fabric and sat down again. He waited for light to flood into the rear of the truck, but it never came.

Tristan heard some further chatter, some complaints, and then the truck driver re-entered the vehicle and turned the engine on. Bauer opened his eyes and looked to the others as the truck began to drive off and through the gates. Tristan kept an eye outside as they drove onwards along the freeway, but began to drift right and then rotate around. They were still in territory claimed and used by the mercenaries with large pitched white tents, makeshift helipads, and parked light utility vehicles, armored personnel carriers, and even tanks. Tristan saw a small platoon of soldiers exiting from a transport helicopter. The entire image passed as the truck left the encampment and proceeded northwards. Tristan took notice and looked away. Bauer was looking out on the opposite side.

"We're going the wrong way," Bauer said, moving towards the rear of the truck and opening the canopy.

Charlemagne followed and looked out with him. They were approximately one-hundred meters from the base of operations of the mercenaries and could see the outer perimeter, a small concrete wall that had been constructed around the encampment with the large monstrosity of a fortress at the head. The fort tower had developed drastically since Charlemagne was last on this side of the river. The concrete structure was approximately the size of his manor and at most five stories tall with defensive guns on the roof with searchlights pointed down. The façade of the fortress was plain. The shape of the fort was rectangular. The surrounding walls that marked the perimeter of the mercenary's encampment were lined with barbed wire atop and had machine gun nests with further searchlights pointed outwards. The truck moved quickly down the freeway, at speeds of up to eighty kilometers per hour, but began to slow down.

"If there's any shred of doubt into the nature of this occupation, one only needs to look at what lies before us," Charlemagne said in a quiet tone. "What a pity."

The truck slowed down even more.

"We can look later," Bauer responded. "We need to plan our escape from this truck."

"We're slowing down… we must be coming to a stop sign," Charlemagne noted. "Kids, come," he said to them in a hushed tone.

The truck stopped and altogether, they jumped off the truck and then hurried to the side and into some bushes. They looked out as the truck then continued down the road, uphill and north. Meanwhile, Charlemagne, Bauer, and the kids sat in the middle of nowhere with plenty of farmland ahead of them to trek through.

Act 4, Scene 4

Charlemagne and Bauer moved into the farmland of the farm behind from where they had previously hid in some bushes.

"We need to go into town and search for a quarantine zone," Charlemagne said. "A reliable target is the school, but defenses may be more abysmal than when I was last here. Of course, going uphill will prove to be more of a challenge without my drone to guide us."

"We'll cross that obstacle when we reach it," Bauer replied. "Keep quiet for now."

"Apologies."

Charlemagne and Bauer led the kids through a cornfield when a helicopter flew overhead with searchlights. The entire team reacted by squatting down and keeping low in the tall field.

"Blimey," Charlemagne remarked, looking up and out. "Do you think they know?"

"You are too paranoid," Bauer replied. "Have faith, you are not the only one out here who seeks to defy the authorities. I overheard the guardsmen speaking of bandits... The courier was being asked if he had seen any suspicious activity since entering the region, if he had spoken to anyone, or if he had made any stops where someone might have tampered with the cargo."

"Interesting..." Charlemagne responded. "I didn't expect it, but it seems that the anarchy that's taken over the town has bred criminals."

Charlemagne and the others stood up and continued through the field until they reached the edge. From there, Bauer kept them low as they travelled to the perimeter of the farmhouse and then crossed over into the neighboring grass field. The grass in the field was tall. The helicopter returned for another pass. Bauer instructed them to go prone in the grass and allow the helicopter to simply pass them.

Once the helicopter had left the immediate area, Charlemagne and Bauer stood up with the kids and then continued forward. Bauer led them through the field when he suddenly stopped and had the others stop behind him. He then looked forward and turned his head from side to side. Tristan took notice of him as he did so.

"We're not alone," Bauer said, looking to the grass ahead.

Tristan looked at him and then ahead. He saw something sticking out from the blades of grass. It was the barrel of a rifle. Bauer looked forward.

"Who's there?" Bauer questioned, pointing his rifle forward.

Charlemagne raised his rifle and pointed it forward too.

"Kids, get down," Charlemagne ordered.

"Kids?" a voice questioned from within the field.

Charlemagne saw as a rifle raised from the grass in one hand and a man appeared from the grass with the weapon raised in surrender. The man holding the weapon was, of course, Miklos in civilian dress, but still armed for war, or at least, insurgency. He wore a brown leather jacket and baseball cap with jeans. He also had his Cabernet-issued assault rifle and a vest underneath his jacket with magazines.

Miklos walked forward and towards Charlemagne and Bauer who lowered their arms. Four others stood up behind him, in civilian dress, and with primitive rifles in hand. The people with Miklos were more than just members of the Protection Squad, but members of the community, including Jock Macmillan, an unrecognizable young man, and another member of Charlemagne's private guard, Hardrada, or Björn Oestring. The unrecognizable man appeared to be the same age as Jock, early twenties, shaven, blue eyes and fair skin.

"It's good to see you," Miklos said, shaking Charlemagne's hand. "I was beginning to fear whether I ever would."

"Even here, work doesn't escape you," Charlemagne remarked. "Where are the others? What are you doing out here?"

"I'll answer all your questions and more, but not out in the open," Miklos replied. "Come with us to a safehouse. A farmer is providing us with some shelter about a click from here. We can take refuge there for the night if you need."

"Perfect," Charlemagne replied, looking to Bauer. "Let's go then."

Charlemagne followed Miklos and the others as they travelled across the rest of the field and reached a fence where they took cover by some bushes on the side. The helicopter made another pass approximately one-hundred meters from the team, requiring them to stay low. Once the helicopter had made its pass, the team continued over the fence and went through the farm on approach towards the freeway above a ridge.

Miklos led the group down the side of the ridge and towards a small tunnel underneath that connected the two sides of the plains. He then led them onwards towards another farm, crossing over to enter a field. The team stopped around the exterior of a small farmhouse, staying low to pass around a barn and then crossing a dirt road to reach another farm. The team crossed the field and reached a larger farmhouse, sticking to the exterior walls to reach some doors that went into a cellar.

Miklos opened the cellar doors at the side of the farmhouse and then led the team inside where they reached a small cellar with a table and some chairs surrounding said table, some beds to the left with some thin mattresses, a cupboard at the back, and shelves to the left with canned foods and other essential supplies. Miklos turned on a light to give a better view of the room. Björn and Jock closed the cellar doors behind them.

"Have a seat," Miklos said to Charlemagne, Bauer, and the kids. "Unfortunately, I don't have much to offer as we don't have much supplies…"

"Nonsense, it's alright," Charlemagne replied, sitting down and lowering his rifle onto the table.

"What are you doing back in Allabrese?" Miklos questioned. "Did you find a cure?"

"No," Charlemagne replied. "I've been unsuccessful in my research efforts…"

Charlemagne explained to Miklos what had happened after he returned with Bauer. His monitoring of Bauer's health and recovery to the attack on the manor. He also explained the reasoning behind the kids being with him and his reason for returning, to continue his research. The kids sat near Charlemagne and kept quiet. Bauer leaned against a wall and didn't speak or add to Charlemagne's story. However, Tristan noticed Bauer looking to him at occasion.

"You can stay here if you'd like, and tomorrow morning, I can take you into town," Miklos offered. "It shouldn't be a problem to find an infected… the number of infected has doubled as have the deaths. The new government established has abandoned efforts to quarantine the infected, and most of them are at their homes with the severe cases and near death in hospital… A couple of my own men have fallen ill, Lukas… Brandan and Maris, but are fighting through. A small group of scientists from the labs have come together and attempted to do their own research at our headquarters, but it's been difficult with lack of equipment."

"Good Lord," Charlemagne remarked. "My heart goes out to all those that have come under, but what do you mean headquarters and a new government? What has become of this town since I was last here?"

Miklos took a deep breath.

"Ever since you left, it only got worse for us. The local army left and were replaced by these mercenaries, the Huntsman that work for Audric Zimmerman. To prevent chaos, the mercenaries attempted to work with the mayor and bring order, but Mayor Grayson refused to work with them. He resigned and was replaced by the police chief, Chief Phillips, who has formed a collaborative government with the mercenaries in face of the small 'uprising' that happened on the night you left. The local police force have been abolished and those loyal to Phillips have formed a small paramilitary group who help the mercenaries track and move around the area. And then there is us. Thanks to you, the fight in front of city hall that scared the army out inspired a small resistance force consisting of myself, Björn, Viggo, and a few civilians and police officers who are loyal to Captain Macmillan – we've formed a militia, who want nothing more than to see these tyrants leave. There is one thing that we are all certain of: this is an occupation and the federal government has no intention of aiding those that are ill, but instead let them die – they'll have all of us die…"

"You are right in that regard, but the true motives of this occupation are a mystery to even me," Charlemagne replied. "All that I know is that these Huntsmen are Zimmerman's men and that he is somehow involved in all this. I need to speak with Mr. Macmillan and these scientists you say are attempting to do some research. Now, if possible."

"Certainly," Miklos replied, "we've just returned from a reconnaissance mission to investigate mercenary activities across the river. I have to return to the warehouse and provide my report to Mr. Macmillan. I will take you to him."

"How has this resistance been travelling from St. Allan's Plains to the heart of the town?" Charlemagne questioned. "I imagine it to be impossible due to the steepness of the hill."

"Easily," Miklos replied, taking out a map and laying it on the table, "we have an alternative route to the north where there is a trail that leads up the cliffs by the base of the mountain. There is a little bit of rock climbing, but it is easier than taking the road."

"Very well," Charlemagne said, looking at the map, "let's not waste a moment then. The sooner I speak with him, the faster we can produce results."

Miklos looked to the kids. He pointed to them. Charlemagne looked.

"If the kids are going to be with us, it would be better if they were armed than unarmed when travelling across the farms," Miklos stated. "The risk of ambush is too high."

Charlemagne looked to Miklos and then to the kids. He gave a sigh.

"I suppose they've both been trained on how to handle a rifle for that reason…" Charlemagne grumbled. "Do you have any spare arms?"

"A few," Miklos said, going towards the back of the room and to a cupboard. "These are bolt-action rifles. They will have to do."

Miklos had his assault rifle fall on its sling and took two in hand. He then brought them over to the kids. He then returned to the cupboard and picked up some ammunition.

"It's better to be armed and pray to never have to use it, than to be unarmed and in danger," Miklos said, putting some cartridges into Tristan and then Diana's hands.

Miklos then turned to Hardrada and the other civilian militiaman.

"Björn, stay here with Barrett for the night," Miklos ordered. "I'll return to the town with Mr. Cabernet and provide my report to Mr. Macmillan with Jock."

"Yes, sir," Björn replied.

Charlemagne and the kids followed Miklos and Jock towards the stairs to return to the surface. Tristan fiddled with the bolt of his rifle as it appeared to be jammed.

"The lock is set," Bauer said to him. "You need to unlock it."

Tristan looked at the lock at the side of his rifle and then back to Bauer.

"Thanks," Tristan simply said, unlocking the rifle.

Tristan uncocked the gun and left it unloaded. He kept the rifle lowered as he walked upstairs with Diana in front of him. Bauer walked behind him. They came to the surface by the farm and proceeded through the field they had just come through and over a separate farm to reach the freeway.

Miklos led them towards the tunnel underneath the freeway. Tristan observed a light utility vehicle and its headlights pass above. Miklos looked up and saw it and rushed the team underneath. They stayed under for a brief minute before continuing along the sides of the freeway to reach the end of the ditch. Tristan saw the LUV had turned to the right and proceeded down the dirt road above the end of the ditch.

"Jock, take point," Miklos said, staggering to lead from behind.

Jock moved forward. The team went uphill and came out of the ditch. Jock stopped them at the top before proceeding across the road to reach the other side. They then proceeded to cross a field that led to a shed. The team took cover behind the shed and Jock looked out around the corner. He then got down on one knee. Bauer was behind him.

"The patrol's stopped at the house behind," Jock quietly said. "They're knocking on the house door."

Bauer concentrated as the six of them breathed quietly. Tristan could barely make out what was being said in English. It sounded like there was a minor argument as the mercenaries aggressively spoke.

"We can't just stand here and listen," Bauer said, turning around and fumbling with a door knob.

Bauer opened the door and entered the shed, moving over to a set of windows so that he could get a better look out. Charlemagne entered while the kids hung back. Tristan could see from where he was that the mercenaries were harassing the farmer, pushing him back. The old farmer was a hunched man in overalls, a brown sweater underneath and a flat cap. The mercenaries were armed with assault rifles.

"If we open fire, there will likely be reprisal against this old man and his loved ones," Charlemagne cautioned to Bauer who observed the mercenaries with focused eyes.

"I know," Bauer replied, keeping focus.

The mercenary at the top of the porch stepped down and moved back to his LUV with the others. They all boarded and then drove around, leaving the farm. The team remained hidden until the farmer returned indoors, afterwards, Bauer and Charlemagne exited to continue across with Jock and Miklos.

"What did they want?" Charlemagne questioned Bauer as they reached some large stacks of hay to take cover behind. "I could barely hear what was being said."

"They were asking about suspicious activity," Bauer simply replied.

The team exited the property they were on, crossed another dirt road, and came to another property. They dashed through the tall crop fields, and then went across the track of land on the other side, around the structures of the farm and over a fence to enter a field of tall grass with some bales set and left throughout, which they used as cover to come across.

From this field, they came to another farm with greenhouses and various barns. Behind this property, they arrived into a small forest which they stuck to the side, along a stone ridge and path that took them east towards the cliffs of the plateau on their right.

Act 4, Scene 5

Jock led them into a small gorge at the base of Huntley Mountain and the plateau. The small ravine was rocky and led uphill to a set of cliffs at the end that went up like three sets of stairs to the top. The top portion of the climb had a set of ropes strewn out. Jock led them forward and they all stopped at the base of the end of the gorge. Jock lowered his rifle and brought it around his shoulder to free his hands. He then started to climb up the cliff to reach the first landing.

"Bring your hands where we bring our, and all should be fine," Miklos said, ushering Charlemagne forward.

Charlemagne followed Jock. Diana followed Charlemagne. Tristan followed Diana up the cliff. Miklos went before Bauer and Bauer stayed behind to come to the first landing. By the time Bauer had come up, Jock was already halfway up the second portion. Charlemagne climbed up and then continued forward to come to the top. Jock helped him up once at the top, and then helped the kids.

At the top of the cliff, the team found themselves at another forest with a rocky pathway ahead for them to follow through. Within a couple minutes, Charlemagne noticed some fences to their right of the houses at the side. By following the park path, they reached a cul-de-sac of a far north neighborhood. They continued along the path until it ended and they were pushed towards the forest natural path.

Within a couple of minutes, the team eventually came to a main road that followed through Downtown Allabrese, past the hospital, and went towards Linz Mountain. They were out of the suburban area of the town and surrounded by forest. The team crossed the road and came to the other side, hiding amidst the trees as they travelled southwards and then entered into the forest to reach a side road. The side road led them into the forest and to a warehouse on the outskirts of the town.

The warehouse looked rundown and abandoned. The structure was constructed of red brick. The overhead windows were cracked and broken. At the front of the warehouse were shutter doors and a side door. There were floodlights around the side of the building and CCTV cameras around the side.

Jock led them to the rear of the warehouse. At the rear of the warehouse was a solid metal door. Jock reached the door and looked to the CCTV camera pointing towards the door. He then knocked on the door and waited. Within less than a minute, the door opened and revealed Holger, or Viggo Schalburg. Miklos stepped forward.

"Welcome back," Holger said, stepping aside as Miklos and Jock stepped in.

"I've got the chief with me," Miklos announced.

Charlemagne followed with the kids behind him Bauer followed them from behind. Holger then closed the door and tracked them from behind. The seven of them walked down a narrow corridor with closed doors to the right. At the end of the corridor, they reached the open space of the warehouse, which was more or less empty with the exception of a few parked vehicles on the far left side and a small station of foldable tables with microscopes, computers, and other equipment. Tristan observed several people in civilian clothes sitting and standing around the station. Miklos looked to the open space and then turned around with Jock to face Charlemagne, the kids, and Bauer.

"I'll take you to speak with Macmillan," Miklos said to Charlemagne. "The kids can wait here and have a rest. It's just about an hour past midnight. We can see about having them sleep here tonight."

"Preferably, somewhere safer," Charlemagne responded, "but I understand that we're not in a position to be making accommodations. I only want them out of harm's way."

"Understandable," Miklos replied. "We're still in allegiance to you; Björn, Viggo and I, I mean. If you need us to protect them, we will."

"I won't go so far," Charlemagne replied with an exhausted expression, "as long as they are safe."

"I'll wait here," Bauer said to Charlemagne.

Charlemagne went with Miklos down the side of the rear of the warehouse towards a set of stairs that were parallel to the brick wall behind them. The kids took a seat at the wooden chairs behind them. Bauer walked towards the stairs once Charlemagne went up and crossed his arms to wait.

"Where's your wife and son?" Charlemagne asked Miklos as they walked up the stairs.

"Tanya is at our home with Mathias, Lukas, and his wife. The women are taking care of him and Brandan and Maris."

"Good..." Charlemagne responded.

At the top of the stairs, Miklos opened a door that led into a large room. There was no one in the room. In the middle was a large wooden table with a map of the county on the middle. The map had been marked with permanent marker. Miklos took them to a door leading into another room. He knocked on it.

"Come in," Mr. Macmillan said from the other side.

Miklos opened the door and allowed Charlemagne to step forward. Mr. Macmillan stood up quickly as he looked at his desk, but slowed down as he saw Charlemagne.

"Charles," Mr. Macmillan said, looking to him.

"Eugene," Charlemagne greeted.

"What are you doing back here?" Eugene questioned as Miklos closed the door behind them. "I thought you escaped back to the other side?"

"I did, but I'm here to help," Charlemagne answered. "I met with Miklos and your son out in St. Allan's Plains and they brought me here to speak with you. We need to talk about the current condition of our town and the status of the virus infecting our townsfolk."

"Have you developed a cure? Did your friend prove to be of use?"

"Unfortunately, no," Charlemagne replied. "He healed and I was unable to isolate the virus that infected him. I need to find another patient to run tests off of. I heard you have your own team of scientists doing some research."

"Yes, well as it seems, the public health authorities weren't doing any of their own research, so I reached out to some of the scientists that attended the Halloween Party, discussed with them the situation, and had them come here to do some research on some of the infected... I would highly suggest you go speak with them to coordinate your research as I've heard they've been working hard, but are far from a solution."

"I will," Charlemagne responded.

The two of them went quiet for a moment.

"How have you held up, Eugene?" Charlemagne asked.

"It's been difficult," Eugene said, sighing. "I miss Elliot and Rosa, but I'm glad they aren't here and are with their grandparents, Esther's parents, across the river. Luckily, neither Jock nor Moira have fallen ill, although the scientists have told me that all of us are infected, but to varying extents... Nonetheless, it's been stressful and also depressing... I would be lying if I said I'm not suffering, but my suffering is nowhere near those who are fighting off the infection."

Macmillan turned his head to the side, out the window on his right and towards the open space below. He then looked back to Charlemagne.

"Thanks to you, I was inspired to do something, because you were right…" Macmillan said, "and even more, thanks to your… private security guards, I was able to bring some expertise to train the few police officers and locals who have volunteered to fight back. Miklos has been a tremendous help, but we are not a stable fighting force… there are less than ten of us and we're too under-armed to expand ourselves."

Charlemagne nodded.

"Unfortunately, all I have brought with me is my own weapon, the man I left with two weeks ago who is a skilled mercenary, and my children," Charlemagne responded. "All I have to offer is a small cache of weapons belonging to my security guards, but that is barely enough to equip another two to four people."

"Thank you," Eugene responded.

"Where is Moira?" Charlemagne questioned. "Who is taking care of her while you and Jock are here? Is she at your home?"

"Moira is downstairs," Eugene answered, sighing. "She'll be happy to know that Diana is here with her."

"Is she helping with the cause?"

"No," Macmillan responded. "We've been cut off from Internet since the start of quarantine, and there's really no use for Moira's particular set of skills. I also don't want her to put herself in a dangerous position…"

"Neither do I for my children even though they are eager to help," Charlemagne responded, "but is this the safest place for them?"

"For now, yes."

Charlemagne frowned. Mr. Macmillan moved over to the window and looked out.

"What do you plan to do with this militia of yours?" Charlemagne questioned.

"To push the Huntsmen away of course," Macmillan answered. "I know it won't cure the ill, but it'll give us our freedom to do justice to those that are ill. To reach out to the outside world and ask for help. Right now, food is rationed and civilians are harassed into line. The sick are comforted in their beds, but no efforts, like you said, are being made to cure them. Nothing is being done except by us... because we dared to act."

Charlemagne nodded and then said, "You know who these Huntsmen are?"

"Yes, but what I don't know is why they've come to our town?" Eugene expressed. "Why has this happened to us of all people?"

Charlemagne took a deep breath and looked out the window with Macmillan.

"I too am familiar with these mercenaries. They harassed my family two years ago in Russia and again last year in Egypt. For all I know, they were also responsible for the attempts on my life and my loved ones during our vacation in France earlier in the year. They are a ruthless lot, paid and owned by a billionaire known as Audric Zimmerman. For all I know at the moment, we are part of an elaborate social experiment. Zimmerman is a man with power and connections to do such a thing. His motives are mysterious to me. However, I ensure you, he will pay for what he has done to us and our town."

Eugene nodded.

"Did you know that this used be a hideout used by the Medicis once upon a time," Eugene expressed. "Back in the day, they would hide here, plotting to strike at Allabrese, but now here I am, plotting to strike at the Huntsmen… Did you also hear that Chief Phillips is now in charge of the entire town? He succeeded Mayor Grayson."

"I did. Miklos told me."

Eugene shook his head and said, "I can believe why he did it. A man has to do what he needs to do to protect his family, and I'm sure if we spoke, he'd rationalize to me that he intended to do so to keep peace and protect the town too. However, Cole was always one that obeyed the law because they were the rules and nothing more. He's intelligent, but also obedient. I am not obedient. I let you convince me to let you pass that night, something I thought I could never let happen because I was scared of the consequences if I didn't. I didn't care about the rules I had broken. For most of my life, I thought I was like Cole. I thought I had become a police officer to enforce the law when in reality, I became one to serve and protect our people."

Eugene sighed.

• • •

Bauer stood by the base of the stairs while Charlemagne was upstairs. He waited patiently and stood still with crossed arms, occasionally looking to Tristan who sat at the other side of the room at the chairs. Diana paced in front of him. She stopped and looked towards the stairs.

"I'm not going to wait to find out what's happening," Diana complained. "I'm going to go eavesdrop."

"Okay," Tristan simply replied, watching her go off and then noticing Bauer looking at him again.

Bauer looked to Tristan as he looked at him in the cellar, with intent and focus. Tristan looked away before looking back as Bauer proceeded to walk towards him. Tristan looked at him with fearful eyes. Bauer was a tall man, most likely the same height if not an inch or two taller than Tristan. He was also far leaner. He walked with his arms crossed and his assault rifle around his shoulder on its sling. He stopped before Tristan and loomed over him. He looked down to him. Tristan looked up to him.

"Who was your mother?" Maxim questioned in his thick, but clear German accent.

Tristan stuttered for a moment. He swallowed.

"Elisabeth Merrick," Tristan answered.

"Hm," Maxim responded, looking at Tristan with a serious face.

Bauer's blue eyes stared straight into Tristan's greens. Tristan looked uncomfortable.

"Are you religious?" Maxim then asked.

"N-no," Tristan replied. "Not really."

"Not really?"

"I was baptized Catholic because my mom was, but I don't pray or really believe in God, or anything like that," Tristan clarified. "I mean, Diana does, and she knows how I feel about faith and religion, but for me, it's never really been something I've had a particular appeal for. I don't see any reason behind it, and it doesn't affect me."

"I see," Bauer replied, raising his chin up. "A tragic circumstance… for any son of mine would have been lavished with the word of God from a young age so that he could speak of God's glory at yours."

Tristan looked at Bauer.

"Do you know how to pray?" Bauer questioned.

Tristan hesitated to respond.

"I don't pray," Tristan simply said after a moment.

"Pity," Bauer replied, "especially since there is something that God needs to tell you, but you have not found the time to stop and listen to what He has to say."

"What does God want to tell me?" Tristan then asked in a dull tone.

"You will need to ask Him and find out," Bauer simply said. "If you'll excuse me, I need to step out for a moment. If Mr. Cabernet returns and requires me, please kindly let him know where I have disappeared to."

"S-sure," Tristan responded, looking to Bauer as he left into the corridor.

Charlemagne came downstairs with Diana. The two of them across the open space and towards the makeshift laboratory in the right corner of the room. Tristan stood up and joined them as they made their way over. Charlemagne looked to them, recognizing each of them, especially one directly ahead. Barry looked up and looked to him.

"Charles?" Barry questioned.

Charlemagne stopped and gave a light smile to him before saying, "I should have known that you would be here, doing good as you only know how. I heard from Eugene that the lot of you have been researching the virus."

"We've been researching... but we're stumped," Barry complained with a tired voice. "We've looked at hundreds of blood smears, tissue samples... We've ran thousands of blood tests, viral isolations, culture tests, antigen tests, but none have given us anything."

"Well, at least I'm not the only one..." Charlemagne responded. "I've ran similar tests at my own lab and wasn't able to find the pathogen in question... and then my patient got better, which is why I find myself here. We are dealing with an elusive pathogen to say the least."

"You can say that again."

"Yes," Charlemagne said, turning around and bringing a hand to his chin. "Can I have a word with you for a moment?"

Tristan looked towards the adults as they left.

"What is it?" Barry questioned.

Charlemagne proceeded to explain the last couple of weeks for him, how he came to Allabrese in search of a test subject and rescued Bauer instead, and also his own findings at the manor. He also mentioned Zimmerman's role in the occupation and probability that they're behind the illnesses as well as Bauer's importance to Zimmerman and probable cause that the town is under occupation because of their hunt for Bauer.

"You cannot let Eugene know of this," Charlemagne warned. "They do not understand Bauer's value and will quickly betray him to set this town free."

"Of course," Barry agreed, stroking his beard.

"Maxim told me that there is no biological weapon in Zimmerman's arsenal that matches the symptoms of this current decease," Charlemagne stated, "but I have my doubts. I'm fearful that we might be dealing with something far more dangerous and new than what Bauer could have been familiar with, but I need your help. I need to know everything that you know before we start to run more tests."

Barry sighed for a moment, adjusted his glasses, and then said, "We've taken careful notes of all the tests we've run and our conclusions drawn. I also have some observation notes of patients given to me by our contact, a doctor at the hospital, who's provided us with details into the late-stage symptoms of the disease."

"What symptoms?"

"The late-stage symptoms include headache, higher fevers, and delirium and hallucinations."

"Hallucinations?"

"Yes," Barry replied. "All patients gradually become delirious, according to our contact, and start to have visual hallucinations that cause them to become anxious and alert. All of the patients that have died have died from cardiac arrest, but in fairness, those that have patient were also patients with poor cardiac health."

"Curious," Charlemagne responded, looking away and taking a deep breath. "What if we've been looking at this the wrong way then?"

"How so?"

Charlemagne explained to Barry the poisonous gas he was exposed to at the manor which caused him to hallucinate being attacked by zombie hordes.

"We know that Zimmerman is behind this," Charlemagne stated. "We know that he doesn't have with him any infectious diseases that would cause symptoms like the one observed, but we do know that he owns a chemical agent that causes hallucinations. Perhaps then, we've been looking at this the wrong way then. We all thought that this was an infection of some kind, most likely viral, however a toxin could also cause a fever and be as elusive as a virus from our sights."

"What then?" Barry questioned. "What caused the town to all become poisoned?"

"Airborne comes to my mind first, but then we'd all be suffering the same symptoms and there wouldn't be such a lag period from respiratory symptoms to hallucinations," Charlemagne stated. "What else do we all share? Food? Water?"

Charlemagne and Barry paused for a moment.

"My Halloween Party," Charlemagne stated. "All was well up to this party, and then everyone came down with the early symptoms..."

"You can't feel guilty about what's occurred," Barry replied. "Here's what I'm thinking: the early symptoms mimic those of a respiratory disease such as the common cold or flu, and in addition, there is a lag period until one becomes delirious. The only other manner of transmission there could have been, and also missed some people, is orally."

"We don't all eat the same food, but we all buy our food from the same grocery store," Charlemagne stated. "However, we're not all infected…"

"What about water?" Barry asked. "Tap water to be more specific. I don't drink tap water. I have a filter at home and only take water from the tap to boil to make tea or coffee. A lot of homes in this county connect to the water grid, but another handful have their own wells or pumps; groundwater. There's a pump right behind where we get out water from here."

"Yes, likewise, the water system at the manor is separate to that of the town," Charlemagne pointed out. "If they were infecting the water, the water at the manor would be unaffected too. This would also explain why Maxim got better while in my care… He wasn't drinking public water anymore, but my own supply. An average of fifteen percent of people only drink bottled water, which could possibly be more with this town's demographics. However, I've heard that supplies are rationed here so that number would shrink and those people who come under, adding to the ill. Nonetheless, a small minority of people filter their water, like you, or don't drink water and instead receive their water from other beverages, such as tea and coffee, or juice and soft drinks in addition to food. Another handful, as you said, have wells and pumps that take water from the ground. My God, and with all these people with fevers and food rationed, they may be drinking enough water to slowly kill themselves just to stay hydrated!"

"If it is the water, there's a central point where the entire town's water supply could be infected easily… the water treatment plant," Barry also stated. "We need to tell Mr. Macmillan and let him know of this… We have to stop them!"

Act 5, Scene 1

"Are you certain that a toxin is responsible for all this, and that this toxin is coming from the water supply?" Eugene questioned Barry and Charlemagne in his office.

"Do you drink tap water?" Charlemagne asked, looking to others in the room.

Charlemagne and Barry were with Miklos, Bauer, Viggo, and Jock. The kids were outside of the office, sitting down by some chairs.

"We have a filter…" Eugene stated with a sigh. "If you're right, how do we help people who are ill get better?"

"Have them boil their water if from the tap," Charlemagne instructed. "Your militia should begin to spread the message to people within town, but keep in mind, recovery won't be instantaneous. The body will need time to flush out the toxins, and since we do not know much about this chemical, there could be penalties or side effects – lasting damage done to organs or tissue. In the future, I would have all of the infected be checked on for at least a year if not more."

"Fine," Eugene responded, scratching his head. "We'll start to spread the word, but we need proof beforehand. We need to go and see for ourselves what is going on at the Nattau Water Treatment Facility. I'm assembling a team to leave tonight."

"Maxim and myself will lead this team," Charlemagne stated. "If I could suggest, with all due respect, I would like to have Miklos lead a separate team for a separate mission."

"What mission?" Eugene questioned.

"A peace mission," Charlemagne explained, looking from side to side. "You said that you needed supplies and manpower, and on the other side of town in *Pianure Calabresi* there is an old crime family who have what you need. If we send a small team and let them know that we need them, they may accept. After all, this is their town too, and despite the divisions and feuds, Allabrese is a town of both Germanic and Roman folk, like a small Holy Roman Empire. I have no doubts that Dino Medici will see reason."

"Perhaps you should attend this peace mission," Miklos suggested. "You have good relations with the Medici family and you are charismatic."

"No," Eugene refused, "I will go. Charles is right, the English-speaking community have a divisive history with the Italians in this town, and if anybody is going to be an ambassador to represent our needs, it better be me."

"Very well," Charlemagne replied. "Let's plan the mission ahead of us."

The group moved from Macmillan's office and into the room behind.

"Your team, Charles, will be responsible with the simple job of collecting information and evidence into possible activities in the county water plant. There are multiple blockades established throughout town, including one enroute to the plant."

"We can bypass that route by travelling through the abandoned mineshaft tunnels at Linz Mountain," Charlemagne said, pointing to its location. "Since my 56th birthday, the mines were more or less condemned, but there are still abandoned sewage tunnels that go straight to the water treatment facility and can provide us with access."

"Once inside the station, I would suggest that you remain hidden and simply observe activities to give us a report. We can always return another day to launch an attack, but our main concerns at the moment are intelligence," Eugene stated. "Meanwhile, I will take my team, including Jock, Miklos, and

Viggo, and we will cross Champion Plains to reach the Medici home. We'll have to travel through the flood plains to avoid the blockades established, but for the most part, it should be a navigable journey."

The group turned to the door as they heard a knock. The door was open, but at the doorway was Moira with Charlemagne's quad-drone in her hands.

"It's ready," Moira simply stated, entering with the drone and stepping towards Charlemagne.

"Lucky," Charlemagne said, taking the drone in hand.

"Lucky?" Moira questioned.

"Yes, that's its name," Charlemagne stated. "Have you kept my drone safe for me?"

"I've kept it safe and made a few modifications," Moira replied.

"How were you able to unlock... Nevermind, perhaps I shouldn't ask such futile questions. I know you are a clever girl. It'll prove useful for our mission," Charlemagne said. "Thank you."

Charlemagne returned to the table and set the drone down.

"Do you suppose your water plants have closed-circuited cameras?" Bauer questioned, looking at the map.

"Yes," Charlemagne said, looking to Bauer. "When my brother held me at gunpoint, the police were able to recover footage of the incident. If we could get our hands on footage of the activities there, we could release them to the world and show them what exactly is going on."

"How would we be able to get access to this footage?" Bauer then asked. "We need an insider for information."

"If I could get my hands on a computer, I might be able to hack my way into the servers and download any footage that you need," Moira pointed out.

Charlemagne looked to Moira and then Mr. Macmillan.

"You are not going with them," Macmillan refused. "It's out of the question."

"I don't need to go with them to help," Moira refuted. "I have a device… if they can attach it to a computer at the plant, I can sneak in through the municipal wireless network and make my way through to find where they store their security footage. I don't need Internet, dad. With Lucky, it can be like I'm there… I'll be able to see, hear, and even be able to control him without having to leave this building."

Macmillan took a deep breath.

"Fine," Macmillan stated.

"If there is nothing more to go over, the faster we leave, the better," Charlemagne stated. "Are there any questions?"

Nobody answered.

"Good."

"My team is to get ready and meet me downstairs in five minutes," Eugene stated. "Dismissed."

Macmillan's team left the room. Mr. Macmillan went to his office. Charlemagne was left with Bauer, Barry, and all three kids. Charlemagne looked to the kids. Moira looked to Charlemagne and left.

"Well, let's get a move on then," Charlemagne said, looking to the others.

"Wait, what about us?" Tristan questioned. "Do we at least get a bed to sleep in? Nobody's really told us anything."

"You won't be sleeping until morning when we return," Charlemagne simply stated. "The two of you are coming with me."

"Really?" Diana questioned.

"Is that a problem?"

"I thought you wanted us to be safe," Tristan replied in a dull tone.

"The two of you being with me and Maxim is the safest option – that's what we discussed," Charlemagne stated. "All we'll be doing is hiking to the abandoned mines, going to the water treatment facility, and then returning with information about their activities. If anything is to happen, the two of you will return via the route we came. Understood?"

"Yes," Tristan replied.

"Good. Let's go then."

Diana and Tristan looked at each other and then followed Maxim and Charlemagne out of the meeting room and downstairs. Once downstairs, they walked towards the exit corridor where they were ambushed by Moira.

"Mr. Cabernet," Moira said, "if we're going to be working together, it'll be best if we're in contact with each other. Here, I'll be using shortwave frequencies to talk with you. I was able to convert the radio system that used to be used by the Medicis in this warehouse for the militia. With it, we'll be in touch."

Moira gave Charlemagne and Bauer two ear-pieces linked to handheld radios.

"Thank you," Charlemagne simply said, taking the radio and clipping it to his belt, "and thank you for your assistance. Are there two more radios that we can take? For Diana and Tristan?"

"Yeah, I can get two more, no problem," Moira responded. "Here, you'll also need this."

Moira gave Charlemagne a device that was similar to a USB drive.

"All you have to do is plug that into a computer for me," Moira explained.

"Very well," Charlemagne replied, putting the device into a pocket.

"Good luck," Moira then said. "I'll get two more radios and meet you by the exit."

Charlemagne nodded and then led his team forward into the corridor, following Moira who disappeared into a side room. Charlemagne opened the door into the outdoors and had his team exit. Once they were out, they stood in the open for a moment as Charlemagne looked around. Moira later came out with two more radios, handed them to Charlemagne who then gave one each to the kids. Moira then left. Once Diana and Tristan were ready, Charlemagne looked to them and then outwards.

"We'll follow the roads to reach the abandoned mineshaft," Charlemagne said, looking around. "Follow me."

Charlemagne led his team away from the warehouse and back into the forest that surrounded it. They went towards the main road and kept hidden within the trees to follow the road north. Charlemagne walked with Bauer while the kids lagged from behind. They walked casually.

"I have an idea that I'd like to run through you," Charlemagne said to Bauer.

"Go ahead," Maxim responded.

"If you are to help me with Zimmerman Corporation, you will need a position within my own organization," Charlemagne stated. "How would you like to become the team lead for my private guard?"

Bauer didn't immediately respond.

"Last year, I was on vacation with the children in Egypt when we were ambushed, beaten up, kidnapped and left stranded in the Eastern Desert. Less than a few days later, we were in the hands of vile terrorists. At the end of the trip, Audric Zimmerman spoke to me and said that I should invest in a personal defense force, which I did. I hired a man named Henry Heavner and various other consultants, and they formed my very own protection squad who provide tactical security for Cabernet Industries. My own team accompanies me on my foreign trips, keep an eye on the kids, and on their down-time, assist with Cabernet security operations in the Nattau County. Currently, Miklos Horvath, the man you met in the warehouse, holds the position I am offering you, but Miklos needs to retire from the field. I plan to promote him to become a security consultant. You on the other hand, are younger than Miklos... I assume. You appear to be young."

"I am thirty-eight," Maxim said.

"A good age still," Charlemagne said. "Miklos is almost forty-five, and he has a young son. I would hate to see something happen to him... I would hate to feel responsible for his son to lose his father..."

Bauer continued to walk with Charlemagne for another two minutes before saying, "Let us first handle this occupation before we make plans for the future. I am a man of my word, and I cannot make a promise that I cannot guarantee to fulfil. I will help you with Zimmerman and his men; that as much I can promise to you right now."

"Of course," Charlemagne replied.

Charlemagne, Bauer, and the kids continued to travel along the road until they reached the intersection that went towards the abandoned mineshafts. Within a couple minutes, they reached the rim of the large canyon that was the outskirts of the old mine. In the last two years, the old structures of the mine camp had been replaced with the skeleton of a large facility under construction. There were additionally various construction vehicles parked around. A chain-link fence with barbed wire surrounded the entire area with a warning sign on the front. A gate at the end of the road was locked with steel chains and a padlock. A sign on the right of the road advertised a future expansion of the water pump station set for 2022. Charlemagne immediately went to working on the padlock with his toolkit in his backpack. Bauer provided some light with a flashlight.

Once the padlock was removed, he led the team downhill and down into the canyon where they went towards the gate into the mines. Diana and Tristan looked around as Charlemagne fiddled with the second lock. Once this lock was unlocked, the team continued inside. Charlemagne led the team down the mineshaft where it was dark and damp.

The tunnels of the mineshaft were large – large enough for a Tiger II and some cars to navigate through. Tristan looked around. The tunnels averaged approximately five meters in width and height. In the last two years, the tunnels had received limited reinforcement as part of the construction project in which the mineshaft was to become cylindrical in shape, but the construction was far from completion as only parts had been modified and the rock walls of the mineshaft could still be seen. Charlemagne led the team down the tunnels.

The descent into the mine followed a curved tunnel before straightening out. They walked for almost ten minutes to reach the end of the tunnel at a T-intersection. At the end of the tunnel, they reached some wooden rubble. Charlemagne looked at the ruins for a moment. Tristan looked into the darkness at the right. Instead of a wooden shack, he saw a parked excavator. Charlemagne continued to lead them to the left where they walked for another ten minutes before reaching the end. Just before the end, the tunnel intersected with a small enclave. Charlemagne shined his light towards the enclave.

The trench with the large pipe that connected to the water treatment facility had been replaced with a low cylindrical pit that was approximately four meters tall. A metal staircase to the right went into the bottom of the pit. Tristan could see the wide

3.7 meter diameter pipe protruding from the left-side of the wall. The entrance of the pipe was guarded with a metal grate. Around the outskirts of the pit was some wooden fencing. Charlemagne led them around the fence, down the stairs, and towards the pipe.

Act 5, Scene 2

Charlemagne shined his flashlight down the long tunnel of the pipe. He then examined the lock on either side of the grate and proceeded to forcibly unlock them. Once the first lock was off, Bauer helped him lower the grate to the ground. He then worked on the second. After the second lock was taken off, Tristan rushed over to help Bauer lift the metal grate and set it aside. Charlemagne and Bauer went ahead and led the kids onwards towards the water treatment facility.

Within five minutes, Tristan began to notice the sound of rushing water in the distance as well as a source of light. After another couple minutes, the team had reached the end of the tunnel and entered the water treatment plant. Specifically, they were in the large room with a canal immediately below them. Pipes beneath a metal floor on the left of the room had a gentle flow of water entering the canal. There were additional pipes along the walls on the left and right. The room was dim, but lit by LED lights hanging from the ceiling. In contrast to when Charlemagne and the kids had last entered this room, there was a gentle stream of water in the canal flowing downwards and forward ahead of them. In addition, there was a metal catwalk before them that allowed easy entrance into the water transport pipe.

Charlemagne and Bauer stepped off from the transport pipe and onto the catwalk where they looked around the room. There was no sign of the mercenaries from the room they were in. Charlemagne led Bauer and the kids down the catwalk and to a ladder that brought them onto the right platform above the canal. Charlemagne paused his movement as he reached the bottom of the ladder. He waited for the kids to stop climbing down to pause. He could hear the distant sound of movement and Russian chatter.

"We're definitely not alone," Charlemagne advised, listening to the chatter.

"Yes," Maxim affirmed, looking around the room. "I will take point from here."

Bauer went forward and towards the staircase that went up and over to the other side of the room. It was in this area where the mobsters had held Charlemagne, Salmar, and the kids at gunpoint in the canal below. Bauer reached the top of the stairs and looked around on one knee. He then stood up and motioned the others to come up as he went down. Charlemagne and the kids followed from behind as Bauer crossed the room to the other side and other staircase that went up again. He looked either side and then went to the right towards a corridor that went deeper into the facility.

From the chamber they were in, Bauer led them down a concrete corridor that was sloped downwards. In the middle of the corridor was a metal fence with a metal gate. Bauer reached the gate and then opened it. The gate had an obnoxious creak to it. Once the gate was open, he continued to lead the team forward down the plain corridor. At the end of the hallway, Bauer lowered himself down on one knee as he came to the reservoir room.

The corridor entered the room from a tall height and onto a metal grated platform. Bauer signaled the team to stay back as they hid at the start of the corridor and avoided stepping onto the metal. Charlemagne came up and got down on one knee next to him. The kids lingered behind. The two of them could see movement ahead atop of the platform in the middle of the room where two mercenaries were armed with assault rifles and looking around.

Charlemagne took the opportunity to properly examine the enormous room. From the platform where Charlemagne was, the platform wrapped around and connected to a platform in the middle via the right-side. On the immediate left-side, railing marked the end of the platform as the canal poured out from the room they were just in and into the reservoir room. Below them, a similar platform existed at water level which wrapped around on the left to a set of metal stairs that connected to the same platform, but on the left-side. The platform in the middle had access to two ladders on either side at the center that went down to platforms at the water level. There were various pipes that stretched above the center platform from one end to another. The middle platform itself acted as a bridge between an exit corridor and a corridor that went deeper into the facility where water filtration occurred. The platform before Charlemagne and Maxim was mimicked at the other side of the room, which led to a separate area of the filtration plant. A gentle cascade of water poured from the circular transport pipes, which were approximately 3.7 meter in diameter just like the ones they had just travelled down from the mineshaft. At the opposite side of the room, there was another outlet just like this one, but with a lot more water gushing out. The noise level in the room was moderate and Charlemagne and Maxim were able to slightly hear the mercenaries chatting in the center of the room. The lights in the room were dim and the railings were solid like the ones in the boiler room of the channel ferry.

"We can't fire," Maxim remarked to Charlemagne. "We'll break our stealth and they can't see us."

"I reckon we move around and make our way upstairs," Charlemagne stated. "Moira said that any old computer will do, so let's go find one upstairs where I know there are office spaces."

"Copy that," Maxim replied. "I'll take point. Keep low."

"Aye," Charlemagne affirmed, turning around to get the kids to follow.

Charlemagne then paused his hand.

"Stay 'ere and keep watch," Charlemagne ordered. "You have your radios, so use them."

"Okay," Tristan simply replied.

Charlemagne then continued to follow Maxim as they slowly and quietly went around the reservoir room by hiding behind the railings. Bauer stopped him halfway. Charlemagne looked over and saw the mercenaries moving around. The two of them were smoking and walking towards them at a casual pace. They were distracted by their own chatter. Bauer looked at them with concentrated eyes. A mercenary suddenly turned around to the other with a loud voice. He pushed past his comrade and went to the other side with his back to Charlemagne and Maxim. The other followed. Charlemagne followed Maxim as they went around and then up the set of stairs that left the reservoir room. Charlemagne took point as they went up the set of wide stairs that went to two set of double doors at the top.

On the other side of the door, the atmosphere shifted as they were brought into a modern office space. Immediately behind the door, they entered a corridor with a rectangular archway at the end on the left and right. Bauer kept to the wall and went to the corner of the archway. He peaked around the corner and then turned to Charlemagne.

"Hostile ahead," Bauer reported.

Bauer moved out from where he was and went forward. Charlemagne stepped forward and took his place. He looked as Bauer crept forward towards the mercenary with his back turned. Behind the corridor was a large foyer entrance with glass windows looking out to the parking lot and outside. There were also stairs that went to the offices above them and a front desk on the immediate other side of the wall. Bauer approached the mercenary and brought him into a chokehold, covering his mouth with his glove.

Charlemagne watched as the man struggled for a gasp of air before giving in. Bauer immediately let go and laid the man down on the ground. He then looked around and relaxed.

"It's clear," Bauer announced.

Charlemagne came around the corner and went towards the computer at the front desk. He switched it on and took off his backpack to release the drone. He turned it on and set it to hover next to him as he waited for the computer to boot. Meanwhile, Charlemagne inserted the USB device into the computer.

"Charlie-Actual, this is Oracle, do you copy?" Moira questioned over the radio.

"I copy," Charlemagne responded, looking to the drone. "How is that you know my call sign?"

Charlemagne didn't get an immediate response.

"Never mind," Charlemagne said, shaking his head. "Do you copy?"

"I copy," Moira affirmed. "I saw you put the USB drive in. I'm going to manually activate the worm over the municipal network, which will allow me to bypass the firewall and hack into the computer system. Stand-by."

Charlemagne looked to Bauer as the two waited for a moment.

"Okay," Moira said within a couple minutes. "I'm in. I did a quick search and couldn't find any archives of any surveillance footage…"

"Is it a problem with the computer?" Charlemagne questioned.

"Possibly," Moira replied. "However, I was able to find some useful information, such as floor plans of the facility you're at and controls over some functions."

"I feared we might need to seek out a computer used by security," Charlemagne stated. "The city contracts security operations at this site, and if that's the case, they'll be using their own computers to store footage."

"I'm taking a look at the floor plans and it appears that there's a security room attached to the command center in the back of the plant," Moira stated. "Can you get there?"

"We can if you give us some directions," Bauer replied. "Which way?"

"Well, from where you are, you'll need to go into the plant and cross the reservoir room to reach the water filtration plant. From there, the command center can be reached by some catwalks around the side."

"Reaching that part of the plan will be a tad difficult given the guards in the reservoir room," Charlemagne pointed out.

"Not unless we can deafen the sound of our gunfire…" Bauer suggested. "You said you had access to plant controls? Can you increase water flow into the reservoir?"

"Uh… I should be able to…" Moira replied. "Now that I'm in, I'm in. Be sure to unplug the USB drive. You'll need that virus to penetrate through other systems."

"Okay, take a look and get back to us," Bauer responded. "We'll return back to this reservoir room and see what can be done."

"Sure thing," Moira agreed.

"Let's go," Bauer said to Charlemagne.

The two exited from the front desk with the drone following them. They went back downstairs, but stopped halfway down the stairs.

"Okay... I think I found a way to increase water flow," Moira said. "Let me know if this does anything..."

Charlemagne and Bauer waited. Within a minute, the noise volume in the reservoir room had doubled. Bauer looked to Charlemagne. He then continued down the stairs and reached the bottom of the stairs. He hid behind cover. Charlemagne followed.

"On my mark," Bauer warned.

Bauer then turned around and opened fire towards the guards. The noise of the assault rifles shooting was loud, but slightly masked by the water. Tristan watched from the corridor as the two went down. He perked up from his sleepiness at the sudden onslaught of gunfire. The two mercenaries went down with ease. Charlemagne and Bauer and then rushed towards them, checking on them before continuing forward. Tristan moved forward and looked over to Charlemagne and Bauer as they crossed and then left.

The facility continued via a long corridor that ended at the entrance into the filtration room, which was at a raised platform that surrounded the entire room. Charlemagne and Bauer looked out and saw that the filtration area was wider and larger than the reservoir room with various individual cells, or stations plotted around for the purposes of coagulation of small particles, flocculation, and filtration. Each station was rectangular and pool-like with a catwalk surrounding the entrenched pool. The cells existed in a five by three grid. Each catwalk was raised by approximately three feet above the ground with similar railings that blocked line of sight. From where Charlemagne and Maxim had entered, a room could be seen on the other side with downward slanted glass windows looking out below. There were a few a patrolmen walking around with assault rifles mounted with flashlights that were on. Charlemagne took a deep breath of the chloramine in the air as he looked around.

"Control room is on the other side from here," Moira explained, moving the drone around. "Follow me."

Bauer and Charlemagne followed the drone around the side of the water treatment room and came to a set of three stairs that went into the command center. The stairs were next to a short corridor that went deeper into the facility. The door into the room was locked and had a proxy card reader on the side. Charlemagne examined the door knob and saw that it took a key. He proceeded to pick the lock.

Once the door was unlocked, the team entered into the control room and looked around. The control room had various desks lined against the walls with windows looking into the filtration room. Each station had at least four computer monitors with additional TV monitors above the windows pointed downwards. There were approximately three large desks in total with six computer stations. At least two of the computers were on and all of the monitors projecting the main software used to control the water system. The graph on the monitor was actively creating a line as time went forward. At the back of the room directly opposite from where Charlemagne and Maxim had come in was a solid black door with the word 'Security' in front.

Charlemagne went to the door and saw that it had a proxy card reader on the side as well as an individual deadbolt lock with a keyhole. He proceeded to pick the lock and open the door. Maxim stopped Charlemagne as he brought a hand to his shoulder. He then placed a hand over the door and brought his forehead to gently rest against the surface of the door. He paused for almost a minute before moving his away.

"There is no one inside," Maxim stated.

Charlemagne continued to pick the lock and once he had the door unlocked, he opened it and walked in with Maxim and the drone behind him. On the other side of the door was a short corridor that led into small room with a desk and various computer monitors. All of the monitors were black as the entire security system appeared to be offline. Charlemagne went to the chair and sat down. The drone moved over. Charlemagne looked for the computer hardware and popped the USB widget in.

"Can you turn the PC on, please?" Moira requested.

"Certainly," Charlemagne replied, turning the computer on.

The computers flashed a blue screen and then loaded up. Bauer took point at the end of the corridor and looked out for Charlemagne as he sat at the desk with his back turned. The main computer screen displayed a log on console.

"Alright, give me a moment," Moira said.

Charlemagne and Bauer waited for a couple minutes. In that time, Moira bypassed the log on and managed to sign on to the computer. She was then able to bring up the security footage console and give them eyes on the entire facility with a map in the corner. Charlemagne studied the map before looking to each screen. He did not see anything suspicious at the time.

"Hm," Charlemagne grunted, looking at each camera view. "I suppose one ought to think where they would pour any chemicals if they were doing so."

Charlemagne's eyes went from each point of view to the next. He then pointed to a view of a section behind the filtration station.

"Here," Charlemagne said, "have footage rewind in this area for last several days."

Moira did not immediately respond. The footage of the clearwell, which was a reservoir immediately behind the filtration room where filtered water was stored for the entire town was kept. The footage began to play backwards at 0.25x the speed. The clearwell was simply a large room, smaller than the other reservoir with raw water from the river and with more catwalks above it with railings. The cameras in this room were pointed at various angles. Charlemagne had his focus at a larger platform where the entrance doors were.

"We'll be here for ages," Charlemagne remarked. "We're going four minutes for every minute we have. Have a scroll through the footage until we see what we need."

Moira proceeded to scroll through the footage, going back to earlier in the day. Charlemagne saw people moving around in patrols until around five o'clock in the evening when there were various mercenaries at work pouring some unknown liquid from some barrels into the reservoir.

"Stop there," Charlemagne said.

Moira stopped and then played the footage. Charlemagne watched as he saw Huntsman mercenaries poison the water with the hallucinogen. He shook his head. Bauer turned around and looked.

"I've seen enough," Charlemagne said after a couple of minutes. "Can we rip this footage?"

"Give me a moment," Moira replied, typing into her keyboard at the base. "I need to find where they store their footage."

Charlemagne took the mouse and continued to scroll backwards around the same points of view to see the regular patrols conducted as well as other moments throughout the week when the mercenaries poured the hallucinogenic compound into the water. He went all the way back to the start of the month to before the occupation occurred. He went so far that he reached footage where regular civilian workers were at work in the plant. He then went forward to see the exact moment everything changed, but was unable to see any sort of hostile takeover. Instead, he stopped to the start of the month, the same night as the party in town, and focused on the clearwell after hours.

At approximately four o'clock in the morning, Charlemagne was able to observe various men in reflective vests and hardhats pouring the contents of unmarked metal barrels into the clearwell. Charlemagne went further and just prior to the arrival of these men on recorded footage. He looked at the parking lot and then to the shipping and receiving area at the back, just behind the clearwell where a vehicle arrived at the plant with men dressed in reflective vests and hardhats. They unloaded barrels from their commercial truck on pallets, which were transported on a pallet jack from the truck and into the compound. The men were able to enter through the back doors with a proxy card they had. The operation was simple and they were stopped by no one.

"Okay, I've found the footage. I'm going to start to transfer the footage from today to the USB drive, but it'll take a while. It's almost two gigabytes large."

"Once you're done, I would also like you to download footage from the loading bay and clearwell on October 5th," Charlemagne requested. "It had important footage of the Huntsman before the occupation."

"Sure thing."

Charlemagne and Bauer waited for a couple of minutes. Charlemagne sat back in the chair as he waited for the footage to download. He thought for a moment and then looked towards the main reservoir as he saw mercenaries arrive at the bridge where the corpses were.

"Oh no," Charlemagne said under his breath. "Maxim."

Maxim turned around and looked.

"Damn, the kids!" Charlemagne remarked, picking up his radio from his belt and pressing down the button so that he could talk. "Children, retreat! I repeat. Children, if you can hear me, retreat back to the tunnel at once!"

Tristan perked his head up and looked around. He and Diana were sat against the wall in the corridor and hadn't noticed the mercenaries discovering the bodies. The small patrol was alert to their presence, but not their location. Tristan stood up, but stayed down with Diana. Diana tugged at Tristan's sleeve, causing him to step back and for the couple to have their exeunt.

"There they are," Charlemagne pointed out, pointing to the footage. "We need to leave."

"I'm not done transferring the footage," Moira stated. "We'll be a little short."

"I'm sorry, but we'll have to make do with what we have," Charlemagne replied, pulling the USB drive device. "We're going."

Charlemagne led the way out of the CCTV console room and back to the control room. Him and Maxim then went to the door, exited, and took cover by the railings in the filtration room. They heard some shouting from below met with the spark and clash of bullets on their location.

"We're compromised," Charlemagne grunted.

"Go around to the other side," Maxim ordered. "I'll keep you covered!"

Charlemagne nodded, kept low, and went around towards the exit to the reservoir. Maxim kept his head down for another moment before opening fire below as he attempted to keep up with Charlemagne. Charlemagne went around to the corner and laid down some shots towards the Huntsman mercs below. Bauer caught up and Charlemagne took cover around the corner of the corridor to the main reservoir. He looked behind and saw mercenaries ahead who opened fire to them.

"No good," Charlemagne stated. "We can't return this way. We'll have to go around, through the clearwell, and past the washwater clarification area."

"I'll cover you then," Maxim replied.

Charlemagne kept low and returned towards the command room. He laid down some covering fire for Bauer to catch up before the two went towards the clearwell. They stopped at the end of the corridor and looked into the room. The clearwell was right behind the command room. To the right of the room was a corridor that went towards the washwater clarification area where backwash was treated.

Charlemagne and Bauer dashed to the other side of the room and reached concrete corridor that went forward. A freight elevator in the middle of the corridor opened just as they reached it to have a small squad of mercenaries come out and open fire towards them. The mercs stood in the open for a moment as the two got into cover around the corners of the corridor. Bauer shot at the mercs with Charlemagne, bringing them down within a moment as the mercenaries behind them caught up.

"Go on!" Maxim told Charlemagne. "It's clear!"

Charlemagne went forward while Maxim slowly went back, shooting at the mercs behind as Charlemagne went forward to a narrow room where washwater flocculation and clarification occurred. The room consisted of platforms above the pools of water below. Charlemagne took cover behind a concrete pillar as he spotted mercenaries ahead. Bauer caught up and joined Charlemagne in firing towards them. Charlemagne was a poor shot in comparison to Bauer, who had excellent aim and precision.

The mercenaries went down with ease for them to continue forward towards the end of the room that brought them into the initial room they were in before. The pair followed a short corridor that brought them to a catwalk that overlooked the canal that poured into the main reservoir. Charlemagne looked to the left. The catwalk they were on did not connect to the other side of the room, but instead consisted of a stairway that went down. A separate stairway was then needed to go up and over to the other side.

"Hostiles ahead!" Maxim shouted.

Charlemagne turned to the right. Another squad of mercenaries had arrived from the main reservoir and pinned them down. The two moved to the left slightly, but were kept in cover as they opened fire towards them.

"We're being suppressed!" Charlemagne remarked.

"We're being surrounded," Bauer complained.

"Moira?! Is there anything you can do to help?!" Charlemagne questioned.

"Uh… let me take a look…"

Tristan and Diana were at the transport pipe that went back to the mines. The couple could hear the gunfire on the other side of the room, but could not see anything. Tristan looked around and brought his rifle from around his shoulders. He then set off towards the stairwell that went up and over to the other side of the room. Diana followed.

"We need something," Charlemagne demanded as he felt the heat on them.

Bauer kept silent as he and Charlemagne kept their heads down. Charlemagne looked over for a brief moment and saw mercenaries closing in on their position. Bauer continued to return fire down the corridor to keep the mercenaries behind them at bay. He came to the end of his magazine and checked his vest for another, but he was out.

"They're closing in on us," Charlemagne warned. "What are we going to do?"

Bauer moved away from the corner of the corridor and towards the railing. He looked over and then lowered his head.

"Hold my rifle," Bauer simply said, resting the rifle on the railing.

Charlemagne's eyes widened as Bauer let go of his weapon. His ears then twitched as he heard footsteps come from behind them as someone walked up the stairs. Diana and Tristan walked up the stairs on the other side and came to the top. They remained low and looked as the mercenaries were about to close in on them.

The mercenary made his turn around the corner of the railing and brought his weapon towards Charlemagne and Maxim. Maxim extended his arm towards the man and caused him to drop his weapon and clench his head. The man shouted in pain. Tristan observed as the gunfire towards Charlemagne and Bauer stopped for a moment. The mercenary fell over the railing and onto the ground. Bauer then stood up and clenched a fist as he extended it towards the mercenaries.

"Charles, take point at the hallway and give me covering fire!" Bauer requested.

"Yes," Charlemagne replied, switching places and then going around the corner of the corridor to shoot at the mercenaries behind them.

Tristan watched as the mercenaries below all clenched their heads as if they had a terrible headache. The mercenaries were hunched over and staggered around. Some of them fell over. Diana looked at Maxim directly as this happened. His eyes glowed purple. Bauer held his right hand in a fist, flexed his arm and then threw his arm forward, opening his fist. The men in distress and pain on the floor below him fell over unconscious as he did so.

"The room is clear," Bauer stated. "Go!"

Charlemagne turned around and sure enough, the room was clear. Bauer moved aside and pointed his arm towards a mercenary ahead. Charlemagne saw as the man was raised up with his face pointing upwards as if a giant was grabbing him by the jaw. The man screamed in pain and hovered as he was raised up and then let go. Once the man touched the ground, he began to shoot his gun into the air, startling his comrades.

"Go!" Bauer shouted to Charlemagne again.

Charlemagne looked to Bauer and saw the purple in his eyes. Without hesitation, he left and went down the stairs before going to the other to go up and over. Tristan saw Charlemagne move and moved down the stairs with Diana. The two regrouped with Charlemagne by the tunnel.

"In the pipe! Hurry!" Charlemagne barked at the kids.

Tristan helped Diana in before he went inside. The two went forward while Charlemagne hung back, waiting for Bauer. Bauer soon ran over the stairs and caught up with Charlemagne. Charlemagne climbed into the tunnel and then turned around to wait for Bauer to join him. Bauer climbed into the tunnel and hurried along, behind Charlemagne as they made their escape from the facility.

Act 5, Scene 3

Diana and Tristan reached the end of the tunnel and came out into the pit in the mines. The drone eventually lost connection with the outside world as they ventured through the tunnel and fell to the ground. Charlemagne picked it up and placed it in his backpack. At the end of the tunnel, Charlemagne turned around to Bauer as he exited. Bauer caught up with them. Charlemagne observed that Bauer had a hand at his shoulder. Once he exited, Charlemagne waved a hand to Tristan.

"Help me put the gate back," Charlemagne said to him.

Tristan helped Charlemagne lift the large metal gate and hold it in place so that he could put the locks back. Once that was done, they went to the stairs and walked up to take a moment to catch their breath. Charlemagne looked at Bauer's shoulder and saw that his glove was bloodied.

"You're injured," Charlemagne stated. "Let me touch that up before we leave. We can rest here – I think we have time for that."

Bauer nodded and knelt down. He removed his glove from his shoulder and Charlemagne saw that a bullet had grazed him. Charlemagne removed his backpack and fetched a first aid kit. Diana and Tristan took a moment to sit down as Charlemagne knelt down and proceeded to treat Bauer's wound.

The entire group was silent until Tristan uncrossed his arms and said, "So, what the hell was that?"

Maxim looked to him. Charlemagne turned around and looked at him too.

"Are we all going to pretend like we didn't see what we just saw?" Tristan questioned.

Charlemagne went back to treating Bauer's wounds.

"We'll talk about it when we return to the warehouse," Charlemagne simply said. "We're not out of the heat yet."

"No, perhaps this is the best time to talk," Maxim instead replied. "I have not been entirely honest with you, Charles."

"You don't need to say much, because I already know…" Charlemagne said. "I'm not an idiot. I knew you were…"

Bauer unzipped a pocket from his jacket and produced a necklace. Charlemagne looked at the thin platinum chain and the tiny rock attached to it. His eyes widened.

"Is that…?" Charlemagne questioned.

"A piece of the stone," Bauer confirmed. "Yes. You were right to assume that I was no ordinary soldier, but in addition to that, I kept my piece that was given to me. I didn't want to say anything," he grunted as Charlemagne applied an antiseptic, "because all of this… is it because of me?"

"What do you mean?" Tristan questioned.

"Perhaps I should explain what you children don't already know," Charlemagne said instead, putting down a cloth.

Charlemagne explained to the kids how Bauer came to him during the Halloween Party with intel that Zimmerman was plotting something big. He explained that Zimmerman had been experimenting on a group of select humans to unveil psychic powers within them and train them to use their powers as psionic supersoldiers with Bauer being one of them. He also explained that the necklace gave those with the gift of psychic powers the power to teleport, and that was Zimmerman's intent with the Amulet of Ra and the great extent he went to retrieve it in Egypt. Charlemagne finished off with saying that the supersoldiers were part of a larger scheme of Zimmerman's, of which both Bauer and Charlemagne were unsure of.

"So, you were a part of the Huntsman then?" Tristan questioned.

"I was loyal only to Zimmerman," Bauer replied. "I was never a part of the Huntsman, but it was a part of my duties to know everything about them. The Huntsman Legionnaires are a group completely separate and independent of the Zimmerman Corporation. They are a private military company owned by Bogdan Alexandrov, a former Spetsnaz GRU operative. They are contracted by Zimmerman to help him with large-scale operations, but that was intended to change. Zimmerman intended to build his own armed forces with these psionic soldiers like me in his inner circle, controlling the armed forces."

Bauer sighed.

"All of this – the effort to contaminate the water supply, the panic over an inexistent pandemic, was all an effort to exert control over this town because I came here looking for Charles to help me return home to Switzerland."

"If you can teleport, why not teleport to Switzerland?" Tristan questioned.

"Alas, a shortcoming in Zimmerman's design. When his scientists broke the stone down, he made each individual piece weaker than the entire orb was as a whole. If I had the original crystal, I could, but I cannot," Bauer explained. "Nonetheless, my former cohorts are looking for me and won't end this occupation until they have found me. I should never have come here…"

"You are here, and we cannot let them get to you," Charlemagne affirmed as he finished dressing his wound. "You are with us now."

"But they *are* here…" Bauer replied in a frightened tone, looking up to the ceiling. "Ever since I arrived at your home, Charles, I have felt the presence of the others nearby."

Bauer then looked back down to the ground.

"Perhaps I should explain a little more before we leave…" Bauer stated. "The powers that I possess I have had since I was perhaps a child, but I never knew I had them until Zimmerman awakened them within me. It is likely that more exist like me, out here – I am not sure of the exact percentages, but they do exist, and have existed throughout history. To become awakened comes at a great cost. What they did to make that happen was nothing more than torture. I was subjected to months of endless agony… to break me so that I would do as I was told by them and their leader… In total, I spent at least five months in a chamber where they played with me until I was theirs. I was the last of three others… I remember their names, even if they don't remember theirs: Sven, Knut… Harald."

Bauer sighed.

"At this moment, Zimmerman has this crystal and all its power, but he is in search of the other… the second artefact," Bauer stated, putting the necklace around his neck. "I intended to escape from all this, but I now understand that this is not my fate and that instead I am to aid Charles in a quest to stop Zimmerman because I and the others are a small part of many dastardly projects… I brought this entire occupation onto your beloved town. I am sorry for that."

"But you will help us. You will redeem yourself, and that starts and ends by helping us end this occupation. With the footage we have recovered, we can expose to the world what is going on to the masses. Macmillan has his own ideas, particularly in insurgency, and you will help me help him in that regard. However, your secret is safe with us," Charlemagne said, turning to the kids, "because Macmillan cannot know that the root of this occupation is Bauer's presence in this town. Am I understood?"

The kids nodded.

"Thank you," Bauer responded.

Bauer stood up and fixed his weapon. Charlemagne handed him some ammunition clips from his backpack. Once he was ready, the four of them continued through the mines.

Act 5, Scene 4

Charlemagne and Bauer led the kids out of the mines and to the outside. Dawn was upon them as the skies were dark, but looked brighter than they were throughout the night. Charlemagne looked to his watch and saw that it was just past seven o'clock in the morning. He fumbled with the lock of the gate and then opened it for them to exit. Bauer and the kids stepped out. Charlemagne then closed the gate behind him. He then turned around, but stopped as he saw before him, a peculiar purple orb of bright light appear out of thin air and emit a wave of light that almost blinded him and the kids.

"Hide!" Bauer shouted. "It's one of them!"

The orb was small, approximately the size of a baseball, but soon expanded and burst as a soldier in a similar uniform to Bauer, but with a ballistics vest on and matching helmet and tinted visor that prevented one from seeing his face. The soldier was armed with an assault rifle behind his back. His hands were free and he had a similar necklace to the one that Bauer had just shown them around his neck.

The supersoldier stepped forward as Charlemagne and the kids rushed off into the construction site. Bauer charged towards the soldier and immediately engaged him. The supersoldier blocked Bauer's immediate blow. Tristan was unable to witness what happened next as Charlemagne pulled him and Diana behind the structure of the future pump station.

"Are you going to help him?" Tristan questioned as Charlemagne entered into the unfinished structure.

"I intend to, but first I need to get the two of you out of here," Charlemagne replied, waving them over. "Come on."

Tristan vaulted over a concrete barrier and entered the unfinished building with Diana. The two rushed through the unfinished rooms of concrete and came out to the other side with Charlemagne.

"Go! Up the ramp and to the top of the gorge!" Charlemagne ordered the kids. "Go!"

"Alright..." Tristan whispered under his breath, taking Diana's hand.

The couple ran off and went up the slope to the top while Charlemagne returned to the corner of the unfinished structure and readied his assault rifle. Diana and Tristan stopped at the top of the slope and looked down as Bauer continued to engage the supersoldier in close quarters hand-to-hand combat. Charlemagne turned around and saw a ladder for him to climb up to the second floor where there was no ceiling or roof.

Bauer and the supersoldier took a defensive stance with their arms in front of each of them, watching the other's moves. The supersoldier crept forward and took Bauer's left arm and threw him back onto the floor. Bauer quickly pivoted himself around and stood up, moving away from the supersoldier and maintaining his stance. The supersoldier backed up. Bauer moved in with a kick, but the supersoldier deflected and grabbed Bauer from under the arm pit, bringing his right arm up and around to drop Bauer onto the ground again. Bauer rolled out of the way and stood up. He returned to a defensive stance and lunged forward to grab the supersoldier by the neck.

The supersoldier retaliated and kicked Bauer in the abdomen whilst holding his neck and shoulder to flip him around. The supersoldier maintained Bauer's arm. Bauer raised his legs up and attempted to kick his foe with both of them. He deflected either one, but Bauer gave himself a chance to back up as the two separated again.

Charlemagne took cover behind an unfinished window and aimed his rifle towards the supersoldier. He then opened fire towards the supersoldier as the two were apart. The supersoldier pushed Bauer forward and then ducked. He raised a hand towards Charlemagne. Charlemagne's head turned back for a moment and he shouted out in pain.

"Charles!" Diana shouted.

Bauer took out a knife and grabbed the supersoldier by around the neck, turning him around and maintaining the knife at his neck. The supersoldier countered and took the knife off of Bauer, kicking him onto the ground. The supersoldier lost focus on Charlemagne. Charlemagne collapsed onto the ground and dropped his rifle. The supersoldier took the knife from the ground and attempted to stab Bauer with it. Bauer caught his arm and before his foe could stab into the chest, Bauer vanished with a pulse of purplish-pink light.

The supersoldier stabbed the ground and shouted in annoyance. The kids ran towards a bush and hid from sight while the soldier turned around and went towards the unfinished structure. Charlemagne brought a hand to his head from where he was and slowly stood up. He picked up his rifle and looked down, seeing that both the supersoldier and Bauer were gone. Charlemagne then turned around with his rifle ready as he heard shots fired from below him. He quickly went to the ladder and returned down and then around to enter past a plastic sheet that went into a room below where he was.

There, the two were fighting again, more violently than outside as the supersoldier threw punch after punch towards Bauer who had his arms flexed to deflect the punches before grabbing the supersoldier's arm and locking it in his grip. The supersoldier attempted to break free with his other arm, but Bauer evaded the attempt to strike back at him twice before knocking the supersoldier away. He then went forward and attempted to kick at him, but the supersoldier deflected. Bauer followed up the kick with a punch, but it was deflected, and then another punch with his other arm, but it was deflected. The two disappeared into the next room and Charlemagne followed, entering the corridor with his rifle raised and aiming forward towards the pair.

In an instant, the supersoldier disappeared this time. Bauer rushed forward and grabbed Charlemagne as the supersoldier appeared behind him. Charlemagne had only time to react by turning around. The supersoldier brought a hand to his rifle, but that was it, not making contact, as Bauer disappeared with Charlemagne. The two appeared elsewhere in the unfinished structure. Charlemagne looked around and saw that it was a large space and they were on a balcony on the second floor. Tristan could see them from where he was with Diana.

Bauer looked to Charlemagne for a split second, nodding to him, and without uttering a single word, Charlemagne took point towards an entrance on the ground floor ahead while Bauer ran down the balcony aisle. The supersoldier appeared from the entrance Charlemagne was aiming at and opened fire. The supersoldier extended his arm towards Charlemagne, causing him to lower his weapon and bring his hands to his head. Bauer went forward and jumped over the concrete railing to attack the supersoldier.

The supersoldier deflected and jumped back. Charlemagne recuperated from the psychic attack and raised his rifle again, aiming towards the psychic soldier, but avoiding to fire. Bauer continued to engage him in close-quarter combat, throwing kick after kick towards the soldier who deflected them. Bauer then attempted a jump kick, but the supersoldier grabbed him and picked him up. Bauer struggled and looked to Charlemagne. Charlemagne opened fire towards the psionic soldier who threw Bauer aside.

Before Bauer could land on the ground, he disappeared and Charlemagne fled away. Bauer ran towards Charlemagne across from where Charlemagne was running to, and the two then disappeared together out of the structure.

Charlemagne and Bauer appeared outside and behind the structure, between the walls of the cliff and the exterior surface. Tristan could see them again as they hid behind an excavator. Bauer left Charlemagne and went to take cover. He then turned around and looked to Charlemagne, into his eyes, and then over towards the exit where the supersoldier appeared, wielding his assault rifle. He opened fire towards them. Bauer disappeared and appeared next to the supersoldier.

The supersoldier turned upon Bauer's arrival and Bauer deflected the barrel of the assault rifle downwards, making it move in an arc and grabbing the rifle off of him. He then pushed his cohort back who promptly disappeared and re-appeared behind Bauer. Bauer turned around and used the rifle in his hands to block the pistol that the supersoldier had. A shot had fired from the pistol and then Bauer used the rifle to knock the supersoldier back onto the ground. Bauer aimed the rifle towards him, but he blinked again and disappeared.

Charlemagne repositioned onto the other side of the excavator as the supersoldier reappeared further to the side. Tristan and Diana had lost visual of the commotion and proceeded to move to get a line of sight again. Bauer re-engaged the supersoldier with a punch, but it was deflected. He threw another and it was deflected. Bauer then attempted to grab ahold of the soldier's arm and in the process, he grabbed the necklace and ripped it from the supersoldier's neck before he could teleport again. The soldier then attempted to charge at Bauer, but Bauer flipped him onto his back and kept him on the ground. Charlemagne took this moment to open fire, but not at the soldier and instead at the fuel tank at the side to cause gasoline to spill at his feet.

Bauer moved out of the way and retrieved the rifle he had dropped that belonged to the supersoldier while he stood back up onto his feet. Before he could flee into cover, Bauer extended a hand towards him and caused the gasoline to ignite. The supersoldier's clothes doused in fuel caused him to light up and scream in pain. He staggered to the side before the fuel tank behind him erupted. The supersoldier fell to his knees and shouted in pain as he stood next to the explosion. Charlemagne lowered his rifle while Bauer raised his to shoot at his cohort, killing him and causing him to collapse forward.

Charlemagne stood up and looked towards the corpse of the fallen soldier. A storm of light span around the corpse met with a terrible low-pitched scream that caused Charlemagne and the kids to cringe. The noise was followed with a blast wave with a pulse of light that hit back all the way towards the kids as if there had been an explosion originating where the corpse of the soldier was. Charlemagne and Bauer shielded their eyes as did the kids, and as they looked back towards the corpse of the soldier, it continued to be there as lifeless as it was.

Diana and Tristan looked at the corpse with a troubled face. Charlemagne also looked at the corpse with a troubled face. He stepped forward towards it and met up with Bauer. Bauer looked at the corpse for another moment and then turned around to leave. Charlemagne followed so that they could return to the base.

Act 5, Scene 5

Charlemagne, Maxim, and the kids returned to the base just before sunset and briefly debriefed with Macmillan before retiring to get some sleep. The beds in the living quarters of the warehouse were not the most comfortable and Charlemagne could not sleep. He laid in bed for three hours before getting out of bed and returning into the warehouse at noon. Charlemagne went upstairs to the meeting room where he was with several other militia members, including Bauer, listening to a radio. Cole Phillips was speaking.

"… as a result of this senseless attack against our infrastructure, I am left with no choice but to instill harsher measures towards those that disobey and resist against our emergency government in this time of crisis. Our heart goes out to those that were injured and killed at the Nattau Treatment Facility, but as a result of their brave actions, we were able to identify a root to the cause of our problems, which lies in this insurgency who are not only insurgents against this town, but terrorists who have brought this chaos onto us."

Macmillan looked to Charles as he crossed his arms.

"The Public Health Agency has announced the transmission of this deadly virus to have originated in an agent sent to this town to infect us and weaken us, but let it be known, that we may have suffered, but we are as strong as ever."

There was a moment of claps.

"And so, I must set a bounty for the capture of one, Maximillian Magnus Bauer, who came to this town at the start of the month and is a deadly member of the militia. For once we capture this man, dead or alive, the Public Health Agency has stated that we will be able to develop a cure to the deadly disease. For those of you, listening from home, you will be able to identify this man through posters that will be appearing throughout town, put up by our brave guards who have kept us safe."

There was a short pause and some inaudible mumbling before Phillips continued.

"The death toll is at one-hundred citizens... almost ten percent of our entire population has perished, and many more will continue to die if this man is not captured. I urge citizens, to not approach this man, but to let your local constable know immediately if seen. In addition to the development of a cure, there will be a handsome reward for information that leads to the arrest of this man."

Another pause took place with further inaudible mumbling.

"Alright, I've heard enough," Macmillan complained. "Turn it off."

Jock turned off the radio and then sat back down at the table.

"Well?" Jock questioned, looking at the others as they sat in silence.

Eugene looked at his son and then to Charlemagne.

"It's going to get worse out there for sure," Eugene stated. "We can't run a propaganda campaign large enough to compete with the Huntsman. We don't have the manpower or equipment to even communicate with each other, let alone the town. Even if we could, why would they believe us? They think we're terrorists..."

Macmillan sighed and scratched his head.

"We need to end this occupation then," Charlemagne stated. "Tonight."

Macmillan looked at Charlemagne.

"Thanks to your team," Charlemagne said, "we have the Medici family at our side and thanks to my team, we have vital footage that can expose this entire occupation to the masses of the world. What we lack is an access point, and I will guess that we'll find an access point in the fortress at the Nattau Bridge."

"Are you mad? We can't storm their castle! You may have just gotten here, but I've had the militia running reconnaissance missions since the start of the occupation, and we are severely outgunned and outmatched. They have tanks, armored cars, and the defenses on their base is too hard to crack! We'd need more manpower and equipment than we currently have, even with the Medicis at our side."

"I propose that we get the equipment you need then," Charlemagne replied. "If I remember correctly, the Nattau County Police Department headquarters has an armory with enough weaponry to fight back. If we can take the police department, we can not only have the weapons and armor we need, but a centralized point that divides the Huntsman in half."

"If we attack the police department, the Huntsman will send everything they have to that exact point and flush us out..." Eugene grimaced.

"Which is why we don't attack just the police department, but we launch a distraction at the furthest point away from their headquarters..." Charlemagne responded, walking over to the map. "With the Medicis on our side, we have them organize all of their available manpower to attack the checkpoint at the Carella River. The Huntsman will respond by sending at least half of their army to assist, and during the ensuing battle, we will take to the streets and have our uprising. It's now or never, Eugene, we won't be any more stronger than we are now..."

Mr. Macmillan did not respond as he thought. He then looked to the side.

"We need more men to launch an offensive like that," Macmillan replied, "there's not enough of us in this room to fight."

"Then let's recruit every laid off policeman, every able-bodied man and woman who can hold a rifle, and take to the streets..." Charlemagne encouraged. "We won't have another opportunity like this."

Mr. Macmillan walked over to the map and took a deep breath.

"With the police armory, we could tackle the blockades enroute to the bridge..." Macmillan stated. "We'd be able to easily mobilize and strike back... Who do you personally know, Charles, who would be willing to fight?"

"I know of some brave souls, particularly some people who owe me a favor for bringing them to Canada, but also others... I know that you know of some policeman who may be willing to partake in this last attack."

Macmillan looked at the map.

"Raise me an army, Charles, and you'll have your assault. We have enough weapons for thirty fighters... with the police armory, we'll be able to double our numbers and upgrade from this equipment borrowed from the Medici family. I'll get into contact with Hudson and see who we can call up from my end."

"Very well," Charlemagne replied, nodding.

Macmillan looked to the others, and then said, "Dismissed."

The others left the room until it was only Mr. Macmillan, Maxim and Charlemagne.

"I hope you're in the right about this," Eugene said to Charlemagne, "not because half of my current militia consists of your own men, but because I trust you and not them, I won't ask about why the Huntsman are after him."

Macmillan looked at Maxim.

"I won't give you a reason to resent that," Charlemagne assured him.

Later in that same day, by evening, the militia was busy making preparations for the oncoming assault. Tristan found Maxim sitting on a chair in the main space of the warehouse, against a wall, cleaning his rifle. Diana was with Moira and he was alone. Tristan approached Bauer sheepishly and looked at him. Bauer looked back at him.

"Can I tell you something?" Tristan questioned. "Something personal? But if I tell you, you can't tell anyone, including Charles and Diana. It's about something that's been bothering me, and I need to tell someone because it's driving me insane..."

Bauer looked at Tristan as he spoke with hesitation, but also anxiety and distress. He walked back and forth as he spoke.

"What is it?" Bauer questioned.

Tristan went ahead and told Maxim about what occurred at Northumberland-Berwick Park and how he had lost his most intimate friend. He explained to him who Finn was to him. He also explained to him the last two months he's had to endure the trauma of losing Finn. All Bauer could do as he listened was to nod. At the end of the story, Bauer set down his rifle and looked to Tristan.

"When I was twenty-one, I was in a deadly blast that took the lives of my entire team," Bauer explained. "I lost my most trusted comrade in that incident who I had known since I had joined the Swiss Guard. For months, even years, I wept for him... because to lose a brother, is never easy... All you can do is overcome your emotion and turn that sadness and grief into willpower to strike forward, because life... is a struggle. All of this negativity within you will pass, but not if you are passive about it because look at what is going on here... An uprising is about to take place and that is *action*. You must act and fight back. You must rise against your misery and become anew like the phoenix who rises from his ashes. Your suffering will shape you into a man – a changed man at that as you come to learn, and you will be stronger. I guarantee that, but only if you fight back in the right direction and don't fight against that of which attempts to aid, and that is the truth and the way. If you fight against the truth, you will only find yourself in a greater misery – an endless hell. Pray, Tristan. Pray to God that He may inspire you onto the right path because if not you will be lost and it is not guaranteed that you will eventually find the right path. Only those that are fortunate enough eventually find the right path, while others… never live to ever find the path that awaited them. God has given you all that you need to go on, but it is up to you with your mind to set yourself into that path."

"But what am I fighting for?" Tristan questioned. "Myself?"

"Fight for that which you love," Bauer encouraged. "We fight for what we love, and we hate that which threatens what we love. We do not stop, because the fight never stops, it only gets easier when you've developed that spiritual muscle of your mind."

Tristan gave a depressed sigh.

"I don't want to fight though," Tristan complained. "I just want to… not live anymore."

"Do not surrender," Maxim instructed in a strict tone. "You never surrender. You pick yourself up after every fight, and you fight again. You hold on and stay put until the end because all of this, this is to the end. Do you understand?"

"Y-yeah," Tristan lied.

"Maxim," Charlemagne stated, walking towards the two of them. "We're almost ready. We have two teams equipped to aid us on the streets. We're having our final briefing in fifteen minutes. Tristan, you and Diana will remain here with Moira and Lukas.

With that, Bauer stood up and left Tristan. Tristan watched him as he walked off with Charlemagne who went to get ready for the upcoming battle.

Act 6, Scene 1

A small team consisting of Charlemagne, Maxim, Hardrada, Holger, Lacplesis and Brandan had set off from the base once the sun had set and come into the town via the streets. A second team consisting of Macmillan, Miklos, Jock, Barrett, Lukas, and Tanya had split up to rendezvous with a third team consisting of policemen led by Sergeant Hudson whereas Charlemagne's team set off to meet with the fourth team consisting of Greenlanders led by Kristoffer Kristoffersen.

Charlemagne's team walked down the main street from the warehouse and through the forest. They travelled with the drone hovering over Charlemagne's shoulder. Each team leader had been given one of the four radios available to coordinate with each while Moira acted as a liaison. Charlemagne's team was split as they travelled on the sidewalk with Charlemagne leading one half and Maxim the other. In the distance, one could hear shouting in Russian.

Maxim stopped the two teams as they went forward. He had Hardrada take a scoped rifle and aim forward. Charlemagne had Holger do the same.

"Contacts ahead," Holger remarked.

"Open fire," Charlemagne ordered, looking through some binoculars as they spotted a small patrol of Phillip's guards ahead at the street corner.

The paramilitary group that was established to replace the police force dressed in similar uniforms to police officers. Holger shot a round. Hardrada shot another round. The two went down with ease and the team continued forward. The team was armed with the small cache of supplies Charlemagne had available for the entire Protection Squad as well as with glass bottles filled with gasoline and tied with rags. The team made their approach past the downed patrol team and continued forward. They had entered the outskirts of the town and were passing a small residential area of condominiums.

Maxim stopped the team again. Charlemagne looked out with his binoculars and spotted two more of Phillip's guards on approach from ahead.

"Contacts ahead!" Charlemagne shouted.

Maxim, Holger, and Hardrada got ready to open fire as the two hostiles made their approach. The team got into cover and opened fire. Holger shot from his scoped rifle. Charlemagne lowered his binoculars and readied his assault rifle to open fire.

"Target neutralized!" Hardrada called out.

"Targets down," Maxim confirmed. "Move up!"

Maxim got out of cover and led the team forward, down the street where they reached a blockade at the intersection. A wall had been constructed that blocked access further down the street, so the team rerouted westwards. Sirens could be heard in the background. The team moved faster as they went down the street, but were cut off by an approaching police car. The team split up again into cover and opened fire as the constables scattered. A second police car turned up with additional sirens in the background.

Once the zone was clear, Maxim led the team forward and southbound where they reached another police car that unloaded with two more officers. The team were able to comfortably handle the two constables before they continued onwards and reached another intersection. They turned down and Maxim moved into cover.

"Sniper! Rooftop! Right-side!" Maxim shouted.

Hardrada got down on one knee and looked out with his scope. Charlemagne shot back with some suppressing fire.

Hardrada took a shot. The constable fell over the rooftop and landed in the bushes before the apartment complex.

"Move up!" Maxim shouted.

The team continued down the street and reached the intersection with the hospital on the east side. Maxim led the team around the right-hand sidewalk and to the street corner where he peaked out the corner.

"Huntsman," Maxim said in a low voice, returning fire.

Maxim then rushed forward and found cover by some parked cars. The rest of the team moved forward and spread out into cover as they came up with Huntsman mercenaries ahead. Charlemagne shot back towards the hostiles when he noticed a vehicle turn around the street corner. A Huntsman APC vehicle turned across the street corner with a Huntsman mercenary riding atop and manning the turret. The APC shot a powerful machine gun towards the team. Charlemagne aimed at the vehicle and shot his assault rifles towards it. The bullets merely bounced off the heavy-duty armor of the craft. Charlemagne stopped firing and reloaded.

"You two, get on the flank and get ready to throw petrol bombs," Maxim ordered Lacplesis and Brandan. "Everybody, stay low!"

Maxim shot towards the mercenary manning the turret. He was able to get him, but the vehicle continued to fire the smaller guns towards them. A second mercenary from inside soon replaced the other. Lacplesis and Brandan continued to move forward. At least three other mercenaries were spread around ahead. Once Lacplesis and Elegast were in position, they lit the rags of the petrol bombs and threw them towards the vehicle.

The Molotov cocktails splashed flames onto the surface of the vehicles, but did little damage against the armor. The APC did stop for a moment. Lacplesis and Elegast launched another bombardment. Charlemagne noticed Maxim concentrating with his hand forward. He then moved around the side and ran forward with his back bent over. Once Charlemagne was in-line with the APC, he readied a petrol bomb and moved around. The other mercenaries ahead had been taken care of, allowing Charlemagne to move out into the open and throw the Molotov cocktail into APC. The Huntsman mercenaries shouted out in pain and began to retreat without their guns. The team moved forward.

"Let them run," Maxim stated. "We need to move forward."

Maxim led the team onwards and towards the local fire station on the left and some shops on the right with an arcade of stone pillared arches. The team spread out again to face up with the mercenaries hiding behind the stone pillars. Charlemagne could see the back gardens of the library past the shops. The team quickly dealt with the mercenaries, forcing them to retreat so that they could push forward. Maxim led on and Charlemagne observed that it was clear for them as they reached the library and thus heart of the town.

Ahead, across the intersection with the local café on the street corner, Charlemagne observed gunfire coming down the street and towards retreating mercenaries going towards central park. Maxim pushed up and kept the team covered by the foundation of the library. The team had met up with one of the other teams led by Sergeant Evan Hughes consisting of police officers who were loyal to Macmillan.

Maxim and Charlemagne came to the intersection and met with the sergeant for a brief moment. They shook hands.

"Glad you could make it," Charlemagne remarked. "We have a short ways to go to the police department – so let's get on with it."

The two teams travelled together, past the cinema and grocers, as they cut through the city park. Up ahead, in front of town hall, was an APC strolling down northbound.

"Contact!" Maxim shouted.

"APC!" Lacplesis added.

The teams spread out and opened fire towards the mercenaries using the municipal center and its many windows as cover. The APC opened fire towards them. Charlemagne saw snipers on the roof of the hotel on the street corner between the library and city hall.

"Snipers on the roof!" Maxim also shouted.

Charlemagne could see mercenaries on the roof of the civic center as well. He and Maxim were using the fountain in the center of the park as cover. Charlemagne laid some fire down and kept his head down when he needed to reload.

"How are we going to handle that halftrack?" Charlemagne questioned Maxim.

"We need to get closer and then we can concentrate some petrol bombs on it."

The two teams continued to return fire towards the town hall. The APC began to turn and face the team from the left flank. Maxim stopped firing towards the mercenaries and extended a hand towards the vehicle. The APC stopped. Charlemagne moved forward to get in position to throw a petrol bomb towards the APC.

With the amount of cover available in the park, it was difficult to safely navigate towards the vehicle. Charlemagne could only get so close as it was a long distance between a half-wall and the pedestals at south entrance into the park. He threw a Molotov cocktail towards the halftrack and it splashed flames onto the surface.

"Oracle, see if you can immobilize that halftrack," Charlemagne said.

"I'm on it," Moira responded.

The drone moved towards the APC and the APC began to fire towards the drone. Charlemagne saw this and ran for the pedestal. He quickly readied a Molotov cocktail and threw it towards the turret of the APC. The turret was unmanned, but was open. The bottle hit atop of the APC and splashed flames onto it. Charlemagne threw another for good measure, but he could hear the screams of the Huntsman as they abandoned and ran off. Charlemagne regrouped with the drone and used the abandoned APC as cover as he stood in front of his offices.

Gunfire began to die down between the militia and Huntsman in the town hall. The teams pushed forward and past the town hall to go down the highway and make their way to the Nattau County Police Department headquarters two blocks away. The team passed the back gardens of the town hall and shops on the left. The mercs had retreated and cleared the way for them to rush through.

Once the teams had crossed through to the final stretch, the mercenaries drew the line in the sand and took cover just before the police headquarters, on a street with shops on either side. The teams scrambled into cover once more and opened fire against the Huntsman who were determined not to give in. The two sides laid heavy fire against one another, but soon caved. Maxim led the teams forward and towards the intersection ahead where police sirens were flashing.

The local guards had aligned three police cruisers on the street to act as cover. The Huntsman took cover behind them and fought with the remainder of Phillips' private army. Charlemagne observed gunfire coming from the street to the right, or north, which meant that the other teams had arrived.

A Molotov cocktail was thrown from that side and hit one of the police cruisers as well as several hostiles. Both sides continued to fire at each other until Charlemagne noticed the Huntsman give in and begin to retreat westward, down the highway and away from the fight. The teams pushed on and the guards, instead of following the Huntsman, retreated into the headquarters where they continued to fight.

Charlemagne and Maxim took cover behind the police cruisers and continued to lay down fire. Macmillan and Miklos soon joined them.

"Sorry we're late," Eugene apologized. "We ran into an APC in front of the community center and were bogged down for a bit."

"No worries," Charlemagne responded. "Looks like the two factions have split and the headquarters are under siege. What now?"

Mr. Macmillan moved around to open the police cruiser and unlock the trunk. He then went around and got a megaphone out, which he turned on and then began to speak.

"Officers of the Nattau County Police Department, this is Captain Eugene Macmillan. You have sworn to serve and protect the civilians of this town, and yet you have done nothing more than aid and abet a foreign enemy. Sworn peace officers, surrender and you will not be found guilty of treason against the county. Please, I beg of you, fellow constables… Surrender because this occupation is over and we can ensure the health and safety of those of whom you love."

Macmillan turned off the microphone and dropped it to the ground. He then looked to the others.

"I'll take point and you two, follow behind?" Macmillan suggested, referring to Miklos and Bauer. "The rest of you," Mr. Macmillan shouted, "hold until further orders."

"Will do," Miklos replied to Macmillan's former suggestion.

"Wait!" Kristoffer shouted, pointing.

Charlemagne saw a corporal exit from the police department with a rifle held up.

"We surrender!" the corporal announced.

Macmillan looked ahead and held an expression of relief. He went forward with Charlemagne and entered the police department. Inside, dozens of constables and guardsmen sat around with lowered arms. The rest of the militia followed and joined these officers while the corporal took Macmillan and Charlemagne as well as Miklos and Bauer upstairs.

At the third-floor, they exited the stairwell and walked across to reach the double doors into Phillips' office. The corporal led them through and Chief Phillips rose from his chair and looked to them. He had a tired face and a bruised eye. He was at his desk with two of his guards at either side.

"Eugene," Phillips simply said, "Charles…"

"Cole," Macmillan responded.

Chief Phillips took off his hat and set it down on the desk.

"It's yours Eugene… all of it," Phillips remarked. "Do what you need to do to end this occupation. I concede to you and am stepping down. You're the Chief of Police now."

"You'll have time to step down when this is over, Cole," Macmillan responded. "Right now we need you more than ever. Have the armory opened, your men and my men equipped, and ready the briefing room. We're going to strike at the heart of the occupation."

Act 6, Scene 2

Once everybody was equipped and ready to continue, the teams, two additional teams formed out of the police officers that had been loyal to Phillips, set off to continue the fight. Charlemagne's team exited from the west-side of the police headquarters from a fire exit. They took with them from the police armory some tear gas and smoke grenades as well as gas masks. Maxim led the team across the parking lot and towards some hedges at the edge where they stopped. The drone kept up with Charlemagne as it flew around his right shoulder.

Maxim prepared a grenade and tossed it overboard, unleashing a cloud of smoke. Charlemagne saw gunfire coming from the eastside of the freeway via friendly units. Maxim then walked towards the exit from the parking lot and opened fire towards the blockade at the intersection ahead. He then moved forward as the blockade cleared due to the overwhelming firepower from nearby. Charlemagne moved out from cover and joined Maxim as they entered the intersection.

The blockade consisted of sandbags placed in each corner of the intersection in a slight U-shape with a machine gun turret in the middle, facing inwards, but able to angle from left and right. Effectively, the militia would come face-to-face with two turrets as they made their approach with another two facing the direction they needed to go. The turrets facing west at the blockade they were at though had been damaged and dismantled by the Huntsman, rendering them out of service.

Macmillan joined the team as they entered the intersection and took cover by the sandbags to fire back at the retreating Huntsman ahead. Captain Macmillan was not dressed in his regular police uniform, but in a tactical riot uniform with a helmet. The police officers changed into this uniform, which provided extra protection against gunfire. The civilians, Charlemagne's Protection Squad not included, that volunteered with the militia were given bullet proof vests, helmets, an assault rifle, and gas mask.

"You, you, and you," Macmillan ordered to some militiamen, "take point here and man those turrets. The rest of you," he addressed to another crowd, "are with me. We're going to take Clifford Street."

"Charles, Kristoffer, I want you to take the freeway and continue on," Macmillan said. "We'll aid from the left-side and regroup at the final blockade."

"Understood," Charlemagne confirmed.

"We need these blockades cleared so that our armored personnel carriers can mobilize through town – so let's go!" Macmillan shouted, going off and north towards Clifford Street.

Charlemagne and Maxim continued down the freeway and towards the next intersection, which was a T-intersection with the left street going towards Lord Phoenix Secondary School. On the right were multiple residential homes that were vertical, whereas the homes on the left were horizontal.

Huntsman mercenaries were spread throughout in small groups of three as they pushed forward towards the next intersection. The fights were typical and similar as they were in town, each side would exchange fire until the mercenaries would retreat due to weak numbers. The only superiority the militia had was its strength in numbers.

Once the team was at the next intersection, Charlemagne saw the next blockade ahead where the Huntsman had made their defense and were firing back at them. Charlemagne exchanged fire with Maxim. He lowered his head behind a mailbox and reloaded his rifle. He had spent half of his magazines by now. Charlemagne was about to continue to return fire when he noticed a loud noise in the distance. He then looked up into the sky and saw a volley of projectiles launch from the west and make their way towards them.

Immediately, canisters with a greenish-brown gas emitting from them hit behind the teams. Charlemagne immediately took his gas mask from behind him.

"Gasmasks!" Charlemagne yelled.

The militia hurried to put on their gas masks. Charlemagne shook his head as he felt some of the gas come on him before he was able to put on his mask. He staggered for a moment and simply shook his head as he looked to the ground. He then looked up and towards the sky. He looked towards the blockade and saw a reddish-black sky in the background as well as flashes of light coming from the muzzle fire of the turrets.

Charlemagne looked to the south and saw some creatures crawling about. He re-focused his attention to the street where the school was and could see some Huntsman in the area as well, mixed in with the zombies.

Suddenly, a creature jumped from the hedge nearby and pounced atop of Charlemagne. The creature was shot immediately, allowing Charlemagne to recover.

"Are you alright, Charles?" Maxim asked.

"I'm alright," Charlemagne affirmed, "but we have hostiles on the left flank!"

Charlemagne moved forward and towards a parked car on a driveway. He returned fire towards the encroaching enemies. He then ducked his head to reload.

"Maxim, I'll take a team and push these guys back. We'll hit the blockade from the left-side and press them harder!"

"Very well! I'll see you there then," Maxim replied. "Be careful, friend."

Charlemagne pushed on with a small group consisting of Greenlanders. Fridtjof Monrad was among these volunteers as well as other young men that had come from Hvitrnord.

"Back, you scoundrels. Back!" Kristoffer aggressively yelled as he pushed the Huntsman towards the school.

Charlemagne moved up as they reached the intersection before the school. The Huntsman were retreating back. Charlemagne concentrated on them, but was unable to ignore the zombies in the area, firing towards them as he saw them left or right.

Charlemagne's team eventually made it to the intersection and spread out onto the property of the school as they drove the Huntsman into the school. Kristoffer led the charge into the school through the front doors. Charlemagne could hear the patter of footsteps coming from the rooftop of the school. He shook his head and took cover around the other corner of the front doors. He looked in and saw Huntsman inside, taking cover around doors.

The interior of the school had changed slightly where there was now no quarantine zone as the Public Health Agency had seemingly abandoned the site, but they had left a mess in the halls with abandoned equipment and such. Across the halls was a hose and puddle of water as well as various tools laying across the floor.

"You three, go around and enter from the cafeteria," Charlemagne said. "We'll close in on them quickly so we can assist the others."

Kristoffer went into the heat. Charlemagne looked in and gave some covering fire as he rushed in, taking cover behind the trophy cabinet. Fridtjof moved up to where Kristoffer had been. The three of them continued to fire back until Kristoffer decided to push in again.

"Go back to the hell that you came!" Kristoffer shouted like a mad man, rushing in and towards the side of some lockers.

Fridtjof moved inside. The Huntsman retreated back once more. Charlemagne prepared a canister of tear gas and threw it forward. The Huntsman scattered and allowed them to push in as the tear gas leaked out a small white plumage. Kristoffer moved up to the middle corridor that connected with the gym. He opened fire down the corridor and then went down towards the gym. Unable to see what was going on in the corridor, Charlemagne could only hear the sound and screeches of zombies being shot. Charlemagne moved up and took his place, turning around and see the corpses of several zombies.

Kristoffer took cover behind a turned over table. The gym doors were closed. Charlemagne turned around and saw gunfire come from the left hallway ahead. The rest of the Huntsman ahead retreated back. Charlemagne moved up with Kristoffer before quickly turning around at the smashing of metal and appearance of a horde of zombies behind. Charlemagne opened fire towards them, startling the rest of the team as he fired blindly into the open corridor.

"Charles! What are you doing?" Kristoffer questioned. "Are you mad?"

Charlemagne looked to Kristoffer and through the eyeholes of his gas mask. Charlemagne was breathing heavily.

"Sorry, I'm having a bad reaction from the gas from earlier," Charlemagne confessed.

"Stay together, friend," Kristoffer encouraged.

The team regrouped with the other half of the team and then continued across the field as the Huntsman retreated towards the blockade. The militia picked them off before continuing ahead. They crossed the field from the side and then exited onto the street to spread out between the parked vehicles. Up ahead, the blockade was under fire from Maxim's team and Macmillan's team. Charlemagne laid his share of fire and they were able to eliminate the hostiles ahead to push on. The three teams united at the blockade and took control of the turrets.

"Alright, Kristoffer," Macmillan said. "Have four of your men remain here to control this point. We have one more."

"Yes," Kristoffer agreed before speaking in Danish to his men.

Kristoffer and Fridtjof continued with the rest of half of the militia, which now consisted of members of the Protection Squad, Charlemagne and Maxim, Mr. Macmillan, and those officers who were loyal to Macmillan, including Jock and Sergeant Hughes. The rest of the police force were at the police headquarters with Phillips.

"I'll take my share of the men and go around the right flank," Macmillan said. "Take your men and hit them hard."

"Will do," Charlemagne affirmed.

Macmillan left with his son and the other police officers, leaving Charlemagne with Miklos, Tanya, Holger, Hardrada, Lacplesis, and Elegast in addition to Bauer. The team went forward under cover and on towards the last blockade. They shot at the street lights around them to give them some darkness. The Huntsman opened fire to them, but they stayed hidden as they stayed low and took cover around the gardens of the houses nearby.

"Viggo, Björn, take sniping positions from a safe distance and attempt to snipe the gunners," Charlemagne ordered. "The rest of us will move up as a feint."

"Affirmative," Hardrada confirmed, taking his rifle and lingering back.

The rest of the team crept forward and reached the T-intersection before the stretch of the freeway that went to the blockade. Charlemagne took a prone position by a hedge and kept hidden. He looked ahead and saw that there was a moderate-sized force in the last defense before the edge of the plateau.

Maxim and Miklos opened fire, taking shots towards the gunners. A single, loud shot was heard in the air. Charlemagne saw a gunner fall back as one of the two Nords fired a shot from their scoped rifle. The gunner was replaced by the closest man who manned the machine gun. Another scoped shot fired and took the other, but they were soon replaced.

The mercenaries shot back towards them, but Charlemagne's team remained hidden and obscured in the darkness. Within a couple of minutes, gunfire could be heard from the right-side as Macmillan's team pressured the blockade. Hardrada and Holger continued to fire shots until the Huntsman abandoned the machine gun, but continued to return fire as they defended the intersection.

Charlemagne stopped returning fire as he felt the heat from a mercenary shooting towards him. He rolled out of the way and moved towards the side of a house to reload. Once he was reloaded, he noticed at least three mercenaries retreating back and away from the blockade. The other two in the mix were shot dead and with that, the team were able to move forward. Lacplesis and Elegast took to the machine guns facing west and opened fire towards the retreating mercenaries who disappeared forward.

Mr. Macmillan moved up and regrouped with Charlemagne and Maxim at the center of the street. Eugene took a radio from his belt and brought it up to his face.

"Sierra-Six-One, this is Juliet-One," Eugene said. "We've secured the freeway and you can send the armor in."

"Roger that," Phillips responded.

Mr. Macmillan put his radio away.

"Well done," Eugene said to Charlemagne and his team. "We've pushed hard and have a little left on us. Our reinforcements can move in, so how about we move on to the last obstacle?"

"Certainly," Charlemagne replied. "We're with you until the end, so let's move on."

The two teams remained at the final blockade until three armored personnel carriers belonging to the police force drove up to the blockade. Four police officers exited and took over the turret positions.

Phillips exited from another APC. He was dressed in tactical gear and was armed. He walked over to Charlemagne and Macmillan. Charlemagne took his team to the APC where they got inside. Charlemagne turned off his drone and set it on his lap as he sat down inside. Once everybody had taken a seat, Phillips closed the door and sat with them. The APC then moved forward, down the highway, and towards the concrete fortress.

Act 6, Scene 3

"And I've lost connection," Moira said, leaning back in her chair with a sigh. "Good news is that they're two-thirds of the way there…"

Diana sat next to Moira in an office in the warehouse. Moira had set up several computer monitors to one computer. The two weren't alone as the scientists alongside Barry were also with them, assisting Moira with coordination and mapping the efforts of the militia in relation to the Medici family. Tristan sat in the corner of the room, with his hunting rifle at his side.

Tristan's ears poked up and twitched as he heard the noise of some rotors from outside. He straightened up and attempted to listen, but could not hear anything else. He stood up and brought the sling of his hunting rifle around his shoulders to step out. Tristan entered a narrow corridor and walked to the end of it to exit into the exit corridor that went to the rear exit.

Behind him, the floor of the warehouse was dark and empty. Only a single light was lit in the corridor he stood in now. Tristan looked back and forth, and finally decided to go towards the rear exit door where Lukas spooked him. Lukas was still experiencing symptoms from the toxin in the water, but had recovered dramatically in the last several hours thanks to the scientists who've assisted with decontamination. Lukas stepped towards the door and looked out. He then stepped back and looked to Tristan.

"We're not alone," Lukas said to Tristan in his Italian accent. "Stay here and wait for my clear. If it is unsafe, let the others know so that we can evacuate."

Tristan nodded. Lukas left and went down the corridor, into the open space of the warehouse. Tristan followed and knelt down at the end of the corridor. He could see the passing of a beam of light through the broken and cracked upper windows of the warehouse. Lukas went to the main entrance door and looked through the peephole before stepping back.

Before Lukas could return to Tristan, the two of them were met with a loud bash against the shutter doors. Lukas took position around the corner of a truck and then signaled Tristan to retreat. Tristan brought his rifle around from his shoulder and into his hands. The shutters ahead opened by a foot. Tristan could see the boots of the Huntsman on the other side. They rolled canisters of hallucinogenic gas underneath and began to fill the open space with greenish gas.

Lukas opened fire towards them. Some of the Huntsman dropped down and returned fire, Lukas stepped back and then proceeded to retreat as Tristan finally decided to go back and return into the corridor to warn the others. Tristan came to the command room and opened the door.

"We're under attack!" Tristan warned. "We need to get out of here, stat!"

Moira stood up and took a USB drive into her hand before following Diana towards the door. She picked up her rifle before joining Tristan. Barry looked at the scientists.

"Everybody, arm yourselves and let's get out of here!" Barry said. "There's a weapon for each of us – let's fallback to the police department and regroup with the others."

The scientists went to a table in the back of the room where there were spare Thompson submachine guns that had been brought over from the Medici Manor. Once the scientists were armed, Barry led them out and into the corridor. Tristan, Diana, and Moira then followed as they flooded into the exit corridor where Lukas was shooting back at the Huntsman in their defense.

Once Diana and Tristan entered the exit corridor, Tristan looked over to Lukas. Diana grabbed Tristan by the wrist and questioned, "Where are you going?"

Moira stalled as she hung back and watched the couple.

"I have to go help him," Tristan said. "He can't fight them off all on his own."

"Charles wouldn't want you to," Diana argued. "We're in enough trouble as it is…"

"Tristan," Barry said from the rear exit door, "you're leaving," he added in a stern voice.

Tristan looked at him and then back to Lukas. He groaned and then led the girls out of the corridor and into the outdoors. Tristan rushed out and then looked back as Barry and Lukas left together.

The whole group of scientists and the kids ran off together into the forest and went towards Allabrese. They stuck together, but were slightly spread out with Lukas and Barry in the back of the horde, occasionally stopping to return fire against the Huntsman.

Tristan continued to run with Diana and Moira nearby. They went on and on in the darkness of the forest with only the light from the flashlights they had to comfort them. Tristan turned around and began to lose sight of both Barry and Lukas. He then turned forward again and ran into a tree.

Diana stopped and looked to Tristan. Moira stopped too.

"Are you okay?" Diana questioned.

"Yeah…" Tristan replied, shaking his head.

Tristan looked back behind him. He then looked to Diana as they stood in the forest together. It was quiet. Tristan panted. Diana looked at Tristan. He had a fearful look on his face.

"What's wrong?" Diana asked.

Tristan looked around and then to his girlfriend.

"I-I have a sense of an impending doom…" Tristan simply said to her.

Tristan continued to look around before flinching as he saw a shadowy figure rush towards him and cause him to fall backwards as he attempted to strike at the figure with his rifle. A shot fired from Tristan's rifle. Diana tensed her legs as she saw what happened and tried to aim at the figure, but it was gone.

Diana looked around while Tristan recovered and stood up. She looked around and then turned around to Moira as she noticed her raising her arms up with her Thompson gun in hand. She pointed the rifle towards Tristan. Diana looked into her eyes and saw a reddish glow in them.

"Moira, no!" Diana objected, quickly interfering and causing Moira's gun to shoot into the air above.

Tristan looked for a brief moment and ducked his head as soon as he saw Moira pointing her gun at him. Diana struggled with her bewitched friend as Moira fought back. Tristan then jumped around as he saw the shadowy figure rush around again. His eye's focused around as he attempted to see where the man was. Tristan had his rifle pointed out.

The figure jumped out of the trees above and towards Tristan. Tristan deflected the man with his rifle and then pushed him back. The man was none other than a supersoldier, dressed in an identical garb as the other they had encountered in the morning.

The supersoldier disarmed Tristan and grabbed him by the neck. Diana managed to disarm Moira and saw what was happening with Tristan as the supersoldier choked him, raising him up and causing him to struggle with hands at the supersoldier's hand, feet thrashing around. Diana opened fire towards the supersoldier, breaking his focus and causing him to drop Tristan onto the ground.

Moira brought a hand around Diana and held on to her in a chokehold. Diana struggled. The supersoldier grabbed Tristan and dragged him across the forest floor before he went to put a hand on Diana. Before Diana could react, the four of them disappeared as they were brought out of the forest and travelled miles away.

Act 6, Scene 4

Charlemagne rode in the body of the armored personnel carrier that drove along the highway and made its way towards the Nattau River. The inside of the APC was dark and they sat in two rows along the sides of the vehicle. Most of the men inside were hunched over and silent.

"We have one chance to make this happen," Macmillan spoke to those he was with, "but if we don't end this now, we'll only have died later. Let's remember what we're fighting for because it's more than just our liberty if it even is about that… It's about our families, and our community – the people we care about and love, and their wellbeing which is under threat. If we don't the make the effort now, no one else will… because we're all that they have, and to be honest, we're all they should ever need. We're a community, so let's defend our home and our families."

Charlemagne nodded.

"Godspeed to all of us…" Mr. Macmillan then said, broadcasting over the radio.

Charlemagne took a deep breath. The APC began to vibrate and he could hear some ruckus outside consisting of machine gunfire and explosions. The vibration was met with a violent shake before the APC tilted over. Everybody inside held on as the APC rolled. Charlemagne held on for his life until it was over and he was on the side of the vehicle.

The men inside groaned. Charlemagne looked around and composed himself. Maxim moved and helped a man next to him while Macmillan got the hatch open for them to exit. Once the hatch was open, gunfire could be heard from the outside in addition to the shouting and yelling of men from both sides.

Charlemagne climbed out of the armored vehicle and stepped onto the ground.

The APC had landed in a field a part of a farm near the highway. Macmillan helped the others out while Charlemagne composed himself. He looked up to the grey clouds of the dark night sky, whose thickness was worsened with the smoke of gunfire and the explosions around them. The defenders of the castle fired rocket projectiles towards the militia and the APCs absorbed most of the shock.

Once the last of the policemen inside the APC, the driver, got out, Macmillan took his rifle and went to stand behind Maxim who had opened fire against the outer walls of the fortress. Macmillan attempted to fire from behind him as Maxim was knelt down.

"I'm out," Maxim said, moving out of the way so that Lacplesis could move in. "Their defense is hard."

"We need to push in…" Charlemagne insisted.

"It'll be no use without a way to punch in through their main entrance, but they've got the gates closed…"

"What about an APC?" Mr. Macmillan questioned. "Would that be enough to break the door down?"

"It's possible… I don't think the doors are made of a heavy material," Maxim answered.

"Hold on," Miklos said from his side. "They're opening the doors, I think…"

"That's a tank!" Elegast remarked.

"We need to spread out… that thing will kill us all!" Miklos remarked.

"Spread out then," Macmillan confirmed. "Keep low and remain hidden. We need to take that armor out!"

Miklos and Elegast ran off from their position. Tanya and Kristoffer moved in to give them some covering fire. Maxim and

Charlemagne ran off and went towards a ditch on the side of the freeway. From where the APC was, which was at least fifty feet from the tank, he could see the modern armor with its machine guns firing. The other APCs were parked at either side of the freeway.

"Spread out!" Macmillan shouted. "Spread out!"

The tank made its initial shot towards the crashed APC, causing it to erupt into ball of fire. Charlemagne could feel the heat on his cheeks as they turned red.

"Is there anything you can do psionically to help against that tank?" Charlemagne questioned Bauer.

"I sense there are at least four inside the tank," Maxim replied. "I believe I may be able to mind control the gunner and disable the main turret, but I will need to get in a better position than this."

"Let's move then," Charlemagne responded.

Maxim led the way and went down the ditch. Charlemagne followed and they reached the smashed barrier from where the APC had hit. They used the barrier as cover before moving on over to the other side of the freeway and travelled up it to reach the armored personnel carriers. From there, they moved into some bushes which gave them a sightline to the tank as it moved its turret to the other APCs.

"Cover me," Maxim said, "I need to concentrate for this."

"Copy that," Charlemagne replied, kneeling down and laying some covering fire against the hostiles along the wall of the encampment.

The turret of the tank continued to aim towards the APCs, but did not fire. Instead, the turret began to spin and aim at concrete wall, firing a shell into the right-side of the wall, causing a part of it to collapse and breach the defenses of the Huntsman's base.

Charlemagne saw this and continued to fire towards the exposed mercenaries atop of the wall as they attempted to escape from the damage done. Meanwhile, the driver of the tank began to move away from the wall as Maxim aimed the turret to the other side. He fired a shot and caused a part of the concrete wall to collapse on the left-side as well.

The gates of the wall opened as another tank moved in. Charlemagne saw the tank drive forward with its cannon aimed at the tank under partial control of Maxim.

"Watch out!" Charlemagne attempted to warn him.

The tank fired at the other and caused it to blow up. Maxim opened his eyes and looked forward. He stretched out a hand and began to focus on the other tank. The turret of the tank froze before it began to move to the side, shooting into side of the gate and causing the concrete to collapse atop of the tank.

"Move forward! They're exposed!" Macmillan shouted.

Maxim continued to concentrate before slowly opening his eyes. He picked up his rifle and looked to Charlemagne.

"Let's move!" Maxim suggested.

Charlemagne and Maxim dashed across the grass and went into the wall and into the encampment where they stopped behind some parked light utility vehicles. The remainder of the Huntsman fired towards them. Charlemagne observed that there were no helicopters in the area. The main heat and firepower from the opposing forces were from turrets installed atop of the concrete fortress and a tank atop of the intersecting road that went north and south. Due to the close quarters, the tank was only useful to the Huntsman for its two machine gun turrets, one of which was .50 caliber and the other .24 caliber.

From the gate into the encampment, the freeway ramped up on its way to the bridge as an intersecting road crossed through underneath it and connected via on-ramps and off-ramps at every side of the cross. Maxim knelt down to take control of the tank ahead. Charlemagne observed while he returned fire that the tank began to drive off and move under the tunnel of the freeway so that it couldn't fire towards the militia. Maxim then came to.

"There's another tank on the other side," Maxim reported. "I will try to fight it off, but I need to move back in closer…"

Maxim shot forward with Charlemagne

"What's wrong with the tank you had?" Charlemagne questioned.

"They shot the driver," Maxim replied.

Maxim and Charlemagne moved out from where they were and migrated towards the freeway so that they could cross over. Once there, they dashed across the road and vaulted over the concrete barriers to reach the other side. They took cover behind the white tents and met up with Macmillan and Kristoffer.

"We've got some armor on this side," Macmillan said. "If we can distract it, we might be able to throw some Molotovs onto it, or I can wait for something funny to act up like with those other tanks."

"We can pray for some sort of malfunction," Charlemagne remarked.

"No prayers," Maxim replied, concentrating.

Macmillan moved forward while Charlemagne provided some covering fire. The turret of the tank ahead began to move its turret towards the tank under the freeway. Without hesitation, the tank shot at the other tank and caused it to blow up. Afterwards, Maxim opened his eyes and then closed them again with a deep breath.

Charlemagne observed as the tank began to move off, drive into the concrete barrier and stop there. Maxim opened his eyes again and then closed them. The turret of the tank moved and the tank shot a round into the main guns of the fortress. The turret then moved again before firing another round. Charlemagne looked as he saw mercenaries with rocket-projectile guns fire rockets at the tank. The tank detonated. Charlemagne shot towards the mercenaries with the anti-tank weapons.

Maxim came to and pushed forward with Charlemagne now that the armor had been dealt with. They pushed forward and began to move towards the freeway so that they could make a move towards the front doors. The outer defenses had been mostly dealt with and only a few mercenaries remained. Before the militia could move onto the freeway ramp, Charlemagne and Maxim observed as the front doors opened and another tank drove forward towards them. The two and the rest of those with them moved into cover.

"I'll immobilize it," Maxim stated. "Find an RPG and take it down!"

Charlemagne nodded as Maxim moved around the corner and extended a hand towards the tank. He looked around and soon found a rocket launcher on the floor. He swung his rifle around and picked up the RPG, bringing it towards the freeway. Macmillan saw what Charlemagne was doing and left. Charlemagne moved towards the freeway and aimed the rocket launcher towards the tank, firing at it.

The rocket hit the right front of the tank, causing it to smoke, but it was still able to move. Macmillan returned with two rocket launchers. He passed one to Charlemagne who had tossed his emptied one, while Macmillan moved over the concrete barrier of the freeway with his. The two opened fire on the tank and of the two rockets, one of them hit and caused the tank turret to become obsolete.

"Good riddance," Macmillan said, dropping the rocket launcher.

Charlemagne looked to him and then flinched as a loud gunshot was heard. When Charlemagne opened his eyes, he looked before him as Macmillan was on the floor with a gunshot wound in the chest.

"No!" Charlemagne shouted.

Another round fired towards Charlemagne. He ducked by the concrete barrier and heard the concrete chip as the bullet ricocheted off of it.

"Dad!" Jock shouted from nearby.

"Sniper!" Miklos yelled.

"Man down!" Charlemagne added.

"Sniper! Rooftop!" Maxim confirmed.

Miklos shot towards the roof of the fortress. Charlemagne raised himself to look over to Mr. Macmillan. He bled out and was dead. Charlemagne felt a hand on his shoulder. He looked behind him and saw Phillips.

"Let's not let his death be in vain," Phillips said to him. "Let's push on."

Charlemagne nodded. He reloaded his assault rifle and then opened fire towards the location of the sniper.

"Hostile down!" Maxim confirmed. "Move up!"

Maxim moved out of cover and dashed forward, taking cover by the wreckage of the tank as they continued to deal with mercenaries around the exterior of the fortress. Charlemagne looked behind him and his eyes passed the battlefield. There had been a lot of casualties. Jock was at the body of his father before he was moved out of the open by a fellow policemen. Charlemagne moved his eyes away from the sad sight and towards Maxim.

"Let's move!" Charlemagne shouted to him and Miklos.

Maxim moved out his cover and went towards the gates. He moved down the wall and went towards a small door constructed in the gate for easier access. He tried to open it, but it wouldn't open. Charlemagne stacked up behind him, and behind him was Miklos, Tanya, Phillips, and then Lacplesis and Kristoffer. Miklos moved over to be at the other side. He looked to Bauer. Bauer nodded to him. Miklos then moved and kicked the door open before opening fire inside. The mercenaries on the other side returned fire.

"Throwing smoke!" Miklos remarked, unpinning a smoke grenade canister and tossing it in.

The canister created a cloud of smoke. Miklos led the way in and took cover by a pillar of the foundation of the fortress. Maxim moved in and took cover by some of the concrete barriers that had been moved to provide cover inside. Charlemagne looked in and saw that the pillars of the foundation acted as stairwells to go up to the upper levels. He rushed in and went straight to them.

Charlemagne pointed his rifle up and checked for hostiles before looking out the door.

"On me," Charlemagne said, "this way!"

Kristoffer joined Charlemagne, and Charlemagne began to go up the stairs with caution. Phillips and Maxim later joined him. Charlemagne came up to the second-floor, which led to a catwalk that wrapped around the entirety of the bridge. He went forward and began to provide supporting fire to the militiamen below him. Those behind Charlemagne joined him and spread out to provide supporting fire.

The actual space of the fortress was not that large as most of the body of the fortress was a mere shell for the checkpoint. The only solid space was above them from pillar to pillar and was two-stories in combination.

Charlemagne continued to provide covering fire before moving down the causeway and reaching the other stairwell.

Maxim and Phillips joined him. The stairs led up to an armory with various weapons and munitions inside as this space provided access to two machine gun nests. Mercenaries opened fire from the other side. Charlemagne and Maxim took cover by the corner of the door.

"We'll take point here," Miklos said, moving over with Tanya. "Get Charles upstairs to a computer!"

Charlemagne moved out of the way and continued upstairs with Phillips at his side. Maxim joined from behind and the two moved up to the second-floor, which led to a command center with various tables, consoles, and monitors around. Mercenaries from inside fired back at them as they arrived. Charlemagne could see on the other side of the room, inside the top of the stairwell, there were three chairs with three people to them. It was Diana, Tristan, and Moira. Charlemagne opened fire against the mercenaries inside.

Tristan looked to the side as he saw the fight between the two sides. Maxim went in and took cover behind a desk. He aggressively pushed in with Phillips, and within a moment, they had cleared the room. Charlemagne lowered his rifle and rushed over to untie the kids, freeing their wrists so that they could remove the duct tape at their mouths.

"Children," Charlemagne said, hugging both of them. "What are you doing here? How did you come here?"

"It's a long story, but involves one of those supersoldiers and the warehouse being raided," Diana responded.

Moira stood up as Phillips had freed her. She removed the tape from her mouth and then took out a USB drive from her sweatshirt.

"Come on, let's show the world the horrors that've occurred here," Moira stated, moving into the command center. "While you had the drone on, I recorded some of the fighting because I thought it'd be useful… All I need is a moment to upload the footage."

Moira moved to a computer and inserted the USB drive. Charlemagne walked into the room with her and looked to the computer screen. Moira pulled a seat out from the desk and moved to sit down.

"How's my dad? Is he okay?" Moira questioned, looking to Charlemagne and then Phillips.

Charlemagne cleared his throat and held a saddened look on his face.

"Watch out!" Maxim shouted, raising his rifle and shooting towards the stairwell the kids had been held up in.

A mercenary shot towards them. Phillips grabbed Moira and brought her to the ground while Charlemagne and Kristoffer did the same with Diana and Tristan. A shot had passed between the crowd. Maxim and Lacplesis returned fire and killed the hostiles ahead. Lacplesis and Maxim moved up to take point at the stairwell doors. Charlemagne removed his grip from Diana and looked over as he saw blood on the floor.

Diana looked in horror as her eyes looked at the blood stains on Moira, but her eyes then moved over as she saw the gunshot wound in Phillips who took a bullet to the back in order to save her. Phillips shouted out in pain. Kristoffer moved him out of the way and Charlemagne rushed over to give first aid. Moira watched before she was helped up. Diana brought a hand to her friend's shoulder.

"Moira…" Diana said to her.

Moira looked back at her and then returned to the computer. Charlemagne removed the ballistic vest from Phillips' body and saw that the bullet had pierced through. He removed his own backpack and began to search for gauze to stop the bleeding.

Kristoffer helped him while Moira typed away to upload the footage.

"We've got a connection," Moira stated. "I'm going to need a minute or two to upload these to the right site, otherwise they might get taken down."

Moira worked while Phillips' condition stabilized as Charlemagne was able to stop the bleeding. Phillips squeezed Charlemagne's arm.

"Charles..." Phillips said to him. "I can't feel my legs..."

Charlemagne looked at him with sympathy before looking over to Moira.

"How's the upload going?" Charlemagne questioned.

"Almost there..." Moira replied.

Diana and Tristan looked at the computer screen at the loading bar as the footage was being uploaded to the World Wide Web.

"And it's done!" Moira responded with a cheer.

The footage had uploaded and floated onto an anonymous image board. Moira made multiple posts on different sites, but the footage of the chaos in Allabrese had reached the public. Diana and Tristan took a deep sigh.

"See how the fighting is downstairs," Charlemagne said to Kristoffer. "We need to get Phillips to a doctor."

"Yes, Charles," Kristoffer responded, leaving.

Lacplesis held his position while Moira continued to spread the footage elsewhere. Maxim looked to them with his assault rifle pointed up to the ceiling. He then leaned to the side, dropping his rifle on its sling as he brought his hands to his head and screamed out in pain. Charlemagne looked over and went to him.

"Maxim, are you alright?" Charlemagne questioned.

Tristan looked to him and brought a hand to his shoulder. Diana was holding hands with Tristan as he did this. She held a worried look on his face. Maxim's eyes began to glow purple and in an instant, he straightened up and disappeared with those that were in contact with him.

Act 6, Scene 5

Charlemagne opened his eyes and looked around him. He was in the lobby of Cabernet Laboratories with Maxim and the kids. The lights of the building were turned off, but Charlemagne continued to look up at the eccentric architectural design of the atrium lobby and past the glass to the sky above. Maxim was on one knee, rubbing his head before composing himself and standing up. He walked over to Charlemagne who was looking around the lobby of his research and development company.

"What are we doing here?" Charlemagne questioned.

"I'm sorry, but I had a terrible vision..." Maxim confessed, "while we celebrated our success at the bridge, I caught a glimpse into the near future where all of the land around us was consumed by a nuclear explosion. When I thought how that could be possible, I sensed the activity of Huntsman operating from within this space."

Maxim closed his eyes and took a deep breath.

"I continue to sense them... They are here."

"The other supersoldiers," Charlemagne questioned.

"No, although they continue to linger in this region... I do not sense them nearby..." Maxim replied. "I sense the Huntsman below us, busy plotting their last resort against the occupation."

"They're going to override the fusion reactor and trigger a nuclear explosion," Charlemagne responded. "If they can't control the town and find you, then they'll take anything and everything with it, eradicating all of us."

"We need to stop them," Maxim stated.

"We're only two," Charlemagne responded, looking to him, "but I understand the urgency – I trust you."

"We can help too," Tristan insisted.

"You're unarmed and I won't have you in danger," Charlemagne deflected.

"I will not land them in danger," Maxim responded. "I will not let them be harmed, but with them, we can ambush the team inside without them even firing a bullet at any of us."

Charlemagne looked at Maxim. He sighed.

"Very well," Charlemagne replied. "Let's get a move on then… who knows much time we have before it is too late."

Charlemagne fixed his rifle before taking point to lead Maxim into the laboratory halls. He stopped at the security panel and noticed that all power had been cut-off with the entire security system disabled.

"Hm…" Charlemagne said, opening the door with ease. "The Huntsman have definitely been here, because one must manually disable the auxiliary power to shut down the security system."

"I don't sense anyone immediately nearby," Maxim replied. "Let's keep moving."

Charlemagne continued into the halls and made his way towards the service elevator. He pressed to call the elevator, but it was dead. Maxim lowered his rifle and forced the elevator doors open, exposing the shaft. He shined a flashlight in and saw a ladder on the side.

"Watch your step," Bauer warned.

Bauer grabbed ahold of the latter and started to climb down. Charlemagne assisted the kids over to take the ladder before he joined them down to the bottom. The service elevator was parked at the very bottom where they let go of the ladder to step onto. Bauer moved over to a vent grate and began to pull it off.

"I feel their energy," Maxim stated. "I will lead from here."

Maxim went into the large vent and crouched his way forward. The kids followed from behind and Charlemagne walked behind them. Through the maze of the vent shaft network, Maxim led them to an end where he was able to look out and into the chamber were the fusion reactor was held. Diana and Tristan looked below into the circular room.

From where Tristan was, he was able to observe the layout of the room. The fusion reactor main core existed in the center of the room and had a platform around it with rails. A mercenary could be seen atop of these, walking calmly and keeping guard. Below him were two mercenaries fiddling with the fusion reactor by taking canisters from the bottom of the machine where they were stored and bringing them upwards to insertion point at the middle platform. From the central machine, there was an extension that went below the main control room and connected the platform in the middle with the outer platform that wrapped around the rest of the room. This extension of hardware was large and did not allow anyone to pass through. The control room was connected to the outer platforms by a stairway, which before it was a stairway that went to the ground floor as well. There were two mercenaries in the control room and two patrolling around the outer platform at either side. The last two mercenaries could be seen standing guard at the main entrance into the chamber from the sublevel corridors. Above all of this were three beams that crossed each other at a central pillar that extended upwards from the roof of the fusion reactor and into the ceiling. This pillar contained various tubes and thick cables and went upwards to provide electricity out of the room. From where the vent opening stuck out, to the left was the main entrance and to the right was the control room.

"What's the plan then?" Charlemagne questioned as he caught up.

"Let me tell you," Bauer replied.

Bauer discussed the plan of action with Charlemagne and the kids. He then disappeared and reappeared onto the outer platform, behind one of the mercenaries. Bauer brought the mercenary into a chokehold and took him down, grabbing his rifle and some cartridges before returning to the vent. He handed each of the items to Tristan before disappearing and reappearing behind the other to do the same. Bauer's teleportation made a screeching noise as it happened, but it was not a distraction. Charlemagne took a prone position in the vents and kept an eye on the mercenaries by the main doors.

Diana took the second rifle from Bauer as well as two magazine clips. Bauer then looked down into the chamber, pointing out two mercenaries for each of the kids. One of them on the ground floor was carrying a canister towards the stairs and bringing it to the upper platform, while the other did not have a canister as he was returning to get one. Diana gave a thumbs up to Bauer. He then took Diana's hand and teleported with her.

Bauer brought Diana onto the ground floor and behind some crates. They laid low and Bauer looked out around the corner before turning back to Diana to move into his position. Bauer then teleported and reappeared behind the mercenary who was walking quickly to retrieve a canister. Diana pushed her weight against the crates, causing them to slide and causing the mercenary to stop walking out of distraction. Bauer then grabbed the mercenary and took him down. Once that was done, Bauer disappeared with Diana and reappeared at the roof of the control room where she could hide. He pointed to the mercenary in the middle and then left.

Charlemagne left with Bauer, and the two reappeared behind the two mercenaries at the main entrance. Each of them took ahold of the other in a chokehold, bringing them down and out.

Bauer noticed the other mercenary on approach towards his stockpile immediately before them, and thus teleported with Charlemagne and the bodies, entering the vents with them. Once that was taken care of, Tristan gave a thumbs up to Bauer and left with him.

The two teleported to the ground floor and behind some machinery. Bauer left Tristan around the corner of the cover and then teleported behind the mercenary. Tristan banged a fist against the machine, causing some slight noise and distracting the merc. Bauer then moved in and took ahold of him, causing him to drop his canister. Tristan quickly moved in, jumping and catching the heavy canister while Bauer took care of the merc. Tristan let the canister down gently and then left with Tristan to teleport to the rooftop of the control room where Bauer joined Diana in observing the guard in the center.

The mercenary began to move around, out of sight from the control room. Bauer teleported and took care of him, using the blinding light of the artificial star to cover him. Once the mercenary was down, Bauer kept down and looked over to the control room. He opened fire towards the merc and shot one dead. The mercenaries shouted in Russian as they noticed Bauer. The other shot a pistol at him, but Bauer teleported behind him and took him down before the bullet could even pass by where he was. He smashed his body into the console and then threw him out the window.

Tristan moved out of prone and got onto one knee as he saw the room was clear, but it was not clear for long. Charlemagne saw from the vents as a purple glow could be seen from the main entrance into the chamber. With a loud screech, a supersoldier teleported into the room with two Huntsman mercenaries at his side. The three of them then spread out while Bauer opened fire towards them as did Charlemagne. Charlemagne had shot one of the mercs, while other survived as did the supersoldier.

Bauer exited from the control room and dropped down onto the platform to move around. He moved a hand towards the mercenary and took control of him to open fire towards the supersoldier. The supersoldier instantly killed the merc, allowing Bauer to teleport before the supersoldier and engage him in hand-to-hand combat.

Charlemagne took the chance to break out of the vent and drop down onto the platform below. He moved out of the way and took a shot towards the supersoldier. Charlemagne grazed the supersoldier by the arm and gave Bauer a chance to move forward and bring the supersoldier down. The supersoldier then teleported and disappeared elsewhere within the room where he chose to instead shoot towards Bauer.

Bauer moved into cover and returned fire. Charlemagne moved around and into a better position. The kids remained where they were, observing the unfolding fight as it happened. Tristan quickly moved his eyes back over to the entrance into the chamber as he saw a purple orb glow bright and then spread out as a few more reinforcements were teleported in.

A second supersoldier backed by two more mercenaries had entered the room. Charlemagne opened fire towards them, while Bauer quickly teleported as he had his flank exposed. He reappeared near the control room and continued to lay fire towards the initial supersoldier. The second supersoldier stretched an arm towards Charlemagne.

Charlemagne dropped his weapon and brought a hand to his head. He screamed out.

"Charles!" Diana shouted, opening fire towards the mercenaries on the left.

The supersoldier that Bauer had been concentrating on stretched a hand out towards Diana. Bauer noticed this, and instantly and instinctively shot his rifle towards the supersoldier, piercing his helmet and killing him. A storm of purple energy followed, spinning around and echoing a terrible demonic screech before exploding and expelling the energy outwards.

Diana shook her head and had stopped firing before Bauer had intervened. The supersoldier had died before he could harm her. Meanwhile, Charlemagne continued to scream in pain while Bauer moved around, firing at the Huntsman and supersoldier below.

"G-get out of my head!" Charlemagne shouted as he rolled around on the platform with both hands at the side of his head. "Poulsson!"

Bauer shot towards the supersoldier, distracting him and causing him to let go of Charlemagne. Charlemagne stopped screaming and took a moment to recover from the mental torment he had just endured. Bauer had managed to kill one of the two Huntsman, but the other remained closer to Charlemagne. Bauer focused on the supersoldier more than the other merc.

The supersoldier teleported and reappeared behind Bauer. The two engaged in hand-to-hand close quarter combat. The Huntsman mercenary began to shoot towards Bauer in a distracting manner. Charlemagne slowly stood up and grabbed his rifle. He saw the mercenary shooting towards Bauer and moved quietly around the outer platform to get into the flank of the hostile. He then shot at the merc and killed him.

Once the mercenary was down, Charlemagne lowered his rifle and looked across the room as Bauer fought with the supersoldier. He raised his rifle again and provided some covering fire. The supersoldier jumped over the railing. Bauer followed and landed below. Tristan watched as the two continued to spar. Charlemagne moved around to continue providing supporting fire. He grazed the arm of the soldier and Bauer moved in with a punch.

The supersoldier deflected and stepped back before moving in with some kicks. Bauer grabbed the supersoldier's leg and threw him into the fusion reactor base. The soldier's body hit hard. He quickly recovered and moved out of the way, teleporting as he became exposed to a direct shot from Charlemagne. The supersoldier reappeared on the outer platform and extended another hand to Charlemagne.

Bauer teleported up to the platform and shot towards the psionic soldier. The supersoldier abandoned his effort and instead threw an arm towards Bauer. Bauer's eyes glowed purple as he raised both hands and competed with the supersoldier as if they were struggling psionically with each other. Charlemagne rubbed his head from the attempted mind control. He then took his rifle and shot towards the supersoldier.

The supersoldier broke his concentration, allowing Bauer to overpower him and knock him over. He then moved in, but the supersoldier stood up and the two engaged each other in hand-to-hand combat once more. Charlemagne continued to assist while the two began to move towards the central platform. The two moved apart from each other before the supersoldier moved in. Bauer instead went and took the supersoldier by the throat, picking him up and bringing him into the glass of the fusion reactor, cracking it slightly.

Bauer ripped off the necklace and tossed it aside. He then continued to choke the supersoldier with Bauer's eyes glowing purple. Charlemagne took the finishing shot and killed him. Bauer threw the body below him, allowing it to explode at a safe distance from either of them. The explosion of energy and demonic scream caused some sparks to fly out from the wiring. The ceiling shook.

Charlemagne lowered his rifle and climbed up the stairs into the control room. He looked at the panel and read the error messages.

"What's going on?" Bauer questioned, panting.

"Hold on," Charlemagne replied, typing on a keyboard and looking at various monitors.

Diana and Tristan hopped down from the roof of the control room and entered. Bauer walked around and joined them.

"The mercenaries had been feeding the fusion reactor with an excess of Boron-11," Charlemagne finally explained. "The core is overheating and set to detonate if I don't stop it."

"Is there anything I can do to help?" Bauer questioned.

"Get the kids out of here!" Charlemagne said. "Teleport them to a safe distance."

Bauer nodded and before either of them could object, he grabbed an arm in each of his hands and disappeared for a brief minute before reappearing. Charlemagne continued to fiddle with the console.

"Damn!" Charlemagne shouted, hitting a fist into the keyboard. "The central core is taking in too much energy and I can't stop it! If I can't stop this –"

"It'll detonate," Bauer assumed.

"Worse," Charlemagne replied. "If I can't stop the meltdown, the star in the main chamber will collapse and die. It could then create a blackhole... and possibly consume the entire world, and by extension, entire solar system."

"How long do we have?" Bauer questioned.

"Seconds," Charlemagne responded.

"I'll buy you time," Bauer said, jumping out the window and going to the fusion reactor.

Bauer extended his hands towards the sun as it set off a whirl of solar flares from within its case. He used his powers to control the sun, restraining it.

"You don't understand," Charlemagne replied, moving around to go speak with Bauer, "I can't undo this in a couple of minutes… I need more people… damages need to be patched, and canisters need to be rebalanced. It could take hours…"

"Then it appears that our fate is sealed," Bauer responded.

Charlemagne didn't say anything as he reached him, standing behind him as he continued to control the solar activity in the vat.

"If you can't stop this, then I'll absorb as much of the explosion as possible," Bauer stated, grunting as he focused. "I can do that."

"You'll die," Charlemagne said to him.

"Yes," Bauer responded, "but it's our only hope. I'll contain the blast, minimize the damages done, and reverse the energy to collapse the blackhole."

Charlemagne looked to him with an understanding face. Bauer looked back at him.

"Goodbye, my friend," Bauer said, extending a hand to him.

Charlemagne disappeared from the room, but did not travel with Bauer. Charlemagne reappeared on a couch in his library. He was laying down atop of it and lurched forward. He looked around the darkness of the library and then moved his head over to the curtains of the large window looking towards the front yard and river beyond. A bright light could be seen. Charlemagne stood up and pulled the curtains back.

In the distant night sky, Charlemagne could see an explosion dissipating outwards from ahead in Champion Plains alongside a mushroom cloud in the horizon. The combined explosion lit the region as if it were daytime for minutes, causing nearby lampposts on the street to shatter and turn off. Charlemagne could only look on with reverence as he stood at the window, watching until the light went out.

Epilogue

Charlemagne stood at the edge of the massive crater that had been left behind by the detonation of the fusion reactor. The entirety of Cabernet Laboratories had been consumed. Each of them looked down as Charlemagne held an umbrella between them. Various men in hazmat suits were below, looking around the wreckage that had been left behind. They continued to look until Charlemagne noticed someone behind him. He turned around and looked at Director Black.

"Quite a mess we have here, isn't it?" Ms. Black remarked in her eloquent Londoner accent. "You have no idea of the week it's been."

"You have no idea of the month it's been," Charlemagne remarked back at her.

"Touché," Ms. Black replied, walking towards him. "All that you need to know about what happened, is that it was an unfortunate accident and now it is over."

"Do you expect me to go on with my life just like that then?" Charlemagne questioned her in a hostile tone. "People died."

"Nobody will remember what had happened, because it never happened," Ms. Black stated to him. "You've been manipulated – such is what you think should happen when you invite a stranger in your home, and that stranger possesses psychic powers."

"Are you suggesting that all of that – and the memories that I share with my children, was nothing more than that? An entire day had passed… Chief Phillips was handicapped. Captain Macmillan was shot dead. Many others died that on that Halloween night when we fought back and took down Huntsman who were brutally occupying our town. We have footage of them poisoning our water supply, proving them to be at the root of the problem. There was no virus – there was only a façade of one because they wanted to recapture Bauer who was a test subject of Zimmerman's."

"Chief Phillips and Captain Macmillan were the unfortunate tragedies of the riots that occurred on the night that you came to Allabrese and returned with this Mr. Bauer to your home," Ms. Black replied. "As you told one of my agents, you came here with your Protection Squad and caused quite a bit of havoc against the Canadian Army, but they had never left. The Huntsman were never here – I'm not sure if they were the ones that ransacked your home, but it does appear that you had come into contact with a vile hallucinogenic on Halloween that kept you, your children, and even your maid unconscious. The footage that you describe, does not exist. There was a virus, we cured it, and that was that. Any suggestion that there was something more is nothing more than a conspiracy theory now. Only you and your kids recall the events that you describe to me, everybody else, who was in the area, state a different narrative."

Charlemagne looked to her in disbelief.

"I'm sorry, Charles, but you were manipulated."

Director Black turned around to leave. Charlemagne clenched a fist in his right hand.

"Do you mean to tell me," Charlemagne said, "that the sacrifices of those good men who died to defend this town – men like Macmillan and Phillips, will be lost on their families? You manipulated all of them, didn't you? You made them forget what had happened in an effort to cover up this entire ordeal? To vindicate Zimmermann as if he owed you anything when he was the one that had Selebi killed and stolen the plans for your psionic project."

Director Black did not turn around as she left.

"And what of Poulsson?" Charlemagne shouted. "Where is he? Your friend – our friend who fought with us? He was one of them; one of these supersoldiers. Admit it – he had gone missing. How could I have known that?"

Director Black turned around and looked at him.

"You know it, because the idea was planted in your head, not because you had witnessed anything," Director Black replied. "You are lucky that the council has decided not to punish you for this environmental disaster and the blatant treason against the Canadian government on the night that destroyed two government vehicles and aided a felon escape from a quarantine zone so that you could experiment on him. Not to mention, I know about your secret in that basement of yours. The G.D.P. will be forced to look into your activities even closer, and that begins with your so-called Protection Squad. We seek only to maintain the status-quo. We can't have a billionaire financing his own personal army," she said with a sigh. "I'm sorry, but I am only doing my job and I am trying to be gentle with you given what we went through together last year, and the service you provided to the international community. So, please, go home, Charles, and get some rest. Please."

Director Black left with these final words. Charlemagne opened his fist. His hands were trembling.

• • •

Charlemagne returned to the manor later in the day. He rallied the kids and brought them into the dinette where he sat them down. He laid down some medical devices on the table, including two syringes and sat down. The kids sat at opposite sides of the table. Charlemagne scratched his head and didn't say anything for a couple minutes before he sighed.

"I understand that we are all confused," Charlemagne finally stated with a nervous tone, "but we need to hold an open-mind to the possibilities…"

"Don't say it," Tristan interrupted.

"It is possible… that we may have been manipulated," Charlemagne confessed. "For what purpose, I am not sure…"

"No!" Tristan rejected. "It happened and you know it!"

"Tristan," Diana scolded.

"Nonetheless," Charlemagne said, ignoring Tristan, "I have signed us all up for group therapy sessions at Allabrese General so that we can clear our thoughts and get through this troubling time. I believe that it will be helpful for us to recover and hopefully move on…"

Tristan clenched a fist and looked at Charlemagne angrily.

"In addition, I will be needing a blood sample from each of you to check for possible toxins," Charlemagne said. "I need to have a look at this hallucinogenic and ensure that all of it has left our systems."

Tristan looked at the syringe on the table. He then looked back to Charlemagne.

"Go to hell!" Tristan said to him, standing up. "Bauer was not a bad man! He helped us save the town! All of what happened, happened. Moira's and Aaron's dads were heroes! If you're too unsure of yourself to realize that, then back off because I accept what had happened as truth even if you don't!"

Tristan stormed out of the room. Charlemagne remained seated and simply looked forward. Diana looked at him with sympathy and then over to Tristan as he had left. She gave a sigh.

"You can get my blood in a moment," Diana said, "but I better go and make sure he's okay. He's not coping well, and between what happened last summer and now this…"

Diana sighed and held a saddened look.

"Go," Charlemagne agreed. "He needs you."

Diana left and went upstairs. She went to Tristan's room and opened the door.

"Can you believe him?" Tristan questioned from atop of his bed. "He's so unsure of himself!"

"Are you okay?" Diana instead asked.

"Of course I'm fine," Tristan replied, standing up and pacing the room. "You believe what happened, happened, right?"

Diana hesitated to provide an answer. Tristan turned around and looked at her.

"Well?"

"Tristan…" Diana said, "are you okay?"

"Yes," Tristan replied in annoyed tone. "Why do you keep asking me that?"

"Because I don't believe you," Diana confessed with a tear rolling down her cheek. "I don't think you're okay, because you haven't been okay since you came home from England. You haven't been the same."

Tristan looked at her with a saddened face. His anger had left him.

"Ever since you've come home, you've been acting strange and I'm worried about you. I just want you to be like you were before all of that. At first, I was worried you were going to break up with me, but more than that, I just want you to be you again. Not like this… not vengeful and angry… I want you to return to the boy I fell in love with…"

Tristan blinked and looked away. He then looked back at her.

"You were scared I was going to breakup with you?" Tristan asked.

"Yes," Diana confirmed, "because you've been so distant!"

"I'd never leave you," Tristan said with watering eyes. "You're all I have that is good in my life."

Diana embraced Tristan. He brought a hand around and rested it on her back.

"I'll admit, it hasn't been easy for me since I returned from the forest, but I've been trying to adjust and being near you helps... Sometimes, I just want to be alone and by myself, especially since I've known that it bothers you, and didn't want you to become sucked into my emotions."

"Like it or not, your emotions affect me. Your sufferings are mine," Diana replied, "and that's just the nature of it. I'm here for you."

Tristan didn't respond and simply continued to hug Diana. Rain pelted heavily onto the roof above them, and that was all that could be heard as they continued to embrace and comfort each other.

"Woe to those who make unjust laws, to those who issue oppressive decrees, to deprive the poor of their rights and withhold justice from the oppressed of my people, making widows their pray and robbing the fatherless."

– Isaiah 10:1-2